Susan Warner

Pine Needles

A story

Susan Warner

Pine Needles
A story

ISBN/EAN: 9783744748162

Printed in Europe, USA, Canada, Australia, Japan

Cover: Foto ©Andreas Hilbeck / pixelio.de

More available books at **www.hansebooks.com**

PINE NEEDLES.

BY THE AUTHOR OF

"THE WIDE, WIDE WORLD."

"They that say such things declare plainly that they seek a country."—HEB. xi. 14.

NEW YORK:

ROBERT CARTER AND BROTHERS,

530 BROADWAY.

1877.

Pine Needles and Old Yarns.

CHAPTER I.

The Franklins were coming to Mosswood.

This might have happened, Maggie thought, a good while ago; but however the view had not been shared by Mrs. Candlish, and a whole year had passed away since the joyful coming home of the family to their old possessions. The winter was spent at Mosswood, in quiet gladness and gradual strength-gaining; the spring brought a return to all the favourite out-door amusements and occupations of the family. Summer was the proper time for company, and the house had been filled till the end of September. Then Mrs. Candlish declared she was tired and must run away, or she would be obliged to entertain people till November; and she joined her husband in a trip to California, which, half for business and half for pleasure, Mr. Candlish had resolved upon taking. At that juncture the children begged for the Franklins; and their mother was willing. " As I cannot be here," she said, "it will not be necessary to extend the invitation to Mrs. Franklin. You may have the others, and do what you will with them."

"I should think," remarked Maggie, "if Meredith and Flora heard what mamma said, they wouldn't like it much."

However, they did not hear it, and if they guessed at the substance of it I don't know; but Flora had too much curiosity and Meredith too much affection engaged, to be over scrupulous. So they came, and were welcomed, I was going to say, uproariously. It just fell short of that. For even Esther privately declared to her sister that "nobody was so nice as Meredith Franklin."

Now after seeing them, the next thing was to make them see Mosswood; and many were the consultations Maggie and Esther had already held over plans and means. Nothing could be settled after all till the guests came. And when they came, the whole first evening was spent in joyous talk and recollections. But the next morning before breakfast Maggie and Meredith met at the house door. Meredith had been out walking.

"How do you like it?" she asked daringly, clasping his hand, while her eyes looked love and pleasure hard into his face.

"It is the most beautiful place I ever saw in my life."

"And it is such a nice day," said Maggie gleefully. "What shall we do to-day?"

"Let us be out of doors!"

"O yes, we'll be out of doors," said Maggie; "but where shall we go?"

"Nowhere out of Mosswood—if you ask me. I don't want anything else."

"Well, Mosswood is pretty good," said Maggie, "because, when you are at Mosswood you have the hills and the river and all, *besides* Mosswood, you know—O Meredith! I have thought of something!"

"I dare say," Meredith answered smiling. "That is quite in your way."

"This is something nice. Suppose we go out and have dinner in the woods?"

"I should say it was a capital plan."

"We used to do that in old times, before ever we went away. And we have got a nice little cart, Meredith, to carry our dinner and whatever we want, and—O it's nice! it's nice!" exclaimed Maggie, jumping on her toes for delight. "I'm *so* glad you're here! and I'm *so* glad to go into tho woods again to dinner."

"We want only one thing," said Meredith.

"What's that?"

"Mr. Murray."

"Uncle Eden! I'll write to him."

"Let us all write to him. Every one put in something. That will bring him maybe."

"Yes, that will bring him!" Maggie echoed; and I do not believe that for the rest of the morning she took another flat step. On her toes, was the only way that her spirits could go. The first thing after breakfast was the Round Robin to Uncle Eden. Maggie began it, as the youngest.

"DEAR UNCLE EDEN—Flora and Meredith are here while mamma and papa are gone to California. We are going out in the woods to dinner; and we all want you. Do please come, if you can get away from Bay House. We want you as much as anybody can be wanted.   MAGGIE."

Then Esther wrote—

"DEAR UNCLE EDEN—It is quite true. We do all want you very much. Fenton is coming, and I am afraid nobody will keep him in order, if you are not here.   ESTHER."

Then Flora—

"I think we would all be very glad to see Mr. Murray. I am sure one sincerely glad would be.
    "FLORA FRANKLIN."

Last, Meredith—

"DEAR MR. MURRAY—You know how true is all the foregoing. And yet, though I cannot suppose I should be gladder to see you than everybody else, it does seem to me that I *want* to see you more than any of the rest can—because I have so many questions to ask, and feel that I need so much advice. I hope you may find that you can comply with our joint earnest desire.
    "MEREDITH FRANKLIN."

After all were done, Maggie begged for the paper, to add a word that nobody else must see. This was what she said.

"DEAR UNCLE EDEN—I want to say a *private* word to you. I feel somehow as if it was not just exactly respectful to Meredith and Flora that they should be here with nobody but just us. Don't you think so? But if you could come, it would be all right. We are going in the woods to dinner to-day—O I wish you were here!   MAGGIE."

This joint epistle finished and sealed, and some other despatches for Leeds got ready, it was time to see about making preparations for the woods. Where should they go? Question the first.

"To the old Fort."

"To the Happy Valley."

"No, to the Lookout rock."

"Not to-day, Esther. Let's keep that for Uncle Eden. Suppose—suppose—"

"The Plateau."

"It seems to be an *embarras de richesses*," said Meredith laughing, "and I do not wonder. Let me help you. Suppose we go up on this height just east of us; isn't the view pretty from there?"

"The South Pitch! O it's *lovely* up there," cried Maggie. "You look down on the house, and you look down the river, and it's shady and nice. It's just lovely. That is best for to-day. Then other days we'll take the other places. Now we must get ready."

"What?" said Flora.

"O, you must get your work, or books if you like; whatever you like; and Meredith must find a book too, I suppose; we always take books and work and then we talk; but once when we took nothing, then we didn't do anything. Esther and I must prepare the wagon; cart, I mean."

"What is to go in the cart? Cannot we help you?" said Meredith. "And where is the cart, in the first place?"

"O, it's up in the wood-house loft; we haven't had it out this year yet, you know. Ditto, maybe you'll tell Fairbairn to get it down, will you?"

"Who is Mr. Fairbairn?"

"O, the gardener. He's out there somewhere. Esther and I must go to Betsey for things."

"I suppose I shall know Fairbairn when I see him," said Meredith smiling, as he put on his hat.

In a quarter of an hour the cart stood at the door, and Esther and Maggie and Flora were busily packing "things" in baskets. Meredith came to put his hand to the work.

"It is so hard to remember everything," said Esther. "We always forget something or other, and then somebody has to go back for it. Now here is all the china, I think. O stop! have we put the tea-pot in?"

"Who wants tea?" said Meredith.

"In the woods? O we always have tea in the woods, and sometimes coffee."

"Make a fire to boil the kettle?"

"Why *of course!*"

"How should I know it was of course? Well, tea is very good in the woods, I have no doubt. Don't forget the tea."

"But I should have forgotten the sugar, if you hadn't spoken."

"And the salt! don't forget the salt; we always do."

"We don't want salt to-day; we have nothing to eat it with."

"Yes, we have."

"No, we haven't; there is cold ham, and bread and butter, and apple-sauce."

"Take the salt," said Meredith, "and give me a few eggs. and I'll make you a friar's omelet."

"A friar's omelet! What is that?"

"You'll see. Only I shall want a dish to mix it in, you know."

Delightful! The dish was fetched from the kitchen, and the omelet pan. Ham and apple-sauce Betty had packed for the party already; rolls and butter, spoons and knives and forks, a pitcher of cream, napkins—I do not know what all—went into the other baskets, and were finally stowed in the cart. A light porter's cart, it was; roomy enough; and yet it grew pretty full. The tea-kettle must find a place; then books and knitting and paper. Then thick shawls to spread upon the rocks, to make softer seats for the more ease-loving. Fairbairn carried a tin pail with water. All these arrangements took up time; so the morning was well on its way and the dew long off the grass, when at last the procession set forth. Meredith drew the cart, which he was informed he must do carefully, or the cream would slop over and possibly other damage be done.

It was not a long way they had to go, this morning. Bordering upon the lawn and shrubbery, to the east, rose a little rocky height, which in fact prevented the dwellers at Mosswood from ever seeing the sun rise. But the hill was so pretty, they forgave it. Towards the house it presented a smooth wall of grey granite; on the top it also shewed granite in quantity, there, however, alternating with moss and thin grass, and overshadowed by cedars, oaks, and pines, with now and then a young hemlock. The soil was thin; the growth of trees in consequence not lofty; nevertheless very graceful. No cultivation, hardly any dressing, had been attempted; the purple asters sprung up at the edge of the rocks, and huckleberry bushes stood where they found footing; here and there a bramble, here and there a bunch of ferns. Now the oak leaves were turned yellow and brown; the huckleberry bushes in duller hues of the same; moss was dry and crisp, and ferns odourous in the warm air.

To reach the top of the height a circuit must be made. There was no path leading straight from the house. Through the grounds at the back of the house the way wound along between beds of acheranthus and cineraria which made warm strips of bordering, with scarlet pelargoniums lighting up the beds beyond in a blaze of brilliance. Turning then into a carriage road, the party followed it to the north of the height which Maggie had called the South Pitch, and struck off then southwards into a little mossy, rocky, hardly traced path under the trees.

"This is easy enough," said Meredith, guiding his cart somewhat carefully, however, to avoid severe jolts which would have endangered the cream. "I do not see where the pitch is yet."

"Ah, but you will, when you get to the south end," said Maggie. "Look out, Ditto, here's a rock in your way. And these huckleberry bushes are very thick."

Following on over rocks and bushes, they soon came to the place Maggie meant, and Meredith rested his cart and stood still to look. From the southern brow of the little hill, the ground fell steeply away; so steeply that the eye had unhindered range over the river which lay below, and the hills bordering it, and the point of Gee's Point which there pushes the river to the eastward. Not a tree-branch even was in the way; river and hills lay in the October light, still, glowing, fair, as only October can be.

"Do you like it, Meredith?" asked Maggie wistfully. *Her* opinion of Mosswood had been long a fixed one.

"I have never seen such a place!"

"Uncle Eden had his tent up here one summer,

and he cut away all the branches and trees that were in the way of the view; for he wanted to lie in his tent at night and be able to look out and see the river and the hills in the moonlight."

"And did he have this wall built too?" asked Meredith, seeing that the platform where he stood was held up on the side towards the river by a regularly laid, though unmortared, wall.

"Oh," said Esther laughing, "that wall was laid a hundred years ago, Meredith. Soldiers laid it; our soldiers; all Mosswood was fortified; this is a breastwork."

"Whom do you mean by 'our soldiers?'"

"Why, the Americans," said Esther. "When they were fighting that war, a hundred years ago. You'll find bits of breastwork all over Mosswood."

"Well, that is delightful," said Meredith. "We are historical. Now, what are we to do first? I move, we make our camp just here. We cannot have a better place."

So there a rock under a tree, here a bit of mossy bank, was taken possession of; places were carpeted with shawls, and luxurious loungers were at rest upon them. Fairbairn set down the pail of water and departed; Flora got her worsted embroidery out of the cart, and Esther a strip of afghan which she was ambitiously making. Maggie nestled up to Meredith's side on the moss and laid her little hand in his, and for a little while they were all quiet: these last two enjoying October. But Meredith did not long sit still; he must go exploring, up and down and all round the South Pitch. Maggie followed him, as ready to go as he, and talking all the while. It was nothing but rocks and moss and trees and brambles and ferns; with the delicious river glittering below the rocks, and the glow of the hills coming to them through the trees, and golden hickory leaves falling at their feet, and now and then a chestnut burr or a hickory schale to be hammered open. Warm and tired at last they came back to their place. And then the girls declared it was time for dinner.

CHAPTER II.

A fire was the first thing. Meredith and Maggie gathered dry pine branches and dead leaves, and Meredith built a nice place for the kettle with some stones. Then they found they had no matches.

"We *always* forget something," cried Maggie. "Now I'll run home and fetch a box."

Meredith went too. It was only a little more walk. Then the fire was set agoing and the kettle filled and put over. Maggie sat by to keep up the flame, which being fed with light material needed constant supply. Meredith threw himself down on the mossy bank and opened his book. For a little while there was silence.

"What are you reading, Ditto?" Maggie asked at length. She kept as good watch of Meredith as of the fire.

"You would not understand if I told you. It is a German book."

"Is it very interesting?"

"Yes."

"I knew it was. I could see by your face; when

you pull your brows together in that way, I always know you are ever so much interested."

"Well, I am," said Meredith smiling

"Would it interest me?"

"I think, perhaps, it would."

"Ah, Ditto, don't you want to try? Read us some of it. What is it about?"

"It is a Mission Magazine."

"Missionary! O then we *shouldn't* like it," said Esther. "I don't believe we should."

"And in it are stories," Meredith continued.

"What sort of stories? about heathen?"

"I like stories about heathen," said Maggie.

"Stories about heathen and Christian, which a certain Pastor Harms used to tell to his people, and which he put in the magazine."

"Did he write the magazine?"

"Yes."

"Who was Pastor Harms?"

"A wonderful, beautiful man, who loved God with all his heart and served him with all his strength."

"Why there are a great many people, Ditto, who do that," said his sister.

"Most people that I have seen, keep a little of their strength for something else," remarked Meredith dryly.

"Was he a German?" Maggie asked.

"He was a German; and he was the minister of a poor country parish in Hanover; and the minister and the people together were so full of the love of Christ that they did what rich churches elsewhere don't do."

"And does that book tell what they did?"

"Partly; what they did, and what other people have done."

"*I* should like to hear some of it," was Maggie's conclusion.

"Well, you shall. We'll try, after dinner. Flora and Esther may shut their ears, if they will."

"If you won't read something else," said Flora, "I suppose I would rather hear that than nothing. I can get on with my work better."

"And worsted work is the chief end of woman, everybody knows," remarked her brother. "The kettle is boiling, Maggie!"

All was lively activity at once. Even the afghan and the worsted embroidery were laid on the moss, and the two elder girls bestirred themselves to get out the plates and dishes from the baskets and arrange them; while Maggie made the tea, and Meredith set about his omelet. Maggie watched him with intense satisfaction, as he broke and beat his eggs and put them over the fire; watched till the cookery was accomplished and the omelet was turned out hot and brown and savoury. The girls declared it was the best thing they had ever tasted, and Flora thought the tea was the best tea, and Meredith that the bread and butter was the best bread and butter. Maggie privately thought it was the best dinner altogether that ever she had eaten in the woods; but I think she judged most by the company. It was a long dinner! Why should they use haste? The October sun was not hot; the sweet air gave an appetite; the thousand things they had to talk about gave zest to the food. They were not in a hurry with their tea, and they lingered over their apple pie.

When at last they were of a mind to seek a change of diversion, and really the dinner was done; for talk as much as you will you yet must stop eating some time; the plates and remnants were quickly put back in the baskets and set again in the cart; tea-kettle and napkins cleared away; and the mossy dining-room looked as if no company had been there.

"This is first-rate, exclaimed Meredith, stretching himself on the warm moss.

"And now, Ditto, you are going to read to us."

"Am I?"

"Yes, for you said so."

"An honourable man always keeps his promises," said Meredith. But he lay still.

The two elder girls got out their work again. Maggie sat by and silently stroked the hair on Meredith's temples.

"This is good enough, without reading," he presently went on. "The moss is spicy, the sky is blue, I see it through a lace-work of pine needles; the air is like satin. I cannot imagine anything much better than to lie here and look up."

"But you can feel the air and see the sky,

and smell the moss too, while you are reading, Ditto."

"Can I? Well! your ten fingers are so many persuaders that I cannot withstand. Let's go in for Pastor Harms!"

So he raised himself on one elbow, no further, and laid his book open on the moss before him.

"But it is in German!" cried Maggie, looking over to see.

"Never mind, I will give it to you in English, I told you it was German."

"What is the first story about?"

"You will find that out as I go on. Now you understand it is Pastor Harms who is speaking, only he was a famous hand at story-telling, and to hear him would have been quite a different thing from hearing me." And Meredith began to read.

"'I will go back now a thousand years, and tell you a mission story that I am very fond of. I found it partly in the parish archives of Hermannsburg, and partly in some old Lüneburg chronicles. I say I am very fond of it; for after the fact that I am a Christian, comes the fact that I am a Lüneburger, body and soul; and there is not a country in the whole world, for me, that is better than the Lüneburg heath—'"

"O stop, Ditto, please; cried Maggie, "What is a 'heath'? and where is Lüneburg?"

"Ah! there we come with our questions. Lüneburg heath isn't like anything in America, that I know, Maggie. It is a strange place. There you'll see acres and miles of level land covered with heather, which turns purple and beautiful in the latter part of the season; but in the midst of this level country you come suddenly here and there to a lovely little valley with houses and grain-fields and fruit and running water; or to a piece of woods; or to a hill with a farm-house perched up on its side, and as much land cultivated as the peasant can manage. So the people of the parishes are scattered about over a wide tract, except where the villages happen to be. And for *where* it is—Lüneburg is in Hanover, and Hanover is in Germany. You must look on the map when you go home. Now I will go on—

" 'And next to the fact that I am a Lüneburger, comes the fact that I am a Hermannsburger; and for me Hermannsburg is the dearest and prettiest village on the heath. My mission story touches this very beloved Hermannsburg. From my youth up I have been a sort of a bookworm; and whenever I could find something about Germany, still more something about the Lüneburg heath, and yet more any thing about Hermannsburg, then I was delighted. Even as a boy, when I could just understand the book of the Roman writer Tacitus about old Germany, I knew no greater pleasure than with my Tacitus in my pocket to wander through the heaths and moors and woodlands, and then in the still solitude to sit down under a pine tree or an oak and read the account of the manners and customs of our old heathen forefathers.

And then I read, how our old forefathers were so brave and strong that merely their tall forms and their fiery blue eyes struck terror into the Romans; and that they were so unshakably true to their word, once it was given, that a simple promise from one of them was worth more than the strongest oath from a Roman. I read how they were so chaste and modest that breaking of the marriage vow was almost an unknown crime; so noble and hospitable, that even a deadly enemy, if he came to one of their houses, found himself in perfect security, and might stay until the last morsel had been shared with him; and then his host would go with him to the next house to prepare him a reception there.

"'But my heart bled too, when I read of their crimes and misdeeds, their inhuman worship of idols, when even human beings were slaughtered on bloody altars of stone, or drowned in deep, hidden, inland lakes; when I read how insatiable the thirst for war and plunder among our forefathers was, how fearful their anger, how brutish their rage for drink and play; and when I read further, how the whole of heathen Germany was an almost unbroken wood and moorland, without cities or villages, where men ran about in the forests almost naked, at the most clothed with the skin of a beast, like wild animals themselves; and got their living only by the chase, or from wild roots, with acorns and beechmast; then even as a boy I marvelled at the wonderful workings of Christianity. Only one thing I could not understand; how there should be nowadays in Christian Germany so much lying, unfaithfulness, and marriage-breaking, while our heathenish ancestors were such true, honest, chaste, and loyal men; it always seemed to me as if a German Christian must stand abashed before his heathen forefathers. And when I observed further, how many Germans nowadays are cowardly-hearted, while among our heathen ancestors such a reproach was reckoned the fearfullest of insults, it was past my comprehension how a Christian German, who believes in everlasting life, can be a coward, and his heathenish ancestors who yet knew nothing about the blessed heaven, have been so valiant and brave.'"

"Ditto," said Maggie, interrupting him, "do you think that is all true?"

"Pastor Harms would not have lied to save his right hand."

"And—but—Ditto, do you think people in America are so bad as that?"

Meredith smiled and hesitated.

"Yes, Ditto," said Flora; "you know they are not."

"I don't know anything about it," said Meredith. "There are not any better soldiers I suppose, in the world, than the Germans, nor anywhere such a band of army officers, for knowledge of their business and ability to do it. But there are some cowards in every nation, I reckon; and as there, so here. But among those old Saxons, it appears, there were none. As to truth"—Meredith hesitated—"There are not a great many people I know whose word I would take through and through, if they were pinched."

There was a chorus of exclamations and reproaches.

"And as to marriage-breaking," he went on, "it is not at all an uncommon thing here for people to separate from their wives or their husbands, or get themselves divorced."

"Why do they do that, Ditto?" Maggie asked.

"Because they are not true, and do not love each other."

"So you make it out that the heathen are better than the Christians!" said Esther.

"I do not make out anything. I am only stating facts. What is called a 'Christian nation,' has but comparatively a few Christians in it, you must please to remember. But I do think those old Saxons were extraordinary people. I like to think that I am descended from them."

"You, Ditto!" exclaimed Maggie in the utmost astonishment.

"Why yes, certainly. Don't you know so much history as that? Don't you remember that the Saxons went over and conquered England, and England was peopled by them, and ruled by them. until the Norman invasion?"

"Oh!" said Maggie with a long-drawn note of surprise and intelligence. "But I didn't know those Saxons were like these."

"No, nor did I. It interests me very much. Shall I go on with Pastor Harms?

"'The older I grew, the more eager I was to learn about Germany, and especially about my dear Lüneburg country, with its most beautiful heaths, moors, and woodlands. I can not express the joy I took in the great fights and battles which the German Prince Herman fought with the mighty Romans. Herman was prince of the Cheruski; so the dwellers between the Elbe and the Weser at that time were called. In his time the never-satisfied Romans were bent upon subjugating all Germany, and sent their most powerful armies into the country, clad in iron mail, armed with helmets, bucklers, lances, and swords, and led by their bravest generals. But Herman, with his almost naked Germans, fell upon them, fighting whole days at a stretch, and beat them out of the land. See now, thought I to myself, there were Lüneburg people along with him, for *they* live between the Elbe and the Weser. Or when others of our forefathers, who were in general called Saxons, boldly sailed over the sea in their ships, and chased the proud Romans, together with the Picts and Scots, out of England, and took the beautiful land in possession and ruled it; then I was glad again and thought with secret delight — "our Lüneburg people were there too, for those ships sailed from the mouths of the Elbe and the Weser."

"'But what adoration moved my heart, when I

read that these very Saxons, who conquered England, there came to the knowledge of Christianity and received it into their hearts; and now from England, from the converted Saxons, came numbers of Gospel messengers back to the German country, to turn it also to the Lord Jesus. Among them was Winfried, the strong in faith, who baptized more than 300,000 Germans, and was called the apostle of Germany; there were the two brothers Ewald, who both heroically died a martyr's death, being sacrificed by our forefathers to their idols. After them others carried on the work, especially Willehad and Liudgar, and the good emperor Charles the Great helped them, until at last all Germany was Christianized, and became through the Gospel what it is now. And I have often thought, how stupid are the unbelievers who follow the new fashion of despising Christianity. We have to thank Christianity for everything we are or have. Science, art, agriculture, handicrafts, cities, villages, houses, all have come to us in the first place through Christianity; for before that, as I said, our forefathers ran about naked in the woods like wild beasts, and fed on roots and acorns; and I used to think the best thing would be, to drive the infidels and the scornful contemners of Christianity into the woods and forests, draw a hedge about them, and let them eat acorns and roots in the woods till they come to their senses. In young people's heads a great many queer fancies spring up, which yet are not entirely un-

worthy of regard; and I still believe that would
be the best medicine for infidels.'"

"But Meredith," said Flora, "the Greeks and
Romans had cities and villages, and sciences too,
and arts, without Christianity."

"Quite true, but the Saxons didn't."

"Perhaps they would."

"Perhaps they wouldn't. The Greeks and Ro
mans were wonderful people, and so were the ancient Egyptians; but though they had arts, and
built cities, they had very little science. And science and Christianity have changed the face of the
Christian world. Well, let us have Pastor Harms.

"'But I must go back to my story. Whenever
I happened upon an old library, I searched it
through to see if I could find something about
Germany, and especially about Lüneburg. And I
do not regret the quantities of dust I have swallowed in my way; although I did often lament
aloud to see so many fine old manuscripts almost
eaten up with dust and mice, about which nobody
had troubled himself for who knows how many
years? But also I found many a one that repaid
the trouble of the search. From the sound MSS. I
made extracts diligently. But I had a good many
vexations, too. For example, I have come to cities
and villages, in which last there were baronial
manors. There I sought to come at the books
and MSS. of the olden time. And would one believe it? Old collections of books had been sold
entire, by the hamperful, to trades-people for wrap-

ping their cheese in. I was baffled. So much the
more precious became my extracts. From them I
will tell you something now, which I found about
my beloved Hermannsburg.

"'I may say in the first place to our dear country people, that the whole of northern Germany in
early times was called the country of the Saxons.
How wide that was, may best be seen by the language. So far as low German is spoken, so far
extends the land of the Saxons; for low German
is their proper mother-tongue. So I am never
ashamed of the low German in our country; it is
the true mother-tongue of our land and people;
my heart always swells when I hear low German
spoken. This entire Saxon nation was divided into
three tribes. One tribe, which dwelt for the most
part towards the west, that is, in the Osnabrück
region and further west as far as the Rhine, was
called the Westphalians. The second tribe, which
dwelt mostly at the east, as far as the Elbe and
further, was called the Eastphalians. Between the
two lived the third tribe, called the Enger or the
Angles; for Enger and Angle are all one. We
here in Lüneburg belong to the Eastphalians. The
name is said to have come from the bright or pale
yellow hair of our forefathers. For clear yellow or
pale yellow was called "fal." Our ancestors wore
this bright yellow hair long and hanging down,
something like a lion's mane; what so many young
people nowadays would esteem a splendid adorn-
ment. These forefathers of ours in the time of

Charlemagne were yet mere heathen and held to their heathen idol worship with extraordinary tenacity and devotion. They were further a wild, bold, stiff-necked people, with an unbending spirit, holding fast to everything old, and with that, loving freedom above all else. They had no rulers, properly speaking; each house-father was a despotic prince in his own house, and lived alone upon his territory, just that he might be free and rule his realm independently. Their common name, Saxon, came from a peculiar weapon, the sachs; a stone war-mallet or battle-axe, which was made fast to a longer or shorter wooden handle. In the strong hands of the Saxons this was a fearful weapon, with which they rushed fearlessly upon the foe, hastening to come to a hand-to-hand fight; for they liked to be at close quarters with their enemies.

"Wild and terrible as their other customs were, was also their idol worship. Their principal deity was called Woden, in whose honour men were slaughtered upon great blocks of stone; their throats being cut with stone knives. Not far off, some two or three hours from Hermannsburg, are still what are called the seven *stone-houses;* in other words blocks of granite set up in a square, upon which a great granite block lies like a cover. The men to be sacrificed were slain upon these blocks of granite. Quite near our village too, there stood formerly some such sacrificial altars. How fearful and bloody these sacrifices were, appears from what an old writer relates; that it was the custom of the Saxons, when they returned home from their warlike expeditions, to sacrifice to their idols every tenth man among the captives; the rest they shared among themselves for slaves. And upon special occasions, for instance, if they had suffered severe losses in the war, the whole of the captives would be consecrated to Woden and sacrificed.' That's the Woden we call one day of the week after."

"We? One day of the week!" exclaimed Maggie; while Flora looked up and said, "O yes! Wednesday."

"Wednesday?" repeated Maggie.

"Woden's-day," said Meredith.

"Is it Woden's-day! Wednesday? But how come we to call it so, Ditto?"

"Because our fathers did."

"But that is very strange. I don't think we ought to call it Woden's-day."

"The Germans do not call it so, who live at this time round those old stone altars; they say Mittwoche," or Mid-week. But the English Saxons seem to have kept up the title.

"Are those stone altars standing now, Ditto?"

"Some of them, Pastor Harms says; and what is very odd, it seems they call them stone *houses;* and don't you recollect Jacob called his stone that he set up at Bethel, 'God's house?'"

"Well, Ditto, go on please," said Maggie.

"You don't care for archæology. Well—'The German emperor Charlemagne, who reigned from

768 to 814, was a good Christian. He governed
the kingdom of the Franks; and that means the
whole of central and southern Germany, together
with France and Italy; and all these, his subjects,
had been already Christian a long time. On the
north his empire was bordered by our heathen ancestors, the Saxons, and they were the sworn foes
of Christianity. Whenever they could, they made
a rush upon Charlemagne's dominions, plundered
and killed, destroyed the churches and put to death
the Christian priests; and were never quiet. So
Charlemagne determined to make war upon the
Saxons, partly to protect his kingdom against their
inroads, and partly with the intent to convert them
with a strong hand to the Christian religion. Then
arose a fearful war of thirty-three years' length,
which by both sides was carried on with great bitterness. The Saxons had, in especial, two valiant,
heroic-hearted leaders, called "dukes" because they
led the armies. The word "duke" therefore means
the same as army-leader. The one of them in West-
phalia, was named Wittekind; the other in Eastphalia was named Albion, also called Alboin. Charlemagne was in a difficult position. If he beat the
Saxons, and thought, now they would surely keep
the peace, and he went off then to some more distant part of his great empire, immediately the Saxons broke loose again and the war began anew.
Charlemagne was made so bitter by this, that once
when he had beaten the Saxons at Verden on the
Aller and surrounded their army, he ordered 4,500

captive Saxons to be cut to pieces, hoping so to give a disheartening example. But just the contrary befel. Wittekind and Albion now gathered together an imposing army to avenge the cruel deed; and fought two bloody battles at Osnabrück and Detmold with such furious valour that they thrust Charlemagne back, and took 4,000 prisoners; and these prisoners, as a Lüneburg chronicle says, they slaughtered; part on the Blocksberg, part in the Osnabrück country, and part on the "stone-houses"; where the same chronicle relates that Wittekind, on his black war-horse, in furious joy, would have galloped over the bleeding corpses which lay around the stone-houses; but his horse shied from treading on the human bodies, and making a tremendous leap, struck his hoof so violently against one of the stone-houses that the mark of the hoof remained. Wittekind elsewhere in the chronicle is described as a noble, magnanimous hero; and this madness of war in him is explained on the ground of his hatred of Christians and revenge for the death of the Saxons at Verden.

"'At last, in the year 785, Wittekind and Albion were baptized and embraced the Christian religion. Thereupon came peace, among that part of the Saxons which held them in consideration, for the most distinguished men by degrees followed their example; and it was only in the other portions of the country that the war lasted until the year 805; when at last the whole country of the Saxons submitted to Charlemagne, renounced heathenism, and accepted Christianity. So hard did it go with our forefathers before they could become Christians. But once Christians, they became so zealous for the Christian faith that their land afterwards was called "good Saxony" as before it had been known as "wild Saxony." Charlemagne, however, was not merely at the pains to subdue the Saxons and to compel them into the Christian faith, but as a truly pious emperor he also took care that they should be instructed; and wherever he could he established bishoprics and churches. For example, the sees of Minden, Osnabrück, Verden, Bremen, Münster, Paderhorn, Halberstadt, and Hildesheim, all situated in the Saxon country, owe their origin to him. At all these places there were mission establishments, from which preachers went out into the whole land, to preach the Gospel to the heathen Saxons.

"'Among these Willehad and Liudgar were distinguished for their zeal. With untiring faithfulness, with steadfast faith, and great self-sacrifice, they laboured, and their works were greatly blessed of the Lord. Willehad finally became bishop in Bremen and Liudgar bishop of Münster. They may with justice be called the apostles of the Saxons. In a remarkable manner the conversion of our own parts hereabouts proceeded from the mission establishment in Minden. Liudgar had lived there a long while, and his piety and his ardour had infected the young monks assembled there with a live zeal for missions. One of these monks, who the chronicle tells came from Eastphalia, and had been converted to Christianity through Liudgar's means, was called Landolf. Now when Witte-kind and Albion had received holy baptism, and so a door was opened in the Saxon land to the messengers of salvation, Landolf could stand it no longer in Münden, but determined to go back to his native Eastphalia and carry the sweet Gospel to his beloved countrymen. He had no rest day nor night; the heathen Eastphalians were always standing before him and calling to him, "Come here and help us!"'"

"There!" said Meredith pausing, "that's how I feel."

Every one of the three heads around him was lifted up. "You, Ditto?" exclaimed Maggie, but the others only looked.

"Yes," said Meredith, "I feel just so."

"About whom?" said his sister abruptly.

"All the heathen. Nobody in particular. Everybody who doesn't know the Lord Jesus."

"You had better begin at home!" said Flora with an accent of scorn.

"I do," said her brother gravely; and Flora was silent, for she knew he did.

"But why, dear Ditto?" said Maggie, with a mixture of anxiety and curiosity.

"I am so sorry for them, Maggie." And watching, she could see that Meredith's downcast eyes were swimming. "Think; *they do not know Jesus;* and what is life worth without that?"

"But it isn't everybody's place to go preaching," said Flora after a minute.

"Can you prove it? I think it is."

"Mine, for instance, and Maggie's?"

"What is preaching, in the first place? It is just telling other people the truth you know yourself. But you must know it first. I don't think it is your place to tell what you do not know. But the Bible says, 'Let him that heareth say, come!' and I think we, who have heard, ought to say it. And I think," added Meredith slowly, "if anybody is as glad of it himself as he ought to be, he cannot help saying it. It will burn in his heart if he don't say it."

"But what do you want to do, Ditto?" Maggie asked again.

"I don't know, Maggie. Not preach in churches; I am not fit for that. But I want to tell all I can. People seem to me so miserable that do not know Christ. So miserable!"

"But, Ditto," said Maggie again, "you can give money to send missionaries."

"Pay somebody else to do my work?"

"You can tell people here at home."

"Well—" said Meredith with a long breath, "let us see what Landolf the Saxon did."

CHAPTER III.

"'What did this man do in the daring of faith? He first got permission of his superiors; then he went aboard of a little boat, took nothing else with him but his Bible and his prayer-book, his few tools, a fishing net, and food for several days, and then dropped down the Weser, all alone, intending by that way to get to the Eastphalians. But his chief strength was prayer, in which he lived day and night. When he came to the place where the Aller flows into the Weser, he quitted the Weser and went up the Aller, that he might look at the spot where those 4,500 Saxons were cut to pieces by Charlemagne, and on the ground pray for the murdered men. For at that time it was believed that even the dead could be helped by prayer, as is still the erroneous teaching of the Catholics. Leaving that place, he wished to visit the "stone-houses," that he might pray there too, where the captive Franks had been slaughtered by the Saxons; and so he went on up the Aller and from the Aller into the Oerze, all the while living upon the fish which he caught.'"

"Had he no bread?" said Maggie.

"How should he?—going through wild woods and countries alone in his boat? He would come to no baker's shops, Maggie."

"Just living on fish! Well, go on, Ditto."

"'But all along on this journey he had not only caught fish, but also everywhere preached the Gospel. And then must have been the first time that the sweet name of Jesus was ever heard in our region. Perhaps when you look at the map you will ask, why Landolf went this difficult way by water, which was a very roundabout way besides, to get to the "stone-houses," when he could have come across from Verden by a much nearer and straighter route? Our chronicle gives two reasons: first, the whole interior of the country at that time was almost nothing but thick forest and deep morasses, through which there was no going on foot; and secondly, he had been told in Verden, that if he wanted to visit the "stone-houses," he must first go to the Billing of the long-legged Horz-Saxons, who lived on the river Horz in Harm's "*ouden dorp*." Now this river Horz is the Oerze; and the name, the chronicle announces, comes from the fact that this river runs and leaps like a *Horz*—that is, a horse; and because a great many horses were pastured on its banks. For the chief wealth of our Saxon ancestors consisted in cattle, especially in horses, which they used not only for riding and in war expeditions, but reckoned their flesh a favourite food. And were a horse but entirely spotless

and white, it was even held to be sacred. Such
white horses were kept in the sacred forests of oak,
where they were used for nothing but soothsaying;
for by the neighing of these white horses the heathen priests prophesied whether a business, or a campaign, that was in hand, would turn out happily
or unhappily. For this reason also our Lüneburg
country since the earliest times has borne the free,
bounding horse in its escutcheon; and for the same
reason most of the houses in the country of Lüneburg down to the present times have their gables
adorned with two wooden horses' heads; and it is
only lately that this custom has somewhat fallen off.

"'The Saxons, or as the chronicle writes, *Sahzen*,
were called "Horzsahzen," either because they lived
on the Horz, or Oerze; or because they were almost
all of them horsemen and owned a great many
horses. They bore besides the honorary title of
the "long-legged," for our forefathers were distinguished by their unusual stature. It is remarkable,
that the name "Lange" is still the widest spread
family name of any in our region, so that there are
villages that are almost exclusively inhabited by
"Langen," among whom a goodly number might
yet be called "long-legged"; though many also
have grown something shorter, while they nevertheless bear the name of *Lange*. Well, that is all
one, so they only keep the old, tried faithfulness
and honesty, and the manly holding to their word,
and the beautiful pureness of morals, for which our
forefathers were renowned.

"'But now, what sort of a man is the *Billing?* Our chronicle translates the word into Latin; *curatos legum*, that is, the "guardian of the laws." *Bill*, you see, in old low German or Saxon, was a "law" which had been confirmed by the whole assembly of the people; and the man who proposed these laws, and when they were confirmed had the charge of seeing that they were not transgressed, was called the *Billing*. The Billing of tho Horzsahzen was at this time a man named Harm; that is Hermann; and he lived in Harm's *ouden dorp*—or Hermann's old village. The spot whero this old village of Hermann stood, is now a cultivated field, about ten minutes away from the present Hermannsburg; and this field is still called at the present day, *up'n Ollendorp*, and lies right on the Oerze. To this place accordingly the brave Landolf repaired, and was received kindly and with the customary Saxon hospitality by Hermann the Billing.

"'Hermann's dwelling was a large cottage, surrounded with pens for cattle, especially for horses, which were pastured on the river meadows. There were no stables; the animals remained day and night under the open sky, and even in winter time had no shelter beyond that of the thick forest with which the land was covered. The pens themselves were merely enclosures without a roof. Landolf was entertained with roasted horse's flesh, which to the astonishment of his hosts he left untouched. For by the rules of the Christian Church at that time it was not permitted to eat horse-flesh; they reckoned it a heathen practice.

"'When Landolf had made his abode with the Billing for a while, he found out that his host was in fact the principal person in all that district of country, and as guardian of the laws enjoyed a patriarchal and wide-reaching consideration. He was indeed no *ediling* (or nobleman), only a *freiling*—a free man; but he possessed seven large manors; on which account later writers, as for instance Adam of Bremen, give the Billing family the name of *Siebenmeyer.*' (*Sieben* means seven, Maggie). 'The oldest son, who regularly bore the name of Hermann, was the family head; and after the death of his father the dignity of Billing descended to him. The younger brothers were settled in some of the other manors, remaining nevertheless always dependent upon the oldest.

"'Now Landolf preached the Gospel zealously to the family whose guest he was, and they listened to him with willing ears. But when he would have declared his message also to the Saxons who lived in their neighbourhood, Hermann explained to him that by law and usage he must not do that, until permission had first been given him by the regular assembly of the people. As the house-father he himself could indeed in his own family allow the proclamation of the Christian faith; but a public proclamation must have the decision of the people upon it; that is, of the assembly of all the free men. Landolf had arrived in the autumn; the stated gathering of the commons would not be till spring, and indeed not till May; in the meanwhile he must be contented. Hard as it was for Landolf to wait so long, for his heart was burning to convert the poor heathen to Christ, he yet knew the people and their customs too well to contend against them. So all winter he abode with Hermann. And a blessed winter that was. It was the habit of the family, when at evening a fire was kindled in the middle of the hut, that the whole household, men, women, and children, even the servants and maids, should assemble around it; the master of the house having the place of honour in the midst of them. The house-father then generally told stories about the heroic deeds of their forefathers; about the ancient laws and usages, the knowledge of which was handed down from father to son; and Landolf sat among them and listened with the rest; but soon got permission to tell on his part, of the wonderful things of the Christian faith. So then he profited by the long winter evenings to tell over the whole Bible story of the Old and New Testaments. And with such simplicity and with such joy of faith and confidence he told it, that the hearts of his hearers were stirred. In addition to that, he often sang the songs of the Christian Church, in a clear, fine-toned voice; and presently some among them, the younger especially, began to join in the singing. His Bible stories were in all their mouths; and the people had such capital memories that, he says himself, he needed usually to tell a thing but once or twice, and all of them, even the children, could repeat it almost word for word. This is a common experience among people who have no written literature; they are apt to be uncommonly strong in power of memory. And when he prayed too, and he did it daily upon his knees, he was never disturbed, although he prayed in the cottage, which had only one room for all; instead, he soon had the joy of seeing that many kneeled down with him and with him called upon Christ, "the God of the Christians," as they phrased it. So the winter passed, May came, ice and snow melted away, and everybody got ready to attend the great assembly of the people. It was to be held at the stone-houses. Landolf travelled thither as Hermann's guest, under his protection; Hermann even letting him ride his best horse, by way of doing him honour before all the people. With a noble train of *freilings*—that is, of free men— they set forth.

" 'The first day, however, they went no further than about a quarter of an hour from Harm's *ouden dorp*, to a sacrificial altar which was placed close by what was called the Deep Moor (Deepenbroock, the chronicle says). There Landolf was to be spectator of a terrible scene, which shews as well the frightful savageness and cruelty of the Saxons as their noble purity of manners. By about noon of the above-named day, all the free men of that whole region had gathered together at the altar of sacrifice. This altar consisted, as may still be seen by the so-called *stone-houses* now standing, of four slabs of granite set up in a quadrangle; with four openings, or doors, towards the four quarters of the heaven, broad enough to let a man go through; and covered over on the top with another great, granite block. The young warriors brought up two prisoners, who had been taken in a late campaign and fetched along. One of them was made to go under the sacrifice altar through the north and south doors, the other through the east and west doors. Then stepped forth two priests, having their long, flowing hair bound with a mistletoe branch, and a sharp knife of flint in the hand. You must know that the mistletoe, which is still to be found in plenty in our woods, growing especially on birch trees, was held among our forefathers to be sacred. For since it does not grow upon the ground like other plants, but upon trees, birches particularly, it was believed that the seed of this plant fell down from heaven; and this belief was strengthened by the remarkable manner of its growth, so unlike other plants, with its forking opposite branches and shining white berries. After solemn prayers, which were half sung, half said, to the two gods Woden and Thor, and the two goddesses Hela and Hertha, the captive men were one after the other laid each upon his back on the altar, so that his head hung down over the edge of the altar.'"

"O stop, Ditto!" cried Maggie.

"Why?"

"It is too horrible."

"It is pretty horrible. But men did it, and men suffered it. Can't you hear it?"

"Men were dreadful!"

"Men *are* dreadful, where the light of the Gospel has not come. 'The dark places of the earth are full of the habitations of cruelty.'"

"Tell me about those gods and goddesses."

"Were those Saxon Druids?" Flora asked.

"It sounds so. But I don't know the gods of the Teutons as well as I do those of the Greeks; I can't tell you much about Woden and Thor, Maggie. We'll look when we go home. Now am I to go on?"

"I suppose so. O yes, I want you to go on. But it is dreadful."

"Well, the captives were laid on the altar, as I read, 'and the priests cut their throats with their knives of flint. When the quivering victim had ceased to bleed, the body was taken up by the young warriors and cast into the Deep Moor, where it immediately sunk in the bog. Landolf had not recovered from the shock—for he had never seen a human sacrifice before, having gone while yet a boy into the country of the Christians—when his attention was fettered by another dreadful drama.

"'Some of the young men fetched a long and broad hurdle woven of fir branches; laid it down before the altar, and went away; but came back again presently with a man and a woman, who had been accused and convicted of breaking the marriage vow. An accuser stepped forth, and repeated the charge before the Billing. The Billing then asked the accused whether the charge was true; and admonished them to confess the truth, since never yet had a free Saxon told a lie. And when the guilty people had owned their guilt, first their relations came forward and spat in their faces; then the man's weapons were taken from him, his hands and feet and the woman's were tied together: and so tied they were thrown into the Deep Moor, the hurdle covered over them, and this and the underlying bodies, by their nearest relations first of all, were trodden down into the deep morass. So came the marriage-breakers to a shameful end and received the reward of their sin.

"'Herman told Landolf afterwards that there were three crimes which they punished on this disgraceful wise—marriage-breaking, lying, and cowardice; because such people were not held worthy to die the honourable death of a warrior, and be slain with weapons. Landolf answered, "O Billing, you are terrible people! yet even as heathen you hate the sins that you know. What would you be, if you were once Christians, and the Lord Jesus gave you His light!"

"'And as I write down these words from the old chronicle, I could cast my eyes to the ground for shame and weep tears of blood over the deep, shameful apostasy of the German Christianity of the present day. Christ gives us his light now; we are Christians now; but where have purity, truth, and courage hid themselves? Are there ten in a hundred German Christians that keep a pure life, true lips, and a brave heart? I do not think it. Open and secret impurity, coarse and polished falsehood, disgraceful cowardliness, fear of men and men-pleasing, have infested the whole German Christian nation, and will soon bring down the judgment of God; for "the bruise is incurable, and the wound is grievous." Great and small, men and women, old and young, all are tainted with the plague. Our heathen forefathers were better and cleaner in these things than we Christians; they will condemn us at the last judgment; and we shall have to stand abashed before them. And you that read this, if you prize the name of a German; if, as you should, you prize a thousand times more the name of a Christian; ask your conscience whether it has not been uneasy under the foregoing narration; and if it has, then repent, you degenerate German, you hypocritical Christian; repent in sackcloth and ashes; and on your knees implore your God, the living Saviour: "Jesus my Lord, thou holy God, give me a pure nature, a lip of faithfulness, and a bold heart, through the faith that is in Thee."

" 'And now I must go on to tell what more befell that same day, in which the devilish nature of heathenism among our forefathers was shewn as frightfully as in their murderous sacrifices. Far behindhand as our ancestors at that time were in all civilization, they nevertheless already understood the art of preparing intoxicating drinks. For this purpose they used especially the wild oats which grew all over, and the darnel grass; of which a strong, intoxicating beer was brewed; and to make it yet more stupefying they added a certain marsh plant. And scarce ever was there a sacrifice that was not concluded with a drinking-bout. So it fell out at this time. Many writers tell, how among the old Germans it was even made a boast to spend eight or even fourteen days, one after another, in such carousals. On the occasion of which we are speaking, indeed, they lasted only over the rest of that day and through the night; for tho next day the intent was to go on to the stone-houses. But what horror must Landolf have felt even in that short time! When all of them had got drunk, a quarrel sprang up; and as each man had his weapons with him, his war-axe especially, the quarrel came to duels between man and man; and soon blood was flowing from most of the people, and several corpses lay here and there. The bodies were burned, their ashes buried, and a round hillock of earth thrown up over them; for, as it was thought, they had fallen in honourable fight, as it became men to do. And when Landolf full of astonishment asked the Billing, who of all the crowd was the only one that had remained sober, whether they did not then punish people for murder? the Billing in wonder retorted by the question, where the murderers were? There had been nothing but an open, honest fight, which was to the honour of those concerned in it.

"'Yet another abomination Landolf saw on this occasion; which, however, was in a remarkable manner mixed up with truth and noblemindedness. I mean, that while this drinking-bout was going on, a number of men, young and old, amused themselves with gaming, of which they were passionately fond. To be sure they had no cards, neither dice. But they had little longish, square-cornered, wooden sticks, shaved white, and with certain marks painted on the upper side. Each man took a certain number of these in both hands, shook them, and threw them up in the air. When they fell on the ground, they were carefully looked at to see how many of them lay with the painted side up, and how many with the unpainted; and whoever then had the most sticks with the painted side up, he had won. Upon each throw they set some of their cattle, a hog, a cow or an ox, or a horse; perhaps at last a specially prized drinking vessel, made out of a ure-ox horn; even finally what they held to be most valuable of all, their weapons; and at last Landolf saw a young man, who had lost all he had, cast his freedom upon the last throw; and when this too was lost, he saw how frankly and without grumbling he gave himself up to be the slave of his fellow-player; so fast the German, even amid the bewilderments of sin, held to truth and the inviolable keeping of his word once given. Liberty was truly his most valnable and precious possession, for which at any other time he was ready to die, arms in hand. And yet he yielded this treasure quietly up, when he had lost it at play, rather than break his word and his faith; if he were the stronger, he did not defend himself; he did not take to flight, though he might have a hundred opportunities; the free man who gloried in his freedom, became a slave, that he might keep faith. This was how Landolf found things among the heathen; he wept bitter tears over it; but he never desponded: so much the firmer grew his resolution to preach the Gospel to this people and make the true God known to them. For the thought always rose in him, what might come of a people whom God had so nobly endowed, among whom even in the abominations of idolatry there shone forth such traits of pureness of manners and nobleness of thought, were they but once renewed and born again by the glorious Christian faith.

" 'But if Landolf were to come to light again in these days, when we *are* Christians, what would he say of us? Outward culture truly he would find; the face of the earth would indeed have changed. But if he came into the inns, where drinking and gaming are going on; into the so-called *Maybeers;* into the assemblies for eating and drinking and playing at weddings and housewarmings and christenings; or into the private drinking and gaming parties in people's houses; the gaming hells at the watering-places; the drinking carousals of students; the companies of the noble; the so-called entertainments with which everything must be celebrated in Germany—how confounded would he be, to find that the drinking and gaming devil is still the ruling devil in Germany! but on the other hand, faith and truth are extinguished. It is true, what the old song says—"most are Christians only in name. God's true seed are thinly scattered, those who love and honour Christ and do His pleasure!" Well, God mend it.'"

Meredith shut up his book.

"Ditto," said Maggie thoughtfully, "is it so bad here?"

"How do I know, Maggie?"

"But what do you *think*?"

Flora lifted up her head. "Now, Meredith, don't go and say something absurd."

"What do you want me to say?"

"Why the truth! that there are a great many nice people in America."

"I have no doubt, so there are in Germany."

"Then that talk is all stuff."

"Pastor Harms never talked stuff."

"How do you know?"

"I have read enough of him to know. He was one of those he calls God's true seed."

"Then what did he mean? Or what do you mean?"

"Well, Flora, I will ask you a question: How many people do you know, who live to do Christ's will?"

Flora did not answer immediately. Maggie on her part went to calculating.

"I know—I know—three!" she said slowly.

"*Three!*" said Flora. "Who are they?"

"That's not the question, Flo," said her brother. "How many do *you* know?"

"Well," said Flora, "Mr. Murray is one; and you are another, I believe; but there are other nice people in the world."

"I know people drink," said Maggie, so gravely and sagely that the others laughed. "I do know. I have seen them at our house. You needn't say anything, Esther; I have, once or twice when I have been at dinner, when you were not at home. Not papa, of course; and they don't do it now; papa won't have wine on the table at all; but I saw how they did. Some of the gentlemen began with whiskey and water, and one took brandy and water, before dinner began."

"O stop, Maggie!" Esther exclaimed.

"No, but I want to tell you. Then they took Greek wine or Sauterne with their soup. Then they took champagne with the dinner. Then they had port wine with the cheese—O I recollect, Esther—and then they had Madeira and sherry with dessert, and claret and Madeira and sherry with the fruit. And some of them drank every one. I am glad papa won't have wine at all now. Uncle Eden wouldn't, a good while ago."

"People used in England, not very long ago, to drink a bottle or two of wine after dinner each

man," said Meredith; "but it is not quite so bad
as that nowadays."

Flora was vexed, but silent; she too remembered
bowls of punch and baskets of champagne in *her*
father's time.

"And gaming—" said Maggie, and stopped.

"What?" said Meredith.

"I was thinking how fond Fenton was of it."

"O hush, Maggie! he wasn't!" Esther exclaimed.

"It was just the same thing, Uncle Eden said."

"Where is Fenton?" said Meredith.

"He's coming to-morrow. He likes champagne
too, and other wine when he can get it. And Bolivar—Bolivar put something in his lemonade!"

"Why, Maggie," said Meredith smiling and passing his hand gently over the little girl's head, "you
are taking gloomy views of life!"

"I was only thinking, Ditto. But it seems to
me so very strange that people should be worse
now than when they were heathen Saxons."

"People are a mixture now, you must remember.
The good part are a great deal better; and I suppose the bad part are a great deal worse."

"Worse than the heathen!" cried Flora.

"Well judge for yourself. But darkness in the
midst of light is always the blackest, and not only
by contrast either."

"If you think people are so awful, I should
think you would go to work and preach to them,"
said Esther.

"I will," said Meredith calmly.

"Then what will you do with Meadow Park?"

"O he proposes to turn that into a hospital."

"A hospital!—"

"Flora is romancing a little," said her brother. "There are no infirmaries put up yet. How sweet this place is! Do you smell the fir trees and pines? The air is a spice-box."

"The air a box!" cried Maggie laughing.

"I mean it is full of perfumes, like a spice-box. And these old stones, laid up here by the soldiers' hands of a hundred years ago, just make a dining place for us now. But it's pretty! And the air is nectar."

"You can choose whether you will smell it, or swallow it," remarked his sister.

"By your leave I will do both. Well, shall I go on?"

CHAPTER IV.

"'The morning after the sacrificial feast at the Deep Moor, Landolf with the Billing and the free men travelled on to the May diet which was to be held at the seven stone-houses, and before noon came to the place. There were an enormous crowd of free men assembled; priests, nobles, and commons. The place lies in the middle of a vast, level heath, on the soft declivity of a rising ground, which on the other side falls away sharply down to a boggy dell. I have already described the stone-houses. There are seven of them; a number which must have been held sacred among the Saxons. At least in our country the so-called "Hühnen" graves in which our forefathers lie buried, are always found either alone, or constantly by sevens together in a wide circle. The spot on which the stone-houses stand must have been sacred to Woden; for in the chronicle it is called "Wuotanswohrt," and *wohrt* in Saxon always means a secluded, enclosed, sacred place, especially devoted to the administration of justice; for courts of justice were held under the open sky and always by day; as though to denote that justice is of heavenly origin, courts the light of sunshine and shuns the darkness. The word *wohrt* is connected with *wehren'* (which means, to keep off, Maggie), 'because every thing unholy must be kept off from it, on which account also such places were hedged in. Of the transactions at this May diet it is only told, that a great sacrifice was offered, this time consisting of fourteen men, two of whom were slaughtered upon each of the stone-houses in the manner already described; that then cases of law were decided according to the ancient usage; then the state of things between the Saxons and the Franks was considered; and at this opportunity Landolf, who as guest of the Billing had been present at all the discussions, begged to be permitted to speak, and asked for leave to preach Christianity in the country. Scarcely had he preferred his request, when threatening and distrustful looks were directed upon him from almost all present, and many a hand grasped to the war-axe; for at the word *Christianity*, men's thoughts at once flew to the Franks, those hitherto enemies of the Saxons, by whom after three and thirty years of fighting they had at last been subdued. The Billing immediately observed the excitement, and before any of it could get open expression he himself was upon his feet. He related that Landolf was no Frank, but an Eastphalian, and so of their own people and race; that when a boy he had been taken prisoner by the Franks in the war and carried to the Franks' country, where he had been converted to Christianity and had been a pupil of the good Liudgar, who himself was a Saxon and known by report to all Saxons. That afterwards he had lived with this Liudgar in the country of their brethren the Westphalians; and half a year before this time had come to him quite alone and become his guest. And as his guest he would protect the man, since he had done nothing contrary to the customs and usages of the Saxon people. In his own home he had permitted him to preach Christianity; and now here, in the assembly of the people, according to ancient law and usage, Landolf desired to ask whether he might be allowed to proclaim openly in the country the Gospel of the God of the Christians. This must now be regularly debated in the assembly of the people; and he gave permission to Landolf that free and unmolested he might say out his wishes and tell exactly what the Christian belief was. Then every one might give his opinion.

"'Now Landolf rose up. His tall figure, his noble presence, and the fearless, frank, spirited glance of his eye round the circle, made a deep impression; and in noiseless silence the assembly listened to his speech, the first preaching that ever was held in our country. This short, simple discourse has so grown into my heart and I like it so much, that I shall give it here.' Flora, are you listening?"

"Of course."

"I didn't know but you were too busy counting

your stitches. I want you to hear this speech of Landolf's. It is very fine.

"'"In the name of God, the Father, the Son, and the Holy Ghost, the only true God. Amen. Men and brethren hear my words. One hundred years ago" (A. D. 960, according to the chronicle), "came two pious Christian priests to you, to make known to your fathers the Gospel of Christ, the true God; they were the dark and the fair Ewald. They were your own relations, they came from England; they were your friends, they had left England and come over the sea for the love of you; they were your guests, they had been sheltered in your houses. They wanted to let you know that God has become your Brother, that he might deliver you from your sins. You would not let them preach in your land; you were free not to do that; but you murdered them; here on these stones you slew them in honour of Woden; your brothers, your friends, your guests, you murdered, who had done you no evil. Since that time, the true God, the God of the Christians, has been angry with you. You number as many as the Franks do; you are just as brave as they. Yet Charlemagne, the Frank, has conquered and subdued you. How is that? God fought with Charlemagne; He loved him; he is a Christian. God fought against you, for you have killed his priests; you are murderers. You can kill me too. Do it; I am not afraid of death; I am the servant of God; if you kill me, God will take me up to heaven. God's anger will not depart from you, unless you become Christians. Why will you not become Christians? Your gods are good for nothing; they cannot help you; they have not been able to stand before the Christian's God. Where is your *Irmensul?* Charlemagne has broken it to pieces." (Irmensul was an idol image that stood at Hildesheim). "Where is your *Wodensaak?* Charlemagne has cut it down." (This Woden's oak stood at Verden on the Aller). "Where is your *Helawohrt?* Charlemagne has destroyed it." (The sacred place of the goddess Hela was on the Aller, in what is now the suburb Heelen at Celle). "Where are your brave leaders, Wittekind and Albion? They have become Charlemagne's friends and vassals; they are Christians. Do you think it was Charlemagne that subdued them? No, a greater One, the God of the Christians has subdued them. Charlemagne indeed often overthrew them; but the Christian's God has conquered them. Do you know how that came about? I have heard in Münster, and I will tell you.

""" After the last battle they lost—you know about that, your young men bled there too—before peace was concluded, the brave Wittekind said to his brother in arms, Albion, 'Come, let us go! we will pay a visit to Charlemagne in his fortress, and take a look at his power; for he is the greatest in the land.' So the bold heroes set forth; hiding their strong frames under the dress of beggars; for they wished to remain unknown, and to see and prove for themselves. Fear was not in their brave hearts. They travelled and travelled for days and days; and wherever they came, Christians gave them food. Then they questioned with one another—'Is *this* what Christians are?' They were many nights on their journeyings, and wherever they came the Christians took them in, although they were beggars. Then they asked one another, 'Is this what Christians are?' Many a time they lost their way, in cities, villages, and fields; the Christians set them right, and they said to each other in astonishment, 'Is *this* what the Christians are?' At last they came to Ingelheim." (The chronicle names Ingelheim, and not Aix-la-Chapelle.) "They went through the city, admiring the handsome houses and magnificent streets, till they came to a large house, the largest of all they had hitherto seen. 'This must be Charlemagne's dwelling,' said they; 'for certainly he is the greatest man among his people?' They went in; they heard singing, that sounded as if it came down from heaven. They went further in; there stood up in the chancel a man in a white dress (it was a priest in white church robes) who was speaking: 'Hear, you who believe the glad message; the great God in heaven loves you. He loves you so much that he sent his dear son Jesus Christ to you. Jesus Christ came down from heaven; God's son became your brother, so little and poor that he lay in a manger in the stall for cattle. When he was grown up, he preached everywhere and said, Sinners, turn, and I will save you. He made the lame to go and the blind to see, and healed the sick, and raised up the dead that lay in their graves. He shed his blood for sinners; sinners put him to death. He was still kind to them in his death, and prayed for his murderers, Father forgive them! for they know not what they do. They buried him. But can God stay in the grave? Lo! after three days the earth quaked and the rocks rent; Jesus rose up out of the grave, Jesus went up to heaven, and sits now again upon the throne of his Father, God. He reigns; he commands: Repent and I will save you, you shall come into my heaven and reign with me.'

" ' "So preached the priest. There stood the two heroes in astonishment, but they were to be yet more astonished. Lo! a tall man steps forward through the church up to the altar, where the priest was standing; and a crown was upon his head. It was the King Charlemagne. The two heroes knew him, and yet they did not know him. Was this the mighty hero, whose flashing sword in battle struck and slew? Was this the man whose eyes blazed with the fire of battle? He wears no sword here; his eyes sparkle peacefully; as he stands before the altar, he humbly takes his crown off and sets it on the ground; then he bows his knee upon the steps of the altar and prays to Jesus Christ, the God of the Christians; and all the people fall upon their knees, and the heavenly music of them who are singing praises swells out again—'Glory to God in the highest; and on earth peace, good-will to men.' Then Charlemagne rises and sits down in a chair, and the man in white clothing preaches of Jesus, who came to save sinners; and Charlemagne bows his high head so often as the name of Jesus is named. Then the priest blesses the congregation; the service is over.

"'"It was not Charlemagne's house, in which they were; it was God's house, in which Charlemagne had been praying. God is greater than Charlemagne, and so must God's house be the biggest in the city. The brothers in arms went forth of the church. Before the church door there was a great crowd of beggars, in garments like their own. Gentle and kind, Charlemagne goes to the poor people, giving each one a piece of money and saying, 'God bless it to you, my children; pray for me too.' 'Is that King Charlemagne?' the heroes asked each other by their astonished looks. Then the king steps up to them, looks at them graciously, and says—'You have never been here before, my friends; come into my house, and I will give you your portion.' He goes on and they follow him. They come into his house, which was smaller than God's house. They go into his apartment; there he dismisses the attendants, goes up to Wittekind and Albion, offers them his hand like a brother and says: 'Welcome to my citadel, you brave Saxon heroes! God has heard my prayer; my foes are becoming my friends. Put off your rags. I will dress you as princes should be dressed!' And he had princely robes put upon them, and said further—'Now you are my guests;

and soon I hope, the guests of the Lord my God also.' The two heroes had not expected this, that Charlemagne should know them in their disguise; much less, that he would treat them so nobly, and brotherly. Fourteen days later, the priest in white garments baptized them in the name of God the Father, the Son, and the Holy Ghost; and they swore allegiance to the Saviour, Jesus Christ.

"'"You men, this is the way that your heroes have led the way for you. Saxons, will you forsake your dukes? The curse of sin has been cleared away from them. Now I have come to you; I too am a priest of Jesus Christ; I would gladly teach you and clear the curse of sin away from you, that you may be saved and come to heaven. Say, shall I preach among you? or will you kill me too, as you killed the two Ewalds? Here I am; but in the midst of you I am also in God's hand."

"'Landolf ceased. The whole assembly had heard him in silence; even the heathen priests had listened. Then the Billing lifted up his voice and spoke: "Landolf, my guest and friend, thou hast spoken well, and thou hast been a good man in my house; I will hear thee further. Brothers, let us decide that Landolf shall be free to go about in our country and preach. It is no dishonour to bow the knee before that God who is Charlemagne's God and the God of the Christians; it is no shame to pray to that God who has conquered our brave heroes. Decide!"

"'Then stepped forth an old man with white

hair, who was the oldest man in the assembly, and spoke: "Cast the lot!"

"'The young men made ready seven little sticks, square-cornered, of oak wood, marked on the upper side with sacred signs. One of the heathen priests, the chronicle calls him Walo, shook them in his hands and then threw them up in the air. During this time, Landolf was upon his knees, crying, "Lord, Lord, give the victory, that this noble people may come to know thee!" Then the sticks fall to earth, and behold! six of them lie with the signs up, and only one with the signs down. This is announced, and then the whole assembly cries out—"The Christian's God has won!" and the Billing shakes Landolf by the hand and says, "Now go in and out through the whole land; nobody will hinder you from preaching the name of your God. But do not pass my house by; come back with me; I will become a Christian." And now the assembly broke up; everybody went home to his house, Landolf accompanying the Billing. When they were again passing the stone of sacrifice at the Deep Moor, Landolf said—"Billing, that is your altar-stone; is it not?" "It belongs to me and my house." "There my first church shall stand," said Landolf glad and strong in faith. "May I build it?" "Build it my brother," answered the Billing; "and when it is ready I will be the first to be baptized in it. But the stone of sacrifice we will throw into the moor, that the remembrance of it may be lost."

"'Now did Landolf go to work joyfully; by day he wrought, and at night he preached, and taught in the Billing's house, and in all the country round. No longer than three months after, the little wooden church was done; the first in this whole region; and the same day that Landolf consecrated it, Harm the Billing with five sons and three daughters, and the greater part of the friends of his family and of his farm servants received holy baptism, the water for which was fetched out of the neighbouring Oerze. Now, of course, that church is no longer standing; it was burnt down afterwards by the heathen Wends, and in its place the large stone church in Hermannsburg was built. But to this day the field where that first church stood belongs to the Hermannsburg parsonage, and is still called *the cold church*.

"'This was the foundation of the Christian church in our valley of the Oerze; and as Landolf had come from Minden, the whole Oerze valley was attached to the see of Minden, while the rest of the Lüneburg country came to belong to the see of Verden.

"'Now the faithful Landolf laboured on indefatigably. He sent one of his new converts to Minden and Münster, to get more helpers from thence for his work. Twelve came, who were put under Landolf; and now for the first time the work could be taken hold of vigorously. Landolf must have lived and laboured until 830 or 840, and so blessed was his agency that the whole country of the Horzsahzen was converted to Christianity. It is brought forward as a proof of this, that at the great May diets held at the stone-houses the following laws were unanimously enacted; no more horse's flesh to be eaten; no more human sacrifices to be brought; no more dead to be burned; and all Woden's oaks to be hewn down. And in truth these laws do shew the dominance of Christianity, for precisely these things named were the peculiar marks of heathenism. Of the interior condition of Christianity, little is told; only it is remarked that the entire change in the country was so great and manifest, that the bishops Willerich of Bremen, and Helingud of Verden sent priests to convince themselves with their own eyes whether what they had heard with their ears was true; and these messengers had found not a single heathen left in the whole region. As a good general, Landolf moreover understood how everywhere to seize the right points where with the most effect heathen-ism might be grappled with and overthrown. He always went straight to the heart of the old relig-ion. We have already seen how his first church was built by the Billing's sacrifice stone. West-ward from Hermannsburg is what is called the Winkelberg, upon which was the burying-place of the heathen priests, for the most part cultivated land now, but the twice seven so-called Hühnen graves are still to be seen there. At the foot of this hill he established what was called the *Pfarr-wohrt*, where the spiritual courts should be holden;

and close by this place he laid the foundation stone of the Quänenburg, a house surrounded with a moat, in which the young girls of the country might be taught and educated (Quäne or Kwäne meant a young girl). Both places, Pfarrwohrt and Quänenburg, are arable fields now, still belonging to the parsonage.

"'An hour above Hermannsburg the two rivers Oerze and Wieze flow into each other. At that place, in an oak wood, the idol Thor was worshipped. There Landolf was equally prompt to build a chapel, that the idol worship might be banished. As he had consecrated the church in Hermannsburg to Peter and Paul, so he consecrated this chapel to Lawrence. Around this chapel the village Müden sprang up, so called because the two rivers there flow into one another, or münden. Then he went further up the Oerze and erected a cloister and a chapel at a place which was sacred to the goddess Freija. At that time a cloister was called a munster. The village of Munster grew up around this cloister. In the same way he went further up the Wieze, where there was a wood sacred to Hertha. In its neighbourhood he built a chapel which was consecrated to Bartholomew. Around this chapel Wiezendorf arose. About an hour and a half distant from Hermannsburg, there was a very large, magnificent wood of oaks and beeches; such a forest was then called a wohld. In this forest the heathen priests, the so-called Druids, were specially at home; there too, they kept the white horses which were used in sooth-saying. The wood extended for hours in length and breadth. He could not give that the go-by; and that he might dash right into the midst of it, he built at the spot where it was narrowest a chapel on the one side to Mary *in valle*, and on the other side a chapel to Mary *in monte*. The first means Mary in the valley, the second, Mary on the hill. The villages Wohlde and Bergen have thence arisen. So he grappled with heathenism just there where its strongest points were; and always, by God's grace, got the victory; for the Lord indeed says: "My glory will I not give to another, neither my praise to graven images." And as once the Philistine's idol Dagon fell speechless upon the ground before the ark of the covenant of God, so in our Oerze valley everywhere fell the altars of the idols before the sign of the Cross.

"'Besides all this, Landolf and his companions were skilled husbandmen; who themselves shunned no manual labour nor painstaking, and who knew right well how to eat their bread in the sweat of their brow. So they introduced agriculture univer-sally, of which our forefathers at that time knew little or nothing; and thus they were not only the spiritual but also the material benefactors of the whole district. How much a single man can do, who is wholly given to the Lord, and who is moved by burning love to the Lord and to his fellows! God give all preachers and teachers, and especially all messengers to the heathen, such a mind, such a brave heart, such a single eye, such will to work! that some good may be done.

"'About the next hundred years I have found nothing said in the chronicle. Probably things went on in such a quiet way that there was nothing particular to say concerning them. But then comes the relation of a noteworthy occurrence.'"

Meredith shut up his book.

"Well, aren't you going on?" said Maggie.

"Presently. I want to run down to the shore and see how the water looks."

"Why it always looks just the same way," said Esther.

"Does it? I am afraid something must be the matter with your eyes."

"O, of course sometimes it blows, and sometimes it is smooth; but what is that?"

"Just according to your eyes."

"Aren't all eyes alike?"

"Not exactly. Some see."

"What do you see in the water?"

"There is one peculiarity of eyes," said Meredith. "You cannot see through another person's. Come, Maggie, let us stretch ourselves a bit."

Taking hold of hands, the two ran and scrambled down the steep, rocky pitch of the hill, to the edge of the river. The wind was not blowing to-day; soft and still the water lay, with a mild gleam under the October sun, sending up not even a ripple to the shore. There was a warm, spicy smell in the woods; there was a golden glow here and there from a hickory; the hills were variegated and rich-hued in the distance and near by. Meredith sat down on a stone by the water and looked out on the view. But he was graver than Maggie liked.

"Ditto," she said after a while, "you are thinking of something."

"Of a good many things, Maggie. How good the world is! and men are not!"

"What then, Ditto?"

"One ought to do something to make them better."

"What can you do?"

"What could Landolf the Saxon? I do not know, Maggie; but one ought to be as ready as Landolf was, to do any thing. And I think I am."

"Then God will shew you what to do, Ditto."

Meredith bent down and kissed the earnest little face. "You are the only friend I have got, Maggie, that thinks and feels as I do."

"O Ditto! Uncle Eden?"

"Well, I suppose Mr. Murray would do me the honour to let me call him my friend," said Meredith.

"And papa?"

"Mr. Candlish is very good to me; but you see, I do not know him so well, Maggie."

"Well, he thinks just as you do. And papa goes and preaches in the streets when he is in New York; in those dreadful places where the people live that never go to church."

"*That's* like Landolf," said Meredith. "I almost envy men like that old monk."

"Why?"

"All his strength laid out for something worth while—all his life. And think how much he did! And I fret to be doing nothing, and yet I don't know what to do."

"You can ask Uncle Eden when he comes."

"I hope he'll come! Now don't think any more about it, Maggie. This is the prettiest place I ever saw in my life. I want to get out on that water."

"Now?"

"Not now. Some time."

"O we'll all go," said Maggie joyfully. "We might go in the boat somewhere and take our book and our dinner, and have a grand time, Ditto!"

Meredith laughed and said it was all "grand times"; and then he got up and strolled along by the water, picking up flat stones and making ducks and drakes on the smooth, river surface. This was a new pastime to Maggie, and so pleasant to both that they forgot the book, and the girls left on the height, and delighted their eye with the dimpling water and ricochetting stones time after time, and could not have enough. At last flat stones began to grow scarce, and Maggie and Meredith remounted to the rest of the party.

"Well!" said Flora, "you've come in good time. We are going home."

"Home!" echoed Maggie.

"To be sure. Don't you think we want dinner some time?" said Esther; "and we are tired sitting here. And it is growing late besides. Just look where the sun is."

There was nothing to be said to the sun; and the books and work being stowed again in the cart, Meredith took his place as porter and the little company returned to the house.

CHAPTER V.

A little tired and not a little hungry, it was very good now to have a change, and be at home. The girls went to dress for dinner; while Meredith, whose toilet was sooner made, sat on the terrace in the mellow October light and dreamed. Dinner went off merrily. After dinner, when it began to be dark, they all repaired to the library. A little fire was kindled here, for the pleasure of it rather than from the need. The afghan and worsted embroidery came out again under the bright lamplight; but Meredith sat idly tending the fire.

"Ditto," said Maggie, "can't we see about all those Saxon gods now?—or don't you want to?"

"Of course I want to see about them," said Meredith, springing up and and going to the bookcases. "I want to know myself, Maggie."

"Were they different from the Roman and Grecian gods?" Flora asked.

"It is safe for people who can not keep their ears open, to refrain from questions," Meredith answered.

"Why I heard all you read," said Flora, pouting

a little; "but how should I know but those were the same as the Roman gods, only under different names?"

"If you please to recollect, you will remember that the two nations had nothing to do with one another except at the spear's point. But if I can find what I want, I will enlighten you and myself too," said Meredith, rummaging among the book-shelves. "Here it is, I believe!" And with a volume in his hand he came back to the table and the lamp; but then became absorbed in study. Worsted needles flew in and out. Maggie watched Meredith's face and the leaves of his book as they were turned over.

"Well, Ditto?" she said after a while.

"What?"

"Yes, *what?*" said Maggie laughing. "Have you found any thing?"

"To be sure!" said Meredith straightening himself up. "Yes, Maggie, it's all here—in a somewhat brief fashion."

"Well, who was Woden?"

"Woden was the principal deity. He was the god of the moving air, and of the light."

"Like Apollo," said Flora.

"Yes—more like Zeus or Jupiter. He was the all-father—the universally present spirit; above all the other gods. He was the god of the sky. They represented him with two ravens that sat on his shoulders, which every morning brought him news of whatever was going on in *Midgard.*"

"What's Midgard?"

"Our lower earth. And the abode of the gods was called *Asgard.*"

"We did not read any thing about Midgard and Asgard to-day."

"No, but I thought you might like to know. And then *Walhalla* was the place where Odin put half of the brave men who were slain in battle."

"What became of the other half?" said Flora.

"The goddess Freija took care of them. What she did with them, this book does not say. I have read before of the 'halls of Walhalla,' I am glad to know what it means."

"Who was Freija?"

"Wait a bit; I have not got through with Woden, or Odin. His two ravens were called *Hunin* and *Munin*—which means, Thought and Memory. That's pretty! Woden is painted also as attended by two dogs. He was the chief and head of the gods; you understand. Now Freija was one of his wives. Naturally, she was the goddess of good weather and harvests—a fair kind of goddess generally. Also the dead were in her care; the other half of the heroes slain in battle came into her hands. She is painted riding in a chariot drawn by two cats."

"But, Ditto, if Woden was the sky god, I don't see why those old Saxons should have fancied he would like such cruel sacrifices. Sunlight looks bright and cheerful."

Meredith mused.

"Yes," he said, "it does look bright and cheer-ful—but, it hates darkness."

"What then, Ditto?"

"Darkness means sin."

"O do you think that!" cried Maggie. "To be sure, I know darkness means sin. But do you think those old Saxons—"

"They felt the difference between darkness and light, undoubtedly; and they feared the sun-god."

"But I don't see how they could think he was so cruel, though."

"I suppose that is all quite natural," said Mere-dith musingly. "How afraid we should be of God, if we did not know Jesus Christ!"

"Were the old Hebrews so afraid of him?" Flora asked.

"Terribly. Don't you remember? they always thought they must die, when the Angel of Jehovah appeared to them? And how should people who never heard of Christ, guess that God is so good as he is? They feel that they are sinners; how should they know that he will forgive?"

"But to think to please him by such awful sac-rifices!" said Flora.

"I suppose the idea was, to give him the most precious thing there was."

"I shall ask Mr. Murray," said Flora. "It is all a puzzle to me. In the first place, I do not be-lieve such heathen people know they are sinners."

"Yes, they do. Certainly they do! all the world over; and this is one of the ways they shew it.

'How beautiful' among them must be 'the feet of him that bringeth good tidings, that publisheth peace!—that bringeth good tidings of good; that publisheth salvation!'"

"What a pity you hadn't lived in Landolf's time!" said Flora.

"There are enough heathen left," said her brother; "and worse than those old Saxons. Their's was not a bad specimen of heathen mythology by any means. And yet, think of believing one's self given over to the tender mercies of Woden and Thor!"

"And yet by your account people were better then than they are now!"

"Some people—and some people," answered Meredith. "I must ask Mr. Murray about that. I do not understand it."

"We shall get work enough ready for him by the time he comes. Well, go on with your Saxon mythology and be done with it. I do not think it is very interesting."

"Maggie and I are of a different opinion. But it was rather Norse mythology. Sweden and Norway and Denmark were all of one race and one faith. Norsemen carried it to Iceland; and it is odd enough that from Iceland we get our best accounts of it."

Maggie had mounted up with her knees in a chair and her elbows on the table, leaning over towards Meredith; and now begged he would tell about Thor.

. "Thor was the thunderer."

"What do you mean?"

"The god of thunder and lightning. He was the son of Odin, or Woden. He is represented driving in a car drawn by two goats and with a great hammer in his hand. This hammer was forged by the dwarfs, Kobolds, I suppose, who dwelt in the centre of the earth."

"What did he want a hammer for?"

"To strike withal. And when Thor's hammer came down, that made the thunder, don't you see? and his stroke was the thunderbolt."

"I should think they would have been frightened to death in a thunder-storm."

"Not an expression those old Saxons knew any thing about."

"Well—I should think they would have feared Thor."

"There is no doubt but they did. Those poor captives at the stone-houses were slaughtered in honour of Woden and Thor, don't you remember? But he was also the god of fire, and the god of the domestic hearth. Listen to this: 'Among the pagan Norsemen, Thor's hammer was held in as much reverence as Christ's cross among Christians. It was carved on their gravestones; and wrought of wood or iron, it was suspended in their temples.'"

"Thor's hammer!" repeated Maggie. "Poor people!"

"Nobody worships Thor now," observed Esther scornfully.

"We call one of our days after him yet," said Meredith. "There is a relic of the old Thor worship. Indeed all our days are heathenish in name."

"All?" said Flora looking up. "What is Monday?"   .

"Just the Moon's day, don't you see? Sunday is the Sun's day. Woden's day and Thor's day you know. Then Friday is of course Freija's day—or Freyr's day—I don't know which. Freyr was the god of weather and fruits—another impersonation of Odin. He rode through the air on a wild boar, faster than any horse could catch him. An odd steed! And Tuesday is Tyr's day, or Zin's day—it comes to much the same thing. He was especially the 'god of war and of athletic sports.'"

"Then there is Saturday left," said Maggie. "What is Saturday?"

"I think it must have been Saturn's day—and so not Saxon, Maggie, but Roman. The names of our months are all Roman, you know?"

"Are they?"

"Yes, but wait. Here is something curious, The Saxon devil was called Loki. Now Loki had three children. Listen to this. 'One was the huge wolf Fenris, who at the last day shall hurry gaping to the scene of battle, with his lower jaw scraping the earth and his nose scraping the sky.'"

"What is curious in that?" asked Flora. "It is just like a children's fairy tale."

"But these are not children's fairy tales; and they mean something. How did these old Norsemen know there would be a scene of battle at the last day, and great destruction?"

"How do you know it?"

"The Bible."

"Does the Bible say so, Ditto?" said Maggie. "Where does it say so?"

"Many places."

"Tell us one, Ditto."

Meredith rose up and fetched a Bible and pushed his book of Norse mythology on one side. Then he opened at the nineteenth chapter of the Revelation.

"'And I saw heaven opened, and behold a white horse; and he that sat upon him was called Faithful and True, and in righteousness he doth judge and make war. His eyes were as a flame of fire, and on his head were many crowns; and he had a name written, that no man knew, but he himself. And he was clothed with a vesture dipped in blood: and his name is called, The Word of God. And the armies which were in heaven followed him upon white horses, clothed in fine linen, white and clean. And out of his mouth goeth a sharp sword, that with it he should smite the nations; and he shall rule them with a rod of iron: and he treadeth the wine press of the fierceness and wrath of Almighty God. And he hath on his vesture and on his thigh a name written, KING OF KINGS, AND LORD OF LORDS.

"'And I saw an angel standing in the sun; and he cried with a loud voice, saying to all the fowls that fly in the midst of heaven, Come and gather yourselves together unto the supper of the great God; that ye may eat the flesh of kings, and the flesh of captains, and the flesh of mighty men, and the flesh of horses, and of them that sit on them, and the flesh of all men, both free and bond, both small and great.

" 'And I saw the beast, and the kings of the earth, and their armies, gathered together to make war against him that sat on the horse, and against his army. And the beast was taken, and with him the false prophet that wrought miracles before him, with which he deceived them that had received the mark of the beast, and them that worshipped his image. These both were cast alive into a lake of fire burning with brimstone. And the remnant were slain with the sword of him that sat upon the horse, which sword proceeded out of his mouth: and all the fowls were filled with their flesh.' "

" I do not understand all that, the least bit," said Flora.

" You understand there will be a war, and a battle ? "

" But that's a figure."

" No, it's a fact.   How should it be a figure ? "

" What do you understand by a 'sword proceeding out of his mouth ? ' "

" That is in the description of Christ in the first chapter: 'And he had in his right hand seven stars; and out of his mouth went a sharp two-edged sword.' "

"Well, isn't that a figure? What does it mean?"

"Listen to the description of Christ that Isaiah gives: 'With righteousness shall he judge the poor, and reprove with equity for the meek of the earth; and he shall smite the earth with the rod of his mouth, and with the breath of his lips shall he slay the wicked.'"

"Well?"

"And in Thessalonians; 'Then shall that Wicked be revealed, whom the Lord shall consume with the spirit of his mouth, and shall destroy with the brightness of his coming.' And in Ephesians: 'the sword of the Spirit, which is the word of God.'"

"Well," said Flora, "that is not a real sword, with a handle, and an edge."

"The Bible says it has two edges."

"Nonsense! you know what I mean."

"I know. Certainly Flora, the weapons of that battle may not be weapons of flesh and blood, or for flesh and blood; but the *battle* is real, don't you see? and the awful overthrow and destruction; and what I am wondering about is, how those old Saxons knew there would be such a battle at the end? and how they knew that the mischief would in some sense come from the devil."

"*Did* they know it?"

"The wolf Fenris was one of the devil's children, as they made it out. And another was the serpent which Odin cast into the sea, where it grew and grew till it had wound up the whole earth in its folds. That is very curious!"

"What, Ditto?"

"How did they know *that*?"

"Know what?"

"Why, don't you see? The serpent is one of the Bible words for the devil; here it is a child of the devil; who coming to the earth has enveloped the whole world in his toils. The Bible says, I know, somewhere, that those who are not saved by Christ are '*in* the Wicked one.' How did they know so much, and so little, those old people?"

"Where did you find all those Bible verses just now about the sword, Ditto?"

"References here, Maggie."

"Well, go on, Ditto. There were three children of the devil."

"The third was the goddess Hel or Hela. She was the goddess of the lower world; and was half black and half blue. I wonder! that must be where our word 'hell' comes from. What dreadful old times! And times now are just as bad, for a great part of the world. The goddess Hel was very like the horrible Hindoo goddess Kali, they say here."

"I don't believe those times were so much worse than these times," said Flora.

"You think human sacrifices are a pleasant religious feature?"

"Not to the victims; but I suppose the rest were all accustomed to it, and didn't feel so shocked as you do."

"Landolf seems to have been a good deal shocked."

"Are you going to read us any thing more, Ditto, about those queer old gods?"

"There isn't much more that I need read, Maggie. I have told you about the principal deities. They believed in quantities of lesser ones—really, personifications of the good and evil powers of nature. The elves and their king, and the dwarfs living inside the hills. The dwarfs owned the treasures of the mines, and worked in metals and precious stones."

"I should like to believe in elves and fairies," said Flora.

"Why?"

"O it's pretty and poetical. Fairy rings and all that."

"Would you like to think there were hidden powers in every piece of water, and rock, and hill, which might feel kindly disposed towards you and might not? which might suddenly play you an ill trick and make you most mischievous trouble, for nothing but mischief?"

"Did people believe so, Ditto?"

"Certainly. A great many people, in various parts of the world."

"I would rather believe that God has it all in his hand," said Maggie contentedly.

"So would I, Maggie. And that Jesus has the keys of hell and of death."

"I wonder when Fenton will be here," remarked Esther.

"I hope—he won't come—till—Uncle Eden gets here," said Maggie very deliberately.

"Why not?" said Esther sharply.

"He is uneasy," said Maggie with a corresponding shrug of her shoulders; "I never know what Fenton will take it into his head to do."

"That is a nice way to speak of your brother."

Maggie considered that. "I can't find any nicer," she said at length.

"Then I wouldn't speak at all."

"Never mind," said Flora. "One's brothers are always a mixture of comfort and plague. And that is true of the best of them, Esther; you never know what they will take into their heads to do."

"O, Flora!—" Maggie began, and stopped.

"You think there is a difference between brothers and brothers," said Flora laughing. "Well, my experience is what I tell you."

"Ditto," said Maggie suddenly, "are there any such stones as those queer stone-houses in this country?"

"Not that ever I heard of, Maggie. But in the old world, as it is called, there are a great many, scattered over a great many countries. Not all just like the stone-houses. Some are just single stones set up on end. Some are two laid together, one resting on the other slantwise; the stone-houses in Lüneburg seem to have been made of nine stones, one lying on eight."

"Did people offer human sacrifices on all of them?"

"I fancy not. But I believe it is tolerably. uncertain. Did you never see a picture of Stonehenge?"

Maggie knew nothing about Stonehenge. Meredith went to the bookcases again and got another volume. This contained many illustrations of old stone monuments of various kinds, and he and Maggie were soon absorbed in studying them.

"There!" cried Maggie, as he opened at one of the earliest illustrations, "there, Ditto! that is very like—*very* like—what you read of the stone-houses. Isn't it?"

"Fearfully like," said Meredith. "This is in Ireland. I dare say some of those old Druids sacrificed men on it."

"How could they set it up so? Look, Ditto—the top stone rests just on one point at the lowest end. I should think it would topple down."

"It has stood hundreds of years, Maggie, and will stand for all time—unless an earthquake shakes it down. This Dolmen is made of four stones."

"What is a dolmen?"

"This is one. It says here in a note, that the name comes 'from the Celtic word *Daul*, a table, and *Chen* or *Chaen*, a stone.' A stone table. And it says here that there are probably a hundred of such dolmens in Great Britain and Ireland. How ever did the builders get that enormous block poised on the tips of the other three?"

Slowly and absorbedly the two went on exploring the pages of the book; stopping to read, stopping to talk and discuss the questions of tumuli and stone circles, dolmens and menhirs. The opinion of the author, that the great circles commemorated great battles, and were raised in honour of the dead buried within them; and that many dolmens had a sepulchral character; was somewhat confusing to the Druidical and tragical impressions left from the Saxon chronicle; which, however, at last got an undeniable support. In the stones of Stennis, over which Maggie and Meredith pondered with intense interest, one of the enormous up-standing masses has a hole through it. And this stone, there is no doubt, was dedicated to Woden. And so long had the superstition of Woden's worship clung to it, that until very lately an oath sworn by persons joining their hands through this hole, was reckoned especially sacred; even the courts of law so recognizing it. After that, Woden seemed to Maggie to have strong claim to all the upright stones and altar-looking dolmens that are found where the worship of Woden has once prevailed. Leaving Stennis they went on to Runic crosses, German dolmens, and French dolmens, and on and on, from country to country. When at last they lifted up their heads and looked around them, they were alone. The girls had gone off to bed; the worsted work lay, left on the table; the fire was out, the minute-hand pointed to ten o'clock. Meredith and Maggie glanced at each other and smiled.

"We have forgotten ourselves," said he.

"You see, Ditto," said Maggie, "we've been travelling. O I wish I could *see* the Stones of Stennis, don't you? and the Stone of Woden!"

"Well, now you had better travel to bed, little one, and forget it all. Don't see it in your dreams."

CHAPTER VI.

One expects steady weather in October; so it was really not extraordinary that the next morning should break fair and quiet, with a sunny haze lying over the river. Nevertheless Maggie rejoiced.

"What a pleasant day we had yesterday!" she exclaimed, as the party sat at breakfast.

"Are not all your days pleasant?" said Meredith.

"Yes, but yesterday was uncommon. O Ditto, we didn't look at the map last night!"

"We were looking at stones."

"Yes, but we must look at the map after breakfast. I want to find all those places."

"Take time," said Meredith, "and eat your breakfast. Lüneburg heath will not run away."

But after breakfast indeed the great atlas was fetched out to the sunny terrace in front of the house and laid on a settee, and Maggie and Meredith sat down before the map of Germany with business faces.

"Now here is the Elbe," said Maggie, "it is big enough to be seen; here is the mouth of it, just in a corner under Denmark, where those ships went from."

"What ships?"

"Why, the ships in which the Saxons went over to England—the Saxons that conquered England, Meredith."

"You do remember," said Meredith smiling. "It is worth while, reading to you."

"They sailed from the mouths of the Elbe and the Weser—and here is the Weser. The mouths are pretty near together. Now between the Elbe and the Weser were—which Saxons, Ditto?"

"Towards the Elbe and beyond it, were the East-phalians; those our story belongs to; among whom Landolf went."

"Well here is the Aller, Ditto! they lived *there*, you know; that is pretty far west. And here is Hermannsburg! O I am glad we have found that. And here is Lüneburg—all over here, I suppose. I suppose we couldn't find the stone-houses, Ditto?"

"I suppose not. But here is Verden on the Aller, Maggie, where Charlemagne had those 4,500 Saxons hewed to pieces. And here are Osnabrück and Detmold, where the Saxons beat him again and took the 4,000 captives that they slew at the stone-houses."

"Horrid Charlemagne!" said Maggie.

"It was all horrid, what concerned the fighting. But here is Minden, Maggie, from which good Landolf set out in his little boat and dropped down the Weser to go to the East Saxons."

"And then when he got to the Aller he went up *that;* then he had to row hard, I guess."

"I guess he did a good deal of hard rowing, first and last, Maggie."

"Then to get to the stone-houses he went further up the Aller and turned into the Oerze. Here is the Oerze! Then the stone-houses must be somewhere hereabouts, Ditto; for they are not very far from Hermannsburg."

"There is the little river Wieze, Maggie; and here, where it flows into the Oerze, was that oak wood, sacred to Thor, where the village of Müden now is. And here is the village of Munster where Freija was honoured. All over the land then it was wild country, woods and morasses. And now—think what Germany is!"

"What is it, Ditto?"

"It is the land of Thought, and Art, and Learning, and Criticism."

"Look here!" broke in a lively voice behind them. "Do you know the sun is getting up in the sky? and we have settled nothing. And here are two heads over a map!"

"It would not hurt a third head," said Meredith. "And Maggie and I have settled a good deal, thank you."

"But where are we going to-day?"

"Yes," added Esther behind, "where are we going? I think it is time to be getting ready, because it takes us a good while."

"Esther," said Maggie, "Fairbairn and the men

are going over to the pine terrace to cut down some trees papa wants cut; let us go there and have a big bonfire, and then Ditto will have plenty of coals for his friar's omelet."

"Betsey is making us a chicken pie."

"Well, the omelet will do no harm besides."

"No.   It is a good way over to the pine terrace."

"I don't care how far it is.   So much the better. It is nice walking.   Do you care, Flora?"

"She don't care," said Meredith.   "Come, let us load up.   If we have a journey before us, best be about it."

"And then, Esther," Maggie went on, "we can go to the Lookout rock to read."

"It will be sunny there."

"Well, it's all nice on the pine terrace, and we can find plenty of shade.   Now then, Ditto—if you'll bring up the wagon."

The business of loading up began.   There were always some varieties every time.   To-day a basket of sweet potatoes formed one item, going to be roasted in the great fire-heap which would be left from the bonfire.   A great chicken pie, fresh and hot, was carefully wrapped up and put in.   Meredith provided a hatchet, to trim branches with. Worsted work and afghan of course; but the only book was in Meredith's pocket.   The cart was quite loaded when all was done; for you know, cups and saucers and plates weigh heavy, if you put enough of them together, and the chicken pie in the dish was a matter of a good many pounds, and potatoes are heavy too. Somebody had to carry the bottle of cream, and Fairbairn went laden with a pail of water.

The day was just another like the day before, but the direction of the walk was different. The party turned to the left instead of to the right, and leaving the flower-beds and shrubbery, entered a pretty winding road which curled about through a grove of red cedars. The air was spicy, dry and warm. A soft, rather thick haze filled the air, turning the whole world into a sort of fairy-land. The hills looked misty, the river still and dreamy; outlines were softened, colours were grown tender. The happy little party, it is true, gave not much heed to this bewitchment of nature, with the one exception of Meredith; Flora and Esther were in a contented state of practical well-being which had no sentiment in it; Maggie and her dog were a pair, for jocund spirits and thoughtless delight-taking. They both went bounding about, very much taken up with each other; while Meredith pulled the cart steadily on and feasted mentally on every step of the way. The road brought them soon to the neighbourhood of the river again, and ran along a grassy bank which sloped gently down to the edge of the water. The green sward was dotted with columnar red cedars, growing to a height of thirty feet, with a diameter of two or two and a half all the way, straight as a pillar. On the other hand a low, rocky height grown with oaks and hemlocks overhung the valley, and the rocky ridge seemed to sweep round to the front of them in a wide amphitheatre, giving a sky line of variegated colour, soft and glowing under the haze. Travelling on, they got next into a wood and lost the river. Here all was wild; the ground strewn with rock and encumbered with low growth of huckleberry bushes, brambles, and ferns. The road however was good, and Meredith drew the cart without any difficulty. After a time the ground began to rise, for in fact they were approaching the further end of the rocky ridge before mentioned, where it swept round to the river. Midway of the height the hill shelved into a wide plateau or terrace; at the back of it the sharp, rocky hill-side, in front of it a green slope leading down to the river. The ground on the plateau was gravelly and poor; it gave foothold to little beside white and yellow pines, which in places stood thick, in other places parted and opened for spaces of mossy turf, where the too shallow soil would not nourish them. Here there was a wild wilderness of natural beauty. Now and then a lovely low-growing white pine spreading abroad its bluish-green branches; in other parts scraggy, tall-shooting specimens of the yellow variety; at the hill foot and on the rocky hill-side golden hickories and brown oaks and flaunting maples. The turf was dry and warm, being in fact half moss; the openings and glades allured the party from one sweet resting spot into another.

"We may as well stop here," said Flora at last.

"We might go round and round all day, it is all so pretty. We must stop somewhere, if we are to have any reading."

"Let us go over yonder to the edge of the bank," said Meredith, "where we can have a view of the river."

At the edge of the bank the cedars began to occupy the ground and indeed hindered the view; but a few strokes of Fairbairn's axe set that right; and the party sat down in the shade of some taller trees with a lookout over the pretty conical cedars (not columnar here) down to the water, and across to the green and gold promontory which on the other side of the river closed the view. The girls got out their work. Maggie sat down panting after a race with Rob Roy. Meredith lounged upon the mossy bank and looked lazy. Presently the strokes of a couple of axes began to break the silence. One, two; one, two; one, two—

"It only wanted that!" he exclaimed.

"What!" said Esther.

"That chopping. That ring of the axes. It completes the charm. This is elysium!"

"We have got to make our bonfire!" said Maggie starting.

"Wait,—not yet; they have not cut down a single tree yet.—Hark! there it goes, crashing down. They have got to trim it yet, Maggie, before there will be anything to burn."

"And they must cut and trim a good many trees, before there will be enough to begin," said

Esther. "It is more fun to have plenty to pile on at once."

"Then we shall wait a good while for our dinner," said Maggie.

"Are you hungry? It is only half past eleven."

"No, I am not hungry yet; but a bonfire takes a good while, you know, and I want to get to the reading."

"Come! we might read an hour," said Meredith rousing himself up.

"No, Ditto, that would bring it to half past twelve, and that would never do."

"Well then I will go trim, and we'll have the bonfire going in a few minutes. Where will you have it?"

Maggie sought out a good spot, while Meredith took his hatchet and went to work, clearing the lopped branches of their smaller leafy twigs which were for the fire, and cutting in two the branches which were not worth trimming. There was a nice piece of work then, to drag them to the bonfire place; for it was needful to choose an open, free space for making the fire, where the flames would not mount or be blown into the tops of trees that were to be left standing, and so scorch and injure them. No such open space was at command in the close neighbourhood of the cutting; so the stuff for the fire had to be transported some distance. Maggie and Meredith worked away at it, and Maggie called Esther and Meredith summoned Flora to help; and soon they were all heartily en-

gaged and running· to and fro with armfuls, or
dragging behind them on the ground the heavy
umbrageous branches they might not carry. Presently Meredith stopped and collected a little bunch
of dry sticks and leaves which he heaped together;
tucked paper under, and laid crisp hemlock and
cedar cuttings on top. Then a match was kindled
and fire applied. They all watched to see it; lighting, crackling, smoking,—then the slender upshoot
of flame—and Meredith began to pile on pine
branches thick and fast. At first rose a thick column of smoke, for the fuel was fat and resinous
and the fire had not got under way. Redoubling,
soft, black and brown reeking curls, through which
the sun shot his beams here and there lighting
them up to golden amber. " What tints and what
forms!" Meredith exclaimed. And then another
light and another colour began to come into the
others; tiny up-darting shoots of fire, another illu-
mination rivalling and contrasting with the sunlight which struck the column higher up. Meredith stood still to watch it, while even Flora and
Esther were dragging more branches of yellow
pine to the fire and throwing them on emulously,
till the pile grew and grew, and Maggie was working her cheeks into a purple state with her exer-
tions. Half a dozen thick pine branches flung
on, and the fire would be stifled and the smoke
rise thicker and blacker, with the sunlight always
catching the upper curls; then crackling and snap-
ping and breathing, the fire would get hold, get

the better, mount through the thick, encumbering piney foliage, and dart its slender living spires up into the column of smoke again.

"Do see how he stands!" cried Flora. "Ditto, why don't you work?"

"I am looking."

"Did you never see a bonfire before?"

"Never such a beauty of a one."

"Beauty?" said Flora, coming to his side to look —"where is the beauty? It is just a good fire. You are a ridiculous boy, Meredith. Go to work."

"O don't you think it is pretty?" cried Maggie, throwing down her last burden and panting. "I think it is *lovely!* And do you smell how sweet it is, Flora?"

"She is a poor girl without nose or eyes," said Meredith. "Well, here goes!"

Taking hold of the work again, his powerful arms flung the branches and tops of pine on the burning heap, while the girls ran for more. It took a strong arm now, for the fire was so large and so fierce that one could not come nigh it. Meredith kept the girls all at a distance and himself fed the flames; till all the present stock of fuel was laid on, and the wood-choppers went off to their dinner. There was no more to be done then but to watch the show, and as the fire began to lessen and die down, find a spot where the tea-kettle might be set, at the edge of the glowing heap. It was no use to begin to read, they all agreed, till they had their dinner. And soon the coffee could be made; and the four enjoyed their meal as only those can who have worked for it. They had their chicken pie and their roasted sweet potatoes; the omelet they for to-day dispensed with, being all tired. They took their dinner on the bank, there where they could look away down to the river and see the hilly shores beyond on the other side; and Meredith averred that sweet potatoes never were so sweet before.

"Such air!" said he. "And such colouring."

"And it is just warm enough," added Maggie.

"Well, I have got cooled off now," said Flora; "but I consider feeding bonfires to be hot work."

Then, when dinner was over, and the things packed into the cart, they arranged themselves on the moss in a delicious feeling of resting and re-freshed languor; the girls took out their fancy work, and Meredith opened his book. Maggie, who did not trouble herself about fancy work, crept close to his side and looked with fascinated eyes at the strange characters out of which he brought such delightful things to her ears.

"'It was about the year 940, according to the chronicle, that a boy of thirteen or fourteen years old was herding his father's cattle on the waste land not far from Hermannsburg; when there came along a splendid train of armed cavaliers riding their horses proudly. The boy looks with delight on the shining helmets and coats of mail, the glittering spears and the stately horsemen, and the thought rises in his heart—"Now that looks some-

thing like!" All of a sudden the horsemen quit
the road, which here wound about crookedly, and
come riding across country, over the open land
where he is keeping his cattle. That seems to
him too bad, for the field is no highway, and the
ground belongs to his father. He considers a moment, then goes forward to meet the riders, plants
himself in their course, and calls out to them—
"Turn back! the road is yours, the field is mine."
There is a tall man riding at the head of the troop,
on whose brow a grave majesty is enthroned; he
looks wonderingly at the boy who has dared to
put himself in his way. He checks his horse, taking a certain pleasure in the spirited little fellow,
who returns his look so boldly and fearlessly and
never budges from his place.

"'"Who are you, boy?"

"'"I am Hermann Billing's oldest son; and my
name is Hermann too, and this field is my father's,
and you must not ride over it."

"'"But I will, boy," answered the rider with
threatening sternness. "Get out of the way, or
I throw you down—" and with that he lifts his
spear. The boy, however, stands fearlessly still,
looks up at the horseman with eyes of fire and
says—

"'"Right is right; and you have no business to
ride over this field; you shall ride over me if you
do."

"'"What do you know about the right, boy?"

"'"My father is the Billing, and I shall be Billing after him," answered the boy, "and nobody may do a wrong before a Billing."

"'Then still more threateningly the rider called out—"Is *this* right then, boy, to refuse obedience to your king? I am your king, Otto."

"'"You Otto? our king? the shield of Germany and the flower of the Saxons, that my father tells us so much about? Otto the son of Heinrich the Saxon? No, that you are not. Otto the king guards the right, and you are doing the wrong. Otto don't do that, my father says."

"'"Take me to your father, my good boy," answered the king; and an unwonted gentleness and kindliness beamed upon his stern face.

"'"Yonder is my father's dwelling-house, you can see it," said Hermann; "but my father has trusted the cattle here to me and I cannot leave them, so I cannot bring you there. But if you are King Otto, turn off out of the field into the road; for the king guards the law."

"'And King Otto the first, surnamed the Great, obeyed the boy's voice, for the boy was in the right, and rode back to the road. Presently Hermann was fetched from the field. The king had gone into his father's house and had said to him, "Billing, give me your oldest son and let him go with me; I will have him brought up at court; he is going to be a true man, and I have need of true men." And what true Saxon could refuse anything to a king like Otto?

"'So the brave boy was to journey forward with

his king, and when Otto asked him, "Hermann will you go with me?" the boy answered gladly, "I will go with you; you are the king, for you protect the right."

"'So King Otto took the boy along with him, that he might have him brought up to be a faithful and capable servant of the crown. Otto was allied in the bonds of warmest friendship with Adaldag, the archbishop of Bremen, a man who was distinguished for his learning, his piety, and a lively zeal for the spread of Christianity among the then heathen Danes and Norsemen. Otto could not confide the boy who had become so dear to him to a better teacher; and so he sent him to Adaldag at Bremen. Adaldag, too, recognized the great gifts which God had bestowed on the boy, and had him instructed under his own eye by the most able ecclesiastics; among whom a certain *Raginbrand* is especially named, who later was appointed to be bishop and preacher to the heathen in Denmark, and laboured there with great faithfulness and a great blessing. In Bremen Hermann grew up to be a good young man, loving his Saviour from his heart; but also he was instructed in the use of arms and in the business of the state, for Adaldag was at that time one of King Otto's most confidential advisers. And now Otto took the young Hermann into his court; and soon could perceive that he had not deceived himself when his acuteness discerned the boy's lofty nature. Spirit, daring, and keen intelligence, shot in fire from the young man's blue eyes; his uncommonly fine figure had been grandly developed by knightly exercises; and with all that, he was so humble-hearted and attached to his benefactor with such grateful, touching devotion, that Otto's eyes rested on him with pleasure, and he often called Hermann his truest friend, even called him "his son." But the loveliest thing in Hermann was, that he never forgot his origin; he shewed the most charming kindness to those who were poor and mean; so that high and low at the king's court respected as much as they loved him. So he mounted from step to step, was dubbed a knight, attended the king on his journeys and campaigns, and the king even entrusted to him the education of his two sons Wilhelm and Ludolf. Still later he administered the most important offices of state to the satisfaction of the king; and often travelled through the country of the Saxons as *Graf*, *i. e.*, a judge.

"'That is: The judgment of criminal cases, or the tribunal of life and death, in the whole German fatherland was vested in the king alone. Therefore at certain times the royal judges made a progress through the entire German country. They were called *Grawen*, from the word *graw* or *grau*' (that means, 'grey,' Maggie) because ordinarily old, experienced, eminent men were chosen for the office. These courts for cases of life and death were holden by the Grafs under the open sky, in public, and in full daylight, so that the judgment pronounced could be at once carried into execution. Our chronicle takes this occasion to relate a story about our Hermann Billing, which sets in a clear light the pure character of this admirable man. In his journeyings as Graf, he came also to his native place, to Harm's *ouden dorp.* It was then long after his father's death; and as head of the family he had distributed his seven manor-farms, as fiefs, partly to his brothers, partly to other near relations. The great honours to which Hermann had been elevated had become the ruin of these men; they behaved themselves proudly towards their neighbours, and even took unrighteous ways to enlarge their boundaries, secure in the belief that no one would dare to call them in question about it, whilst they had such a powerful brother and kinsman. Now when Hermann, after the accustomed fashion, was holding the criminal court on the *Grawenberg* (where now the *grauen* farm lies, half an hour from Hermannsburg) there presented himself a certain Conrad, a freiling, that is, a free man; and accused the holders of Hermann's fiefs, that they had by violent and unjust means taken from him half his farm and joined it to their own estates.

" ' Hermann's face, at other times so gentle and kind, grew dark, and with deep sadness but with a lofty severity he ordered his brothers and kinsmen to be brought before him. Conrad's charge was proved to be true, for the Billings could not lie, even if they had done injustice. And what did Hermann? When the acts of violence that his brothers and relations had done were proved, great tears flowed down the cheeks of the tall, strong man, and he cried out with a voice which his tears half choked, "Could you do that, and bear the name of Billing!" He said no more, but was seen to fold his hands and pray with the greatest earnestness. Then he spoke: "My brothers and kinsmen, make your peace now with God; we look upon each other for the last time. You are guilty of death; you must die; you have doubly deserved death, because you are of the race of Billing."

"'The priests, who were always in attendance on the tribunal of life and death where Hermann was the judge, came forward; in the grounds of the court they received the criminals' confession, and upon their penitent acknowledgment of their sin, gave them assurance of forgiveness and then the bread that represents the Lord's body. So, reconciled with God, the seven men came back to the place of judgment; and after Hermann had again prayed with them and commended the penitents to the Lord, he had their heads struck off before his eyes.'"

Meredith stopped perforce, for a storm of exclamations burst upon him. "Horrible!" "Frightful!" "I never heard of such an awful man!"

"I think he was rather an awful man," said Meredith. "I have no doubt all ill-doers would have held him in a good deal of awe."

"But his own brothers!" said Esther.

"They were convicted criminals, all the same."

"But don't you think a man ought to spare his own!"

"A man—yes. A judge—no."

"But a judge is a man."

"I should think it was very disagreeable for a man to be a judge," said Meredith.

"But why?" asked Flora. "I should think it was nice, just for that reason, that a man could spare people he wanted to spare."

"Flora Franklin!" exclaimed her brother. "Is that your idea of a judge?"

"It is my idea of a man."

"But don't you know better? A judge has no business to spare anybody, except the innocent; his duty is to see justice done; he has nothing to do with mercy."

"Nothing to do with mercy! O Meredith!"

"Not as a judge. He is put in his place to see the laws executed."

"Then you think that dreadful old heathen you are reading about, did *right* to have his friends' heads struck off?"

"I think he did just his duty."

"O *do* you, Ditto?" cried Maggie.

"He did not make the law, Maggie; he had only to see it obeyed. The law was terribly severe; but I think the judge was very tender."

"O Ditto!"

"He was what you call a true man. He was no heathen, Flora. But nothing would make him budge from the right. I think he was magnificent.

I wonder how many men could be found nowadays who would be faithful to duty at such a cost."

"You have strange notions of duty!" said his sister.

"I am afraid you have imperfect notions of faithfulness."

"Well, go on. I have no opinion of religion that is not kind."

"'The religion that is from above is *first* pure, then peaceable,'" said Meredith.

"Go on," said Flora. "I suppose you would cut my head off, if you were judge, and I had done something you thought deserved it."

"If the law said you deserved it. But I think I would give my head in that case for yours, Flora. It would be easier."

"What good would that do?"

"Keep the law unbroken and save you. Well, I will go on with my story—

"'When the sitting of the court was ended he sent his retinue to find quarters in the other six of his manors, but he himself passed the night at the principal manor-house on the Oerze, which he had himself built, called the *Bondenhof*, that is, the "peasant's manor;" for in old Saxon *Bond* meant a free peasant. But what a night that was! Sleep never came to his eyes; he passed that night and also the following day in praying and fasting. When at last, by the word of God and the talk of a faithful priest he had got some comfort, at least a little, he vowed to the Lord that he would build a church on this manor, the "Bondenhof," which should be dedicated to the apostles Peter and Paul, like the first one built by his forefathers at the Deep Moor, which in the course of time had become far too small. And as with him to resolve and to do were always the same thing, he did not quit the manor till he had laid the foundation-stone of the new church and given order to have the building vigorously carried forward. That was in the year 958.

"'By this deed of rigid, impartial justice, which nevertheless was found in beautiful harmony with a tender and good heart, the honour in which people held him was raised to such a point, that everywhere they carried him on their hands; and at his return to the royal court he was received with wondering admiration. The great Otto folded him in his arms and called him his most faithful knight, who served his God and his king with equal fidelity.

"'Soon thereafter followed Hermann's greatest elevation. Otto had determined, you must know, in the year 960, to take a journey into Italy, in order to compose certain troubles which had arisen through the godless pope John. But now his beloved Saxon country, out of which Otto himself drew his origin, lay just in the north of Germany; and was bordered on the north and northeast by the Danes and Sclaves, but recently conquered, who indeed were in part nominally Christian, but in part were still heathen, and the whole of them haters of Christianity. Who would take care of Christian Saxony in the king's absence, which it was possible might last for years? Then Otto's eye fell upon the faithful Hermann, and he had found his man. Hermann was appointed to the dukedom of Saxony, so that he might thus supply the king's place and govern in his stead. When this was made known to the good Archbishop Adaldag, who was to accompany the king in his journey to Rome, he rejoiced aloud, and said to the king, "Now we can travel in peace and have no care; for, O king, you can trust him with the land, and I can trust him with my church; Hermann with God's help will protect church and land both." And that is what the faithful man truly did. In the following year the king really set out on his journey to Rome, and Adaldag went with him. Otto set up a stern tribunal in Rome; deposed the godless pope John, and made good Leo pope. Five years Otto spent in Italy; and wherever he came he wrought righteousness and judgment, punished the wicked and relieved the innocent and oppressed; being such a prince as Germany has had few. In the year 962 Otto was solemnly crowned kaiser by Leo at Rome, and thus acknowledged as the earthly head of the whole Christian world. During all this time, the Saxons might count themselves happy that they had such a true and valiant duke in Hermann. The Sclaves ventured again to make a marauding incursion, probably to try whether in Otto's absence they could not accomplish something. One tribe of the great Sclavic race, namely the Wends, dwelt not on the other side of the Elbe only but also on this side, as far as the neighbourhood of Melzen. These Wends, on the hither side of the Elbe, reinforced by a strong party of their brethren from beyond the river, undertook a campaign against Saxony; for they themselves were still heathen and therefore had a hatred against the Christians. This hatred was all the stronger, because the Saxons under Otto had vanquished them. In this campaign, so far as they went, they burnt and laid waste everything, and in especial their aim was directed against the churches and chapels and Christian priests; the former were burned and levelled with the ground; the latter were put to death in tortures. So it befell with that first church which Landolf had built at the Deep Moor; it was burned down and entirely destroyed. Eight priests, who served this church and the chapels lying in the neighbourhood, were slain; part of them at once; part of them were dragged to the Wendish idol altar in Radegast, not far from the Elbe, and there slaughtered in honour of the heathen god; those chapels were likewise destroyed. Hermann was just come to Bremen when this news reached him. He rapidly gathered his warriors, came suddenly upon the robbing and plundering Wends at the so-called Hühnenburg, obliged them to flee with great loss, and pursued them without stay or respite into their own country; whereupon they sued for peace, and promised they would keep quiet and accept the Christian religion. He granted them peace, but went on to destroy their idol temple in Radegast, and then returned in triumph home. He next applied his whole energy to repair the destruction which had been wrought, to rebuild the churches and chapels and establish priests in them. And the better to secure the land, and especially his own beloved inheritance against the like predatory incursions, he built strong fortresses, as for instance the Hermannsburg' (*burg* means a castle or fortress, Maggie), 'the Hermannsburg, around which now the people began to build again, who had fled away before the Wends; the Oerzenburg, the Wiezenburg, etc.'"

"Then *that* is how so many names have come to end with 'burg,'" said Esther.

"Hermann did not build all the castles," said Meredith. "But yes—that is very much how it has come. In those old Middle ages, when the right of the strongest was the only prevailing one, naturally there were a great many castles built. Indeed all the nobles lived in castles, and must. Just look at the pictures of the Rhine, to see what the Middle ages were; see how the people had to perch their fortresses up on almost inaccessible peaks of rock, where it must have been terribly inconvenient to live, one would think. I suppose people knew little of what we call *conveniences* in these days."

"Then round the principal fortresses, naturally,

the villages grew up," said Flora. "They would cluster round the castles for protection."

"Well, I never thought before that one could see the Middle ages through the stereoscope," said Maggie.

"Pretty fair," said Meredith. "Well, let us go on with Hermann. 'Through his unintermitting activity all was soon in blooming condition again, and no enemy dared to shew himself any more. Before his end in the year 972, he had the joy of seeing the church, the foundation-stone of which he had laid at the Bondenhof, consecrated on Peter and Paul's day. That is this same church which is still standing in Hermannsburg, and in which we hold divine service.'"

"O Ditto! is *that* church standing yet? that Hermann built?"

"And the very foundation-stone that Hermann laid is there to this day. I'd like to see it! We have nothing old in this country. Imagine attending a church that has stood for nine hundred years! 'He endowed this church with a tenth, and gave almost the half of the fields and meadows of the above-named manor to the Hermannsburger pastor.

"'Of his remaining great deeds our chronicle says little; which is natural, as it is and proposes to be only a Hermannsburg chronicle. In the year 973, the same year that his great friend and benefactor Otto died, died also Hermann Billing, the freeman's son, who had come to be duke of Saxony.

About his end the chronicle relates only that he was sick but a few days, that he wished for and received the Holy Supper before his death; admonished his son Benno, or Bernhard, who was his heir: "My son, be true to your God and your kaiser, a protector to the church, and a father to your vassals;" laid his hands upon his head and blessed him; and then extended his hand to all his weeping servants who were assembled, commended them to the grace of God; and at last prayed—"Into thy hands I commend my spirit; thou hast redeemed me, Lord God of hosts." Then he softly fell asleep, and the same wonderful sweetness which in life had given such a charm to his face, in death put a very glory around his brow.

"'King Otto the second honoured the true man's memory by confirming his son Bernhard, or Benno, as duke of Saxony.'"

CHAPTER VII.

"Is that all?" said Maggie.

"All in this place, about Hermann Billing."

"I like him very much!" said Maggie drawing a deep sigh.

"Notwithstanding he was such an incorruptible judge?"

"Notwithstanding he was such a hard, cruel man, you should say," said Flora. "Ditto, you are ridiculous!"

"It is a great mistake, you must remember, to judge a man of one time by the lights or laws of another."

"There's a law of nature," said Flora, "in *some* people, which makes them dislike to kill their relations."

"There is a higher law than the law of nature. Nature did not prevent Abraham from making preparations to offer up Isaac. It did not hinder Moses—"

"I do not know what unnatural thing Moses did," said Flora; "but I confess to you, I think

Abraham acted much more like a heathen than like a Christian in that event of his life."

"Which only shews, that if you had been in his place you would have failed to manifest Abraham's faith, and so would have entirely missed Abraham's blessing. 'Because thou hast done this thing, saith the Lord, and hast not withheld thy son, thine only son—' then the Lord went on to heap blessing upon him."

"I don't see how Abraham could do it."

"Because he trusted God. It is not *trust*, Flo, that will not go any further than it sees why."

"Ditto, what are you going to read next?" said Maggie."

"We'll see. Next thing, I think, will be the description Pastor Harms gives of that old church which Hermann Billing built; Hermann the duke, I mean. Don't you want to hear it?"

"O yes. The description of it as it is now?"

"As it is now. But what a wonderful sort of a church is this we are in!" said Meredith looking up.

"Here, this bank, do you mean?"

"This bank; and these pillars of tree-stems; and these wonderful Gothic windows of tree-branches, through which the light comes broken by transom and mullion. And the incense which fills nature's cathedral. And the stillness. And the preaching."

"Don't get highfaluten, Meredith," said his sister.

"No. That would be a pity, here."

"I never heard of silent preaching before."

"The strongest of all."

"Is it? Well, go on and read. My work gets on best then."

"It is too lovely to do anything but look, and breathe. The air is most delicious. And nature seems so wide and free. I have an odd feeling that I am floating with those clouds yonder, and flowing softly with the river, and hovering about generally, like those eagles. Do you see those eagles?"

"Highfaluten again, Meredith," said his sister.

"Well, one good poet has been highfaluten then before me. Don't you remember, Maggie, something your uncle was repeating one day? I have never forgotten it—

 "'My soul into the boughs does glide.'

It is an odd feeling—but it makes me very rich for the present. This is the loveliest place! And now you shall have the Hermannsburg church. So Pastor Harms writes:

"'It is a great thing indeed, and a beautiful thing, to know somewhat of the origin and of the history of the church in which one worships and serves God. When I step into our church, whether it be for holding divine service or that I may pray there alone, every time, I feel my whole inmost soul stirred. The very walk to the church through the church-yard is edifying to me. The church at the beginning was situated upon a little eminence, so that it was needful to mount several steps to get to the church doors. Now one must go *down* several steps from the church-yard to reach the entrance of the church. How comes that! Since the year 972 the church-yard has been the place of burial. The dust of those laid within it has raised the ground level, till now the church lies lower than the church-yard. A hill has grown out of the dust of the dead, and over this hill I go into the church. Does not this walk of itself preach in the most impressive way: "Put thine house in order, O man, for thou must die!" Then when I step inside the church, what a new sermon I get! Since 972 years after Christ, therefore since 880 years ago, men have worshipped there the Father, the Son, and the Holy Ghost; have sung in his honour the church's songs of praise; have thither brought their children to be baptized; have heard the preaching of the divine word there, have eaten and drunk the emblems of the body and blood of the Lord there, have bowed their knees there, where now I bow mine! It always seems to me then, as if the veil were parted which divides the church up yonder from the church down below. Where I am, here have those who are fallen asleep once been and worshipped; and where they are now, thither shall I go also. So in blessed faith I can cry out, "A holy Christian church!" Not a place in the world is so dear to me as the church, my beloved church. I have no paternal mansion; for I am the son of a pastor, and pastors leave no inheritance for their children; and yet I have a Father's house, the best there is in the world, my beloved church; truly that is God's house, and God is my Father, and so it is justly and truly my home.

"'And how wonderfully God has guarded this house of his. What wars have raged since this house has been standing, and it has remained uninjured. Since the thirty years' war, Hermannsburg has been four times burned down; this house has remained standing. Twice lightning has struck the tower, and so shattered the foundations that only a little turret stands now upon the riven walls instead of the slender one-hundred-and-eighty-feet-high spire which was there before; but the church remained untouched. The interior has been altered; the many-coloured paintings on the arched vault of the ceiling are gone; the many-coloured galleries have disappeared; in the body of the church itself gallery over gallery mounts up to the vaulted ceiling, to give accommodation for the hearers; but the church itself has remained unchanged. And when I think of the blessings that have gone forth from this house, what churches, chapels, and cloisters have sprung from here, in Bergen, in Wiezendorf, in Munster, in Müden, and the chronicle mentions many more; yes, when I remember how from the castles founded by Hermann on the Oerze and Wieze, the castellans of Oerze and Wiezendorf marched out, so early as with Duke Bernhard, to help bring the heathen people of Lauenburg and Mechlenburg to Christianity; must not then the zeal of my forefathers kindle my own zeal to bring the Lord's blessing, his word and his sacraments, to the heathen, to the very ends of the earth? And now that seems no longer strange to me, which seems strange to so many, that we from this place should have undertaken to send out a peasant mission. It has not been our own doing; it has come from our church and our history. Did the peasant's son Hermann become duke of Saxony; was the blessing of Christianity carried from here into all the region round about, even into the countries on the other side of the Elbe? why should not Hermann's peasant church preach among the heathen the Saviour who has been their own so long? May such a primeval blessing only make us right thankful, right humble, right kind and loving, only zealous and fervent in spirit. We see well enough that the Lord can use little things; therefore let nobody despise us because we are small, and let us have the joy of serving the Lord with our insignificant gifts and strength, as well as we can. It is written in the Scripture, "Destroy it not, for a blessing is in it!"'"

Meredith ceased reading, and there was a silent pause of a few minutes. Crochet needles worked busily; Maggie sat pondering; Meredith lay back on his elbow on the moss and looked down at the river. Here and there the soft-pointed top of a young cedar rose up between, not hindering, only as it were embellishing the view. In the silence, when the strokes of the wood-cutters halted, little sweet sounds broke in, every one of them coming

like a caress or a murmur of rest; two crows slowly flying over and calling to each other, some crick-
ets chirruping nearer by, a little gentle rustle and
lapping of the water, then a bugle call from the
post opposite. Clouds hardly moved; winds were
asleep; the air, fragrant with the breath of the
evergreens, scarcely stirred, luxuriously warm and
still. The colouring, too, in which all nature
had dressed herself, gave another touch of delight
through every object which the eye rested on.

"What a sky!" said Meredith. "And what air!
It's wonderful."

"Ditto," began Maggie, "have they a *mission* in
Hermannsburg?"

"Yes. They have a mission in Africa."

"Why is it a 'peasant mission,' and what does
that mean?"

"Why, you see, Maggie, the whole people of
Hermannsburg are just a parcel of peasants, part
in the village, and part I believe, farming it here
and there on the Lüneburg heath. They are poor
people; small farmers and the like. They have
not much money to give; but when Pastor Harms
had been with them a while and proposed to them
to set about mission work, a dozen men offered
themselves to go. They were already so filled with
his own spirit."

"And did they go?"

"They had to be put to school first. They were
too ignorant to instruct the heathen or anybody.
So they were set to study, under Pastor Harms'

brother, for three years. While they were studying, Pastor Harms undertook building a ship which
should carry them to Africa. The ship and the men
were ready together about the same time."

"They could not have been a very poor people,
I should think," said Flora.

"They were, though; but you see, they began
by giving themselves to the Lord; and when people do that I guess they generally find that there
is a good deal else to give. O they were poor
enough; but it would cost a great deal, you know,
to pay their passage in a ship belonging to other
people, and the freight on all the goods they must
carry; for they were going out not merely to preach,
but to establish a colony and live among the heathen. And then, whenever new recruits for the
mission were sent out, the expense would have to
be incurred over again; so they thought the cheapest way in the end would be to build their own
ship."

"And they did build it?" said Maggie.

"Certainly. The good ship 'Candace.' And everybody helped in some way. The shoemakers
made shoes, and the tailors made clothes, to go out
with the mission; the women knitted and sewed.
Do you want to hear what Pastor Harms says
about it?"

"O yes, Ditto, please!"

"Yes, read on—anything," said Flora.

"Two men of the first twelve had died, and
two others had proved false. Eight left; to whom

another eight joined themselves, who would go out as colonists. Now I will read:

"'So by God's grace, everything was ready. And now one should have seen the busy industry, the lively expectation, the gleesome bustle, as the last hand, I may say, was put to everything. In the Mission house, what learning and counselling and arranging; in the workshops belonging to it, what smith-work and cabinet-work and tailoring; how our women and girls sewed! Our village shoemaker worked with his might at the foot-gear to be taken along; our village cooper did the same at the great water casks for the ship; my brother went out with the mission pupils in leisure hours and picked berries which were to be taken along. Here people brought dried apples, pears and plums; there buckwheat and buckwheat groats; here rye, flour, peas, wheat; there sides of bacon, hams, and sausages. Then again house-furnishing articles, tools, heather brooms, trumpets and horns, even live hogs and poultry, and even potatoes were hauled along—and all was to go. Even a fir-tree with its roots was planted in a large pot filled with earth, in order that on the ocean the travellers might light up a Christmas tree. Then again came packages of linen made up, and of stuff. And there was a great deal that never came to Hermannsburg. Whatever was prepared on the other side of the Elbe, in Hamburg, Lübeck, Haide, etc., was kept in Hamburg, and we never saw it at all. In Hamburg alone there were handed over from female friends of the Mission, one hundred and twenty-eight cotton shirts, all finished and ready; from Haide forty striped shirts for the natives; from Lübeck and Mechlenburg, besides beautiful under-linen, all sorts of pictures and little things for the heathen; from some children here came writing boxes, pens, and writing books for the heathen children. Also from here, from Osnabrück, Schaumburg, Lüneburg, Bremen and neighbourhood, whole rolls of linen cloth. There was a stir and spring of love that moved people's hearts. Every one of the emigrants was to take a gun with him, for in East Africa there are a great many wild beasts, lions, elephants, serpents, etc. Scarcely had this become known, when guns, rifles, double-barrelled rifles, pistols and daggers came in, till we had enough to leave some for a future party that might be sent out. Then would come our harbour-master, or our captain, from Harburg, to arrange this or that; then our pupils journeyed to Harburg to bring money for the ship. One hardly knew where his head was.'"

"Well, did they go to Africa, Ditto?"

"The colonists and missionaries; yes, sixteen of them."

"Whereabouts in Africa?"

"The east coast, about Natal."

"I haven't the least idea where Natal is."

"You would do well to look it out on the map."

"And are they there yet, Ditto?"

"They went in the year 1853. It is not likely

they are all there now.   But others followed them, Maggie, year after year, till now there are, I believe, between twenty and thirty stations where they are settled."

"All from Hermannsburg! Ditto, it is very curious! So many years ago, Hermann's castles sent out soldiers to bring heathen Mechlenburg to the Christian religion; and now Mechlenburg gives shirts and pictures for Hermannsburg to send to other heathen in Africa."

"What sort of heathen people are those they went to?" Esther asked.

"Quite a good sort.   Here is a description of them, written by one of the brethren who sailed in that first trip of the 'Candace':

"'I cannot make it out, how the heathen can be as they are, although they are day and night before my eyes.   They are powerful, muscular men, with open faces and sparkling eyes; they all go either quite naked or with a very slight covering.   A late law obliges them however to put a shirt on when they are going into a city.   They live in houses which resemble beehives, into which you must creep.   The whole stock of valuables which you find in these huts, is an assaghai (javelin), a club, a mat, a bit of wood for a pillow, and a great horn for smoking.   I have seen nothing else in them. The people have almost no wants.   So many wives as a man has, so many huts has he also, one for each wife, and then one besides for himself.   The women are bought; paid for with cows and oxen;

ten or twenty oxen for a wife. These become then the man's slaves, and the man, when he has got a good many wives, hardly does any more work himself. The women must cultivate the maize and sweet potatoes, which is almost all the people live upon. Once in a while they kill an ox; and then so many come together to eat it that it is all disposed of at one meal. Our German brethren aver that ten Caffres in twenty-four hours will eat up a whole ox, skin and entrails and all, which they roast at the fire; that afterwards, however, they can go fasting four days at hard labour. They are fond of adorning themselves with coral and rings, and snuff-boxes are to be seen in the hands of both men and women. They cork up the snuff in their nostrils with a hollowed-out bit of wood, till the tears run down their cheeks. The women are so hardly used that a mother with a little five-days-old baby must go out to work in the hot sun, with the baby on her back, and the father does not concern himself at all about the child. Of twins, one is almost always killed at once. In short, they are not much above the beasts in their way of life; and the worst of all is, they are almost inaccessible to the truth, and laugh at everything sacred.'"

CHAPTER VIII.

"Well," said Maggie, as Meredith paused, "I should think somebody ought to go to those people!"

"Hopeless work," said Flora, stitching away at her worsted.

"No, it is not hopeless work," answered her brother. "As you would soon see, if all the churches had the matter at heart like Pastor Harms and his Hermannsburg."

"Everybody cannot give himself up to such business," said Flora glancing at him.

"Everybody ought."

"O Ditto!" cried Maggie, "do you think *everybody* ought to go to Africa?"

"Yes," said Flora; "that is just about what he thinks."

"No, Maggie," said Meredith, "neither to Africa nor to other heathen parts; not everybody. But everybody can give himself up to the work of the kingdom, even if he stays at home. Most people must stay at home."

"I don't understand," said Maggie with a shrug of her shoulders.

"Don't you remember—'Seek ye *first* the kingdom of God;'—that's all I mean."

"'First!'" Flora echoed.

"How 'first,' Ditto?"

"Before everything else. The words mean that, if they mean anything."

"*How* before everything else?"

"See, Maggie. Suppose you and I have—"

"Now, Ditto, stop!" said his sister. "I do not want to hear any of that stuff. What is it to Maggie? And Essie and I do not care about it."

"And there comes Fenton," added Esther, springing up to go and meet him. For Fenton it was, bounding up the bank at their left.

Fenton was grown a good deal since our last sight of him; otherwise not much changed. A handsome boy, with a good figure and a bright eye, and also the old, somewhat supercilious upper lip. But he was glad to get home, and greeted the party cordially enough. Then, however, began to criticise.

"What are you all doing, loafing here?" He had sat down on the bank with the rest, and looked from one to another.

"We do not use your elegant expression," said Flora; "partly perhaps because we are not wont to indulge ourselves in that particular amusement."

"What *are* you doing?"

"You do not see anything to engage our attention, in what at present offers itself to yours," Meredith remarked.

"Nothing offers itself to my attention," replied Fenton. "I don't see anything! except our old cart. Anything to eat in it?"

"There is no pie left," said Esther, "for I gave the last of it to Fairbairn; and Flora drank up all the cream. There's some sugar in the sugar-bowl."

Fenton went to get some lumps of sugar, and then stood looking down at the party:

"Aren't you going home to dinner?" said he. "I tell you, I'm raging."

"Four o'clock," said Meredith, looking at his watch. "Just the pretty time of day coming now."

"It'll be dinner-time, by the time you get the cart home, and the girls get dressed. What did you come out here so far for? I haven't had a respectable dinner for six months. I am going to have some wine to-day, if the governor *is* away."

"Governor!" cried Esther. "What a vulgar expression! For Fenton Candlish to use!"

"Wine!" exclaimed Maggie. "You can't have any wine, Fenton; we don't drink wine any more in *this* house."

"What's the matter!"

"The matter is, papa has emptied his wine cellar," said Esther in a rather aggrieved tone.

"Drunk it all up?"

"No, no; sent it off and sold it."

"What was the matter with it!"

"Why I tell you," said Esther; "it is thought improper for good people to drink wine."

Fenton's face was rather funny to see, there was such a blank dismay in it.

"And did mamma give in to that?"

"I don't know what mamma thought," said Esther; "but papa sold the wine; and our dinner-table does not have its pretty coloured glasses any more."

Fenton uttered a smothered exclamation which I am afraid would have shocked his sisters.

"I don't see what *you* want with wine, Fenton!" said Maggie; "papa never let you have it."

"Mamma did though," said Fenton. "That's the good of having two parents. If one is crochetty perhaps the other will be straight. Well, *I'm* not going to live if I can't live like a gentleman. I shall send to Forbes to send me some wine."

His sisters burst out into horrified exclamations and expostulations.

"Papa'll see it in the bill," said Esther, "and he'll be very angry."

"Uncle Eden is coming," said Maggie, "and it will be no use. He'd throw it into the river."

"Uncle Eden coming?"

The girls nodded.

"If I had known that, *I* wouldn't have come!" said Fenton looking very dark.

"I'd think better of it if I were you," remarked Meredith quietly. "There goes more to the making of a gentleman than the drinking of wine."

"What do you mean?"

"Just that. As for instance—self-control, noble thoughts, care for others above himself, indifference to low pleasures."

"Low pleasures!" repeated Fenton. "Do you call wine a low pleasure?"

"Well—it brings people into the gutter."

"Pshaw! not gentlemen."

"I grant you they are not gentlemen after they get there."

"What do you know about it?" said the boy not very politely. "Did you ever drink it yourself?"

"I never will again. A gentleman should be a free man; and wine makes men slaves. I don't choose to be in bondage. And if it would not enslave me, it does other people; and I would not give it the help of my example."

Fenton dropped the subject, but renewed his proposal that they should return home. So shawls and worsted work were stored in the cart, and the little book in Meredith's pocket; and the line of march was taken up. It was indeed coming now to the lovely time of the day. Shadows long, lights glowing in warm level reflections, all objects getting a sunny side and a shade side and standing forth in new beauty in consequence; the day gathering its train, as it were, to prepare for a stately leave-taking by and by. Meredith and Maggie, loath to go, lingered the last of the party; indeed he had the cart to draw, which was heavy, and needed careful guiding in places over and between

9

the rocks; and he could not run on with the heads of the party. And Maggie walked beside him, and put her little hand upon the handle of the cart which she could not help to draw. How sweet it was! The light every moment growing softer, not cooler; the colours more contrasted, as the shadows lengthened; the bugle notes coming over the water now and then. Meredith looked, and drew deep breaths of the delicious air; but Maggie walked along pondering.

"Ditto," she began, "do you think *everybody* ought to do mission work?"

"The dear Lord did not give the charge to *some* of his people, did he?"

"But how can they do it? Everybody cannot go to the heathen?"

"He said, 'in all the world'—so that means at home as well as abroad, doesn't it?"

"Preach the Gospel in all the world?"

"Yes."

"How can *I*, Ditto?"

"You and I, let us say. Well, Maggie, suppose we ask Mr. Murray? But one thing is certain; those who stay at home must furnish the money for those that go."

"Does it take a great deal?"

"Not to send a few. But how long would a *few* people be, about telling the Gospel to all the world? Suppose one man had as much as the whole state of New York, for his parish?"

"He'd never get through."

"Exactly. And so it is nearly nineteen hundred years since the Lord gave the command; and the heathen world is the heathen world still—pretty much."

"But then, Ditto—to send a great many people, it would want a great deal of money?"

"It does. What then?"

"Maybe people cannot afford it."

"Let us ask Mr. Murray about that."

"But Ditto, what do *you* think? I know you think something."

"Maggie, I think we should seek *first* the kingdom."

They were turning into the shrubbery grounds near the house, and Maggie left the discussion. They were all ready for dinner, as far as appetite went, and in a little while the five young people sat down at the board.

"This is jolly," said Fenton, who took the head of the table.

"Roast-beef, to wit?" said Meredith.

"Roast-beef is a good thing, if you are hungry as I am; but I did not mean that. It is uncommonly jolly to be out of the way of the governors."

Maggie looked up astonished.

"'Rulers are not a terror to good works,'" said Meredith.

"They're a nuisance, though."

"Only to one portion of society. I hope you do not class yourself with them."

"Do you mean," said Maggie, making big eyes,

"do you mean, Fenton, that you are glad papa and mamma are in California?"

"No. Only one of 'em. Mamma never interferes with me."

"She leaves it to papa to do," said Maggie, with dignity and sageness.

"I am glad she does. Shews her wisdom. I can tell what is good for me, as well as anybody else."

"Always do it, I suppose?"

"That's just my affair," said Fenton. "There is no use in putting chains round a fellow—all the good of it is, he must just break the chains."

"Do you call papa's commands, *chains?*" said Maggie.

"Don't stare, Maggie; nothing is so vulgar."

"I am glad Uncle Eden is coming, to make you behave yourself."

"If he tries it on, I shall bolt," said Fenton. "I am out for some fun; and if I can't get it at home I'll get it somewhere else."

Meredith succeeded in turning the conversation to a pleasanter subject; nevertheless Fenton's deliverances shocked his little sister several times in the course of the dinner. Among other things, Fenton would go down to the wine-cellar, to see if a bottle or two might not by chance have been left; and though the key was not to be had and he came back discomfited, Maggie could not get over the audacity of his proposition. She was further and exceedingly shocked after dinner when Fenton proposed to Meredith to have a cigar. Meredith declining, Fenton went out to enjoy his cigar alone.

"Fenton is grown very wild!" said Maggie.

"Boys can't be like girls," said Esther.

"I don't see why they can't be as respectable as girls," said Maggie.

"They never are, my dear," said Flora. "Comfort yourself. They will run into what they don't like just to have their own way; because what they do like is ordered or advised by some kind friend."

"Not true without exception, Maggie," said Meredith; "but there is some truth in it. Don't worry about Fenton. I don't believe he means quite as bad as he says."

"But smoking is so disgraceful—in a boy," said Maggie.

"It is not disgraceful in a man," said Esther.

"Well, it isn't nice," returned Maggie. "I always hate to come near that Prof. Wilkins who always talks to me when he is here. He is kind, but his breath is dreadful."

Fenton was not so fond of the company of his cigar but that he soon forsook it. And then his company indoors was hardly an acquisition. He talked big of doings at the school where he was now placed; horrified Maggie by shewing that he was quite as lawless as in old times, and put an effectual bar to any reading or talk either except of the sort that suited himself.

"What's up?" he asked at last. "What shall we do to make the time go?"

"Time does not need any whip with us," said Meredith. "He goes fast enough."

"O we are going out in the woods to dinner," said Maggie.

"You were there to-day."

"Well, we are going to-morrow—and every day. We have a bonfire, and a nice lunch, and the girls work, and Ditto reads to us."

"Jolly slow," said Fenton. "I can't stand much of that. I shall go a-fishing."

"Very well," said Esther. "And come to us for lunch?"

"Same place? It's too far off."

"Then we'll go into the pine wood," said Maggie. "The pine wood is nice—and the pine needles make a beautiful carpet—and we want to go to a different place every day."

So it was arranged.

CHAPTER IX.

The same sweet weather continued again the next day; the air was even warmer still, the leaves of oaks and maples, turning more and more, were growing browner and ruddier and the glow on the hills more deep. The pine wood, however, which lay behind, that is north of the house, at no great distance, was uninvaded by this autumn glow. The soft, blue gleam of the pines alone stood against the heaven's mild blue overhead, and pine needles, brown and thick, carpeted the ground everywhere between the rocks. For rocks were almost everywhere at Mosswood. Only on the skirts of the wood one might see a flaming maple branch, or a golden cloud of hickory here and there, and here and there a cat-briar vine taking a tawny hue, or some low-growing cornus, putting on lovely tints of madder at the edges of its leaves. Through the wood the little party wandered, not knowing where to choose to stop, and Meredith patiently drew the cart along waiting for orders. At last, on a little rising ground they found an open space, yet shadowed enough, from which there was a lookout to the house in the valley; truly no more than the chimneys could be seen; and a wider space of blue sky, and the hills toward the south. This would do. Here were pine needles enough for a carpet, and a felled pine log gave a convenient seat to those who liked it. For Meredith and Maggie preferred the ground and the pine needles. The cart was drawn up under the shade of a tree; afghan and worsted embroidery were taken out; shawls were spread; and the party settled themselves for a morning of comfort.

"This *is* good!" said Meredith, delaying to open his book.

"How perfectly delicious this warm smell of the pines is," said Flora.

"You use strong language, Flo, but for once not exaggerated. We have not got the sound of the wood-chopper's axe to-day."

"I'll tell you what you may hear, though, if you listen," said Esther, "the woodpecker—

"'The woodpecker tapping the hollow beech tree,'

only there are no beech trees on the place. You may hear him on an oak, though."

"This hazy light under the pines—through the pines—is bewitching. O October! O Mosswood!" Meredith exclaimed. "What is so pretty as these autumn woods?"

"What are you going to read us to-day?" said his sister. "Don't get poetical."

"I will read you one or two little bits first, which

touch something Maggie and I were talking of yesterday. We do not want a bonfire to-day; it's too warm."

" No; we will make just a tiny little blaze by and by, to boil our kettle. It would be too warm for a bonfire. And there are no trees here to be cut."

"I should think not!" said Meredith, looking up at the blue-green pine needles over his head. "Well—here's a story for you."

"Heathen?" asked Flora.

"No, Christian. 'There was a man, once upon a time, whom God had richly blessed. He had received a year's income of seven hundred thalers. Four hundred of them he needed and used for his house and family wants, and three hundred were left over. So he thought at first he would put the money out at interest, and enjoy the comfort of receiving rents which were growing while he was sleeping. As he was just setting about this, he read in a mission paper about the wants of the heathen; and the Sunday next following he heard a preaching about how the dear Lord is the safest of all to trust money to, and gives the best interest. So he made a short piece of work of it, and sent his three hundred thalers to the dear Lord for the conversion of the heathen, and said, "Lord, take thou them; I got them from thee, and there is all this left." "Wife," said he, when he came home at evening, "I have done a good bit of business to-day; I have got rid of my three hundred thalers, and am quit of any care of the money, over and above."

"Then you may thank the dear Lord for that," said his wife. "And so I do," he answered.

"'Do I not hear at this point, not merely many a child of the world but also many a believer, secretly half saying, "No, but what is out of reason is out of reason!"—and so do I see a certain compassionate smile playing about mouth-corners. But wait a bit; there is something coming that is more crazy yet. The next year the man was overloaded with such a blessing, that instead of seven hundred thalers he made fourteen hundred thalers, and he did not know where it all came from. Then what does he do but take the surplus, one thousand thalers, and send it to the mission. Is the story true? do you say. You can ask the Lord "in that day"; he knows the story.'"

"I like that," said Maggie.

"Why?" Flora asked.

"I think it is nice," said Maggie with a shrug of her shoulders.

"I don't see it. What good to the man to have twice as much as he had before, if he must give it all right away again?"

"Why he has the pleasure of giving it!" cried Maggie.

"And it shews at any rate that he did not get poor by his first venture," said Meredith. "And the Lord will reckon it 'at that day' as all done for him."

"I don't think people are obliged to give away all they have got," said Flora.

"Suppose they do not reckon anything they have their own? The Christians in the early times did not, if the Lord's work or the needs of others wanted it more."

"Extravagance!" said Flora. "Just enthusiasm."

"Come, I will read you another story. But the poor woman who gave all she had into the Lord's treasury, was not rated as a fool by *him*. I will read you now—

"'A PROBLEM ABOUT STUTEN MONEY.

"'Most of you know, it is true, right well what *stuten* money is, but certainly all do not. Among us, when people go to church on Sunday, the children and younger serving people of the peasants get a groschen to take along; with which they can buy a stuten, that is, a white roll, at noon when they come out of church; by the help of which they can stay in the village and so go to church again in the afternoon. Now there are a boy, a girl, and an old woman known to me, who have no other money but the stuten money they get on Sundays. So each one of them falls to considering how he or she can do something for the heathen. And they arrange it on this wise. One of them every other Sunday eats no roll, and thinks within herself, "I eat as much as I wanted this morning at home, and I can do the same again this evening." The two others buy each a small roll for half a groschen, and lay up the other half groschen every Sunday; and when the year comes round, they have all three of them, counting the festivals, thirty groschen saved up, and bring them with glad, smiling faces to go for the conversion of the heathen. And upon being afterwards asked whether hunger did not often trouble them on Sunday? they say, they have always felt as if they had had enough; and with God's help, they will do the same way next year.'"

"What sort of a story do you call that?" asked Flora, when her brother paused.

"I call it, a story of what can be done."

"And *I* call it, a story of what ought not to be done. Both the children and the old women needed their bread for themselves; it was not good for them to go without it. And what is a groschen? or thirty groschen?"

"What are 'two mites, which make a farthing?'"

"O that is in the Bible."

"But it was in a poor woman's heart first; or we should never have had it in the Bible."

"Well, look at our luncheon," said Flora.

"I will look at it, when I see it. What then?"

"Do you mean that we shall do wrong to eat it?"

"Not at all."

"How can those people be right, and we not wrong?"

"Yes, Ditto," said Maggie. "I do not understand."

"Those people must give their groschen, or give nothing. It was all they could give."

"But we might give more than we do, if we

would live on bread and water," said Flora. "If we are to give all we *could* give. Our luncheon would come to a good many groschen, I can tell you."

"We must ask Mr. Murray. I am not wise enough to talk to you," said Meredith. "I hope he will come! we are getting work ready for him. Meantime I will read you another little story. Maybe we shall find some light.

"'AS POOR, YET MAKING MANY RICH.

"'There was a poor day-labourer who lived by his work, from hand to mouth. He heard it read out of the Old Testament, that under the old covenant every Israelite was bound to give to God the tenth of all his incomings. That went through and through the man's head, and he thought: Could the Israelites do that by the law, and should not we Christians be able to do it by the love of Christ? So, honestly and faithfully, he lays by the tenth of his daily wages; the Lord blesses him, so that many a time he earns sixteen groschen a day; and at the end of the year he comes with his hands full, bringing sixteen thaler twenty groschen for the conversion of the heathen, and with hearty pleasure; and he says, "The love of Christ constraineth me so, I have wanted for nothing."'"

"Not much of a story," said Meredith, in concluding, "but a good deal of a suggestion."

"Suggestion of what?" asked his sister.

"Duty. Certainly, a Christian ought to be able

to do more for love than an old Hebrew did for law; and from this time I will imitate that old German fellow."

"But, Ditto!" exclaimed his sister. "A tenth of *your* income, you must remember, is a great deal."

"Not in proportion—" said Meredith. "He would want every one of his remaining groschen for his necessities; I should not. It seems to me, the richer one is, the larger the proportion should be that should go to the Lord's uses."

"I shall ask Mr. Murray to make you reasonable!" Flora exclaimed. "Stop talking, and go on with your reading."

"The next story is about 'One Groschen and Two Pennies.'

"'It is true, what the Bible says—"The Lord maketh sore, and bindeth up; he woundeth, and his hands make whole." My heart learned the meaning of this word, when a short time ago I had to expel two pupils from the Mission house, who had been led astray by Satan. This gave me great pain, but it had to be done, for their sakes and for the sake of the house; and it was somewhat alleviated in that they came back sorry and penitent and were taken in again.

"'To the honour of the Lord I will here speak good of the balm which shortly after my great hurt he laid upon the wounds. May it have somewhat of the sweetness of that ointment which filled the whole house.

"'Soon after the departure of the pupils was

made known, I had a visit from an eight-year-old boy. He had a groschen in his hand and a reading-book under his arm. He told me that he had found this groschen fourteen days before on the way to church, that he had asked his father to publish the discovery and he himself had announced it in school. But nobody had been found to own the groschen. I said to him: "Well, what do you think, my child? does the groschen belong to you? will you buy something with it?" The boy answered "No, the groschen is not mine, so I am not going to keep it. I will give it to the dear Saviour for the poor heathen children, to get a spelling-book for them." When I questioned him further, he said that once in the church, where his father takes him every Sunday, I had said, "whoever keeps what does not belong to him is a thief; and" —he added with great seriousness, "you said, a Christian child must not be a thief!" I received the groschen now and thanked him. But the boy had not done yet. He asked me if it were true, that two of the pupils had been expelled from the mission house? When with a sorrowful face I assented, he answered, "You need not be so troubled about that. You can send me instead. I can spell already, and I will soon learn to read." When the little fellow with great earnestness had said that, I could not help folding him to my breast in heartfelt gladness. Then I knelt down and together with him prayed that the Lord would some time make a true missionary of him. He went away at last, but could not at first rightly understand how it was that I had as yet no use for him.

"'Soon after this, I received a letter from a dear friend who had been making a lively stir in the matter of the mission among his school and the parish to which his school belonged. The Lord had granted him access to the hearts of great and small, and with cordial pleasure he had been collecting till he should have a full thaler made up, which then should be sent me. Now he wrote, the thaler was made up, and he sent it, and this was how it had come about. In a hospital, where he is accustomed to hold devotional service for an hour, he had mentioned the conversion of the heathen. The next day came a widow, shoved four groschen under one of the books which lay on the table, and then, with a greeting from her children, laid two groschen on the table, saying: "Now the thaler will be made up!" To this mission thaler, which indeed was made up now, a little girl of nine years old had every Sunday contributed two pennies, which she received from her mother to buy rolls with. Some time after, the mother brought the child's two pennies again, silently; but it struck our friend that she had great tears in her eyes. The thing was soon explained. The child had fallen ill. Sunday her mother said to her, "To-day you shall keep your roll for yourself." "No," the child answered, "I could not be easy if I did. I promised my dear Saviour once, that as long as you gave me two pennies to buy rolls with, I would give the money on Sunday for the heathen." How glad that true mother's heart must have been. She had reason to say, "But what a value these two pennies had for me! I could not let them out of my hands at first, for joy." God bless mother, child, and teacher! The mission must indeed thrive when such gifts are offered. From another dear friend of missions, personally unknown to me moreover, I received a contribution for the mission, in the making up of which both men and beasts had given their help. The contributors were specially mentioned, the men at their head; then at the conclusion followed, "A hen, so much and so much."

"Well, Ditto," said Flora, "I will say, you do read the most extraordinary stories?"

"Like them?"

"No, I don't think I do, much. Do you bring them forward as our examples, hen and all?"

"You might do worse."

"But, Ditto," Maggie said anxiously, "you do not think we ought to go without what we *want*, do you? for the sake of the heathen."

"Ask Mr. Murray that question, Maggie. Whose hat is that I see over the wall, coming up to the gate?"

Maggie jumped up to look, and then with a scream of "Uncle Eden! Uncle Eden!" sprang away down the path to meet him. The others dropped book and work and followed her. The pine wood was screened off from the shrubbery and pleasure grounds (but indeed all Mosswood

10

pretty much was pleasure grounds) by a low stone wall, in which wall a little gate admitted to the entrance of the wood. By the time Mr. Murray, skirting the wall, had come to that point, the group of young people had reached it also; and there Mr. Murray received a welcome that might have satisfied any man. Maggie threw herself on his neck with cries of delight; Flora's bright, handsome face sparkled with undisguised pleasure; even Esther looked glad, and Meredith's wringing grasp of the hand was as expressive as anything else. Surrounded by them, almost hemmed in his steps, questioned and answered and welcomed, all in a breath, by the gay little group, Mr. Murray slowly made his progress along the pine walk towards the present camping place. He had got the round-robin, yes, and he had obeyed their summons as soon as he could after clearing away a few impediments of business; he had made an early start and come all the way that morning from Bay House; and he was very glad to be with them. Now what were they going to do with him?

Saying which last, Mr. Murray stretched himself on the soft carpet of pine needles and surveyed the tokens of work and play around the spot.

"From Bay House this morning! And no lunch yet?—That's good!" cried Maggie. "Now, dear Ditto, the first thing is to give him something to eat. He must be ravenous. If you'll build a fireplace, I'll make the fire; and then we can have the kettle boiled in a very little time.—"

Mr. Murray lay on his elbow on the pine needles and watched them, as Meredith built a few stones together to support the tea-kettle, and then he and Maggie ran about collecting bits of pine and pine cones and fuel generally. And then there was the careful laying of dry tinder together, and the match applied, and the blue, hospitable smoke began to curl up under and round the kettle, and an aro matic, odoriferous smell came floating in the air.

"This is better than anything I have seen for some time, children," he said.

"Ah wait!" cried Maggie. "We have got stewed pigeons for lunch."

Mr. Murray laughed. "What are you all doing out here, *besides* eating pigeons?"

"We have set out with the determination to live out of doors," said Flora; "and so we do it. This is the third day; and it is absolutely delightful."

"What are you doing?"

"I see you looking at our worsteds—aren't they pretty colours, Mr. Murray? Esther and I play with these, while Ditto reads to us. And we have laid up a great deal of work for you."

"In what shape, pray?"

"Questions. Somehow, as we read, we get up difficult questions, that nobody can answer, and that we are not all agreed upon; and then by general consent we refer them to you."

Mr. Murray watched the tiny tongues of flame which were darting up round the tea-kettle, where Maggie sat supplying small sticks and resinous

pine cones to feed the fire. The scene was as pretty as possible; Meredith roaming hither and thither collecting more fuel, and the shawls and even
the worsted lying about, with the gay, young figures, touching up the gipsey view with bits of colour. He watched in silence.

"Mosswood is the most delicious place we have
ever seen," Flora went on.

"Almost any place is good in October. How
pleasant this veiled light is. What are you about,
Maggie?"

"This is the pot of pigeons, Uncle Eden; we are
going to get them hot. The kettle boils; now
would you like some coffee, Uncle Eden?"

But Mr. Murray declared himself satisfied with
tea. And in a little while the scene became more
gipsey than ever; except that gipseys are not supposed to indulge in much refinement of china cups
and silver spoons. Everybody was picking pigeon
bones, however; and bread and butter, and cups
of tea, and baked potatoes (which came out hot
from the house, brought in a basket by Fairbairn),
and peaches and pears to conclude with, were discussed with great enjoyment and amidst a great
deal of talk. Fenton arrived from the fishing to
take his share; but I do not think he was as glad
to see his uncle as the others had been; and as
soon as lunch was over he took himself away again.
Then cups and plates and *débris* were packed away
into the cart; the little fire had burnt itself out;
fingers were washed in Eastern fashion, somebody

pouring water over the others' hands; and at last worsted needles and knitting needles came into play again, and the circle was made up around Mr. Murray, who declared himself to be quite refreshed and rested.

"Ready for questions, Uncle Eden?"

"Are the questions very deep?"

"O yes, Uncle Eden; none of us can answer them."

"They had need to be profound! How did they come up?"

"From Meredith's book. Ditto was reading to us some delicious stories about the old Saxons, and their ways and their gods; and we have ever so many questions to ask you, Uncle Eden."

"Have you any more of those Saxon stories on hand, Meredith?"

"Plenty, sir."

"Then I wish you would go on and read another; and so I should perhaps get into the atmosphere of your questions. Besides, I feel like being luxurious and lazy in this warm, spicy air. Suppose we have a story now, and the questions by and by?"

They were all agreed to that. Maggie settled herself to listen comfortably, and Mr. Murray lay on his elbow and looked thoughtfully into the reader's face, or into the blue-green pine wilderness around, or above to the quiet, clear blue which stretched over all; but if Mr. Murray's body was resting, I am inclined to think his mind was busy enough.

CHAPTER X.

" 'The story that I am going to tell you now shall bear the heading, "The Hearts of the Children turned to the Fathers." I read it with a deal of trouble, in an old, yellowed manuscript which the mice had gnawed at. But it bears so entirely the impress of truth that it may speak for itself, although the things happened more than a thousand years ago. I would rather, if I could, give it again exactly as it stood written in that manuscript; but I am unable to do so, because I only made extracts from it. I found the MS. in the library of the Town House at Lüneburg, where I was staying for a few days just then, and with the permission of both the burgermasters of the city, I searched the Town House library through. When later I came to live in Lüneburg for many years, these and other old MSS. were no longer to be found; and I heard that a Jew, to whom the burgermasters had sold a number of old suits of armour and weapons, had probably demanded to have these manuscripts into the bargain, thinking that he might in England dispose of them for a high price.

The MS. was entitled: "Res gestæ Landolfi, Apostoli Salzonum, qui Horzæ ripas ad habitant;" *i. e.,* *"Acts of Landolf, the apostle to the Saxons who lived on the Oerze."* I have told you already many things about this Landolf. It has been mentioned that he built the first wooden church in this whole region of country, there where the heathen god Woden's place of sacrifice had been; which place, under the name of the "cold church," still belongs to the Hermannsburg glebe, ever since the church was burned down in a predatory inroad of the Wends, and Hermann Billing built the stone parish church in Hermannsburg. I have told you too of this Landolf, how he had gradually converted the whole region to Christianity, like a skilful general, consecrating to the Christian faith for the worship of the true God, precisely those places where the heathen had been wont to adore their false idols, so that the triumph of Christianity could in nothing have been more forcibly manifested than in this founding of Christian altars and chapels on the very places where previously the heathen abominations had been enacted.

"'One hour from Hermannsburg above on the Oerze, two little rivers, the Oerze and Wieze, flow into one another. Such meetings of two rivers are called in high German Münden, in low German Müden; so accordingly the village situated at the meeting of the two rivers above mentioned bears the name of Müden. Just a little above the place where the Wieze flows into the Oerze, in the middle of the latter river, lay a wonderfully beautiful little island, almost like an egg in circumference, which had a circuit of perhaps from ninety to a hundred paces. How often when I was a child have I visited that little island, and stayed there for hours at a time. In the whole surrounding region I knew no lovelier place, and it was always a particular delight to me when I could wander that way. On both sides of the island the swift-flowing, clear waters of the Oerze went rushing past, transparent to the very bottom, over the glistening sands of which and among the long, thick, green tufts of the water ranunculus hosts of nimble trout played and darted about. A little bridge on each side connected the island with the two shores. If you crossed the bridge which spanned the left arm of the Oerze, you came into green meadows and the parsonage garden, which extended along the left bank of the river, enclosed with a hedge as high as the trees. If you went from the island over the bridge of the right arm of the Oerze, you were in the court-yard of the parsonage, where the pastor's dwelling stood. This island was entirely framed in with high oaks and alders; and a number of mighty old oaks, with large trunks and lifting their heads high in air, grew on the island and wholly overshadowed it with their green roof of leaves. So still it was, so cool, and so secluded, upon this island that even the fiercest summer had no power over it; it was green and fresh when everything around it was withered and dried up by the hot sunbeams.

And now as I write this it stirs me with pain to be forced to say that this island has disappeared! How can that have come about? It has fallen a sacrifice to the idol of Utility. The fine oaks have been felled, and used for building timber; the alders have been cut down and turned to firewood; the island is no moré, for the two arms of the Oerze have been dammed up, and a straight river bed carries the Oerze now through green meadows which stretch along both shores. Yes, these are beautiful too, these green meadows, and they are very profitable also at the same time; but the wonderful beauty of the island is departed, vanished with no trace of it left; and in the entire valley of the Oerze there is not a place that can be compared to it. See, my dear readers, this is what is done by the much bepraised "Enclosings," which could have originated only in our earthly-minded age ; and which spare nothing, neither right nor usage; respect no old legend, no old custom; have no eye at all for beauty, rate everything only according to its utility, and cannot endure anything round, but favour only straight lines and sharp corners. Even the very unreasoning beasts mourn over the way in which the "Enclosings" are carried on. The valley of the Oerze, once thickly peopled with nightingales on both shores of the river, now has not a single one to show; the poor creatures love the thicket, the dim light, the shade and solitude, where they sing their songs to God and men; but the new-fangled clearings drive the whole away together.

That is no matter; to be sure their singing brings no money in.

"'Well, on this old island in heathen times was the sanctuary of the god Thor, or Donner, as he was likewise called by our forefathers. Among these oaks and alders stood his altar, a big round stone of granite. Near this great stone lay a vast number of what are called thunderbolts; for every thunderbolt that a Saxon found he laid down at Thor's, or Donner's, altar. Now if you do not know what thunderbolts are, go to your pastors or to some other learned folk, and they will tell you, and perhaps she you one. The learned called them Belemnites. They are longish, round, wedge-shaped stones, pointed below, growing broader above; at the point they are quite solid and have a so-called *Peddig*, that is, a fine, round core, as in the middle of a tree-stem, which, however, is entirely turned to stone; towards the other end this core grows thicker and more crumbly, and at last the stone becomes quite hollow. These are petrifactions of sea animals, which have remained since the time of the flood. In my childhood the people still called these stones "thunderbolts," and the belief was generally prevalent that in heavy thunder showers such thunderbolts fall from the clouds upon the earth. That belief had its origin in the heathen time. It was the belief of our heathen ancestors, that Thor, or Donner, the son of their principal deity Woden, was the god of thunder; a man with a handsome, serious face and yellow beard, whose blast caused the thunder, and who in thunder-storms drove through the air in a chariot drawn by goats, and then in the lightning cast his thunderbolts on the earth, so that men might fear and honour him. And he was not only the god of thunder, in the belief of our forefathers, but the god of justice also. Whoever wished to confirm a contract with his neighbour, made it before the altar of Thor; and what ever had been promised "by Thor," could not be taken back. Also, as people believed, he watched over all laws and rights in the land; in the taking of oaths he was the witness appealed to. And woe to him who perverted law and justice, woe to him who swore a false oath; Thor's thunderbolt was sure to fall upon the audacious transgressor and dashed him to pieces. And so, from this it came that every thunderbolt found was laid down at Thor's altar, as witnesses for the god who guarded laws and rights, and punished covenant-breakers and false swearers with his strong hand. He dwelt among oaks, elders and alder-trees; for which reason these trees, which were sacred to him, were always found about the places where sacrifices were offered in his honour. Our forefathers were known for their inviolable truth. Even the heathen historian Tacitus says of them, that the word of a Saxon was worth more than the oath of a Roman, and that among them good customs were regarded with more reverence than good statues among the Romans. From this you can easily imagine in what high honour the god Thor was held by our forefathers, and how sacred was Thor's place of sacrifice. But alas, the full ferocity of heathenism also came out in the worship of Thor; for human victims were slain in his honour, whenever through some failure of faith-keeping or breaking of a covenant a curse rested upon the community. And how often may not yonder little island as well have drunk the blood of slaughtered men!

"'Now in Landolf's time, when he and the Christian doctrine had already been received at old Hermann Billing's, the priest of Thor's sacrificial altar on the island I have described, was a silver-haired old man, whom the MS. calls Henricus; *i. e.*, Heinrich, who also for long years had been a faithful friend of Hermann. However, since Hermann had become a Christian, Heinrich had proudly withdrawn from him; he held him to be a covenant-breaker, and threatened him with the judgment of Thor, which sooner or later would fall upon him because he had forsaken the faith of his fathers. Hermann sought an interview with his old friend, but the proud priest of Thor refused to give it. Now, when in the great assembly of the people at the stone-houses, of which I have formerly spoken, Landolf received permission to declare the Christian faith openly in the whole country, he did not fail to visit among other places also the sanctuary of Thor upon this island, and to preach the Gospel to the people who gathered there for the offering of sacrifices. Heinrich had no liberty or power to hinder the preaching; but when it was done he came out as its most decided opponent; and declared in unmeasured terms that the Saxons who had turned or who should turn to Christianity, were covenant-breakers, on whom Thor's vengeance would speedily fall. In flaming zeal, with these words he lifted one of the thunderbolt stones which lay beside Thor's altar, shewed it to the people, and threatened that with such weapons Thor would punish the apostates. Then arose Landolf's commanding figure, and looking at old Heinrich with a gentle, happy, beaming smile, he spoke:—

"'"Brother, the Christian's God is better than your heathen god. See! all this while he, the only true God, has borne patiently with your heathen ways, has seen how you slew human sacrifices and became murderers of your fellow-men; and instead of punishing you for your sins and transgressions, he has borne with you in great love and patience; and now still, he is not lifting his arm of vengeance against you, but is saying; 'Children, I have overlooked the times of ignorance; but now the time' of salvation has come, I open to you my arms of grace and pray you, be ye reconciled to your God.' But *your* god knows no love. Hermann has not transgressed in anywise; he has only become a Christian; he simply abhors the transgressions which he used to commit. He proves his love towards you; he has kept his friendship for you; he has besought you; 'Brother, come let us talk together about our beliefs, and see whose faith is the right one.' The God of the Christians

has taught him to love like this. But you, you
hate the brother whom once you held dear, who
has done nothing to harm you; you refuse him so
much as a friendly interview; your heathen god
has taught you to hate like this. Men," he went
on, turning to the people who stood around them,
—"which is the right God? the God who loves
and teaches to love, or the God that hates, and
teaches to hate?"

"'The people maintained an agitated silence; it
had become as still as death, so that one could hear
the very breaths that were drawn. Thereupon Landolf raised his voice again, and told the people of
the love of our God, who parted his only-begotten
Son from his fatherly breast and sent him down
to poor sinners to take pity on them; and then he
went on to tell of the love of the Son of God, who
forsook the throne of his Father, came to men, took
part with their flesh and blood, in the heroism of
love went about among men, followed by his faithful apostles; everywhere as the mighty one, God's
champion, overcoming Satan, setting men free who
were fast in his toils, opening the eyes of the blind
and the ears of the deaf, making the lame to go
and the sick to be well; even laying hold of mighty
Death with his divine hand and forcing him to let
go his prey; and how at last this true Hero of God,
in order to save the whole captive world from its
common oppression under the evil one, and that he
might with justice and righteousness set them free,
offered himself up for sinners, for them suffered

death, went down into the grave and Hades to overcome death, hell, and the grave; thence to rise victorious, and to go back to his Father, and to sit down again upon the throne of God, from which he had gone forth. And even there his love and pity never rest; from thence he is constantly sending out his apostles and prophets; and has sent me to you. Not to punish, not to condemn; no, but to pray you, Be ye reconciled to God; to shew you his arms of grace spread to receive you; and to tell you, Come, for all things are ready; the courts of heaven where Jesus reigns stand open to you. His blood has redeemed also you; he will forgive your sins, and has prepared mansions for you to dwell in. Repent and be baptized, that your sins may be forgiven and that you may be the children of God.

" 'After giving such testimony, Landolf kneeled down, as it was always his wont to do after preaching to the heathen, and prayed to the Lord Jesus that he would enlighten the minds of the heathen by his Holy Spirit to receive the word of divine teaching, and that he would open their hearts as once he opened Lydia's; he even had the boldness to ask the Lord to witness for himself, as the living God, among the people there assembled.' "

" What did he mean? a miracle?" Flora asked.

" I suppose, something like the signs that used to be asked for among the Jews in old time. Not a miracle exactly; and yet they were miracles too."

" What, Ditto? I don't remember," said Maggie.

"Don't you remember how Samuel asked for a
sign from heaven once, and the Lord sent thunder,
though it was a time of year when storms never
come. Then Elijah asked for a sign of fire, and
the fire fell and burnt up his sacrifice with the wet
pile of wood on which it lay, and licked up the
water in the trench. Don't you recollect? It was
that sort of sign the Jews used to ask Jesus to give
them, and he never would."

"I wonder why," said Flora.

"We must ask Mr. Murray. I do not know.
Any more remarks? or shall I go on?"

"O go on, dear Ditto."

"'Landolf rose up, quiet and joyous. It seemed
as if every man were pondering in his heart the
preaching and the prayer; all were yet hanging
upon his words; when up rose Heinrich's three
sons, priests of Thor like himself, along with his
only daughter, a priestess of Freija, whose sanctuary was situated about three hours further up
the Oerze. They cried in an open outburst of
rage,—"Our general assembly at the stone-houses
has led the people astray, in suffering the Christian preacher to proclaim his Christian faith. Come
over to us here, whoever is true to the gods of his
fathers! Death to apostates, and the vengeance of
the gods!"

"'The people went over to the side of Heinrich's
children. Landolf stood alone.

"'Landolf folded his hands in prayer, and looked
up to heaven with sparkling eyes; his heart ac-

cepted joyfully the martyr's crown, with which he thought God would adorn him. Once more he fell upon his knees to pray, and cried out in a clear voice, "O Lord, my God, I see heaven opened. Lord, I come gladly, but bless this people. Bless these my countrymen; do not charge their sins upon them; bring them to the true, saving faith of the Christians, make them children of thy church." Then he stepped up to the people and said, "Put me to death. I go gladly to my Jesus in heaven."

"'Upon this, old Heinrich stepped out in front of this faithful witness of the Lord, and with emotion he had hard work to keep down, he spoke: "Thou hast a brave heart. Thou shalt not die a coward's death. I love thee; thou art a hero, and thy Christ is a hero too. He died for sinners, thou sayst, and has vanquished death and the grave and hell. I will see if I can love him. I cannot yet."

"'Scarcely had he finished speaking, when Hermann hastily came up. He had followed after his beloved Landolf, that he might see what turn things would take; for he knew that he was gone to the island. He stretched out his hand to Heinrich, and Heinrich did not turn away, but grasped it. And then the old man brought them both into his house. In the meanwhile the sky became overcast with dark clouds; before anybody was aware, the heavens had grown black, the thunder rolled and the lightnings darted. "Thor is driving in the clouds!" cried the young priests; "he is angry at the Christians!" "The God of glory thundereth; the Lord is upon many waters; the voice of the Lord divideth the flames of fire "—cried Landolf; and with Heinrich and Hermann he went over to the island. The crowd stood there hushed; every eye was fixed intently upon the black clouds and the flashing lightning. Then there came a crash through the air, a blinding blaze darted out of the clouds, passed through the crowd, and shattered to pieces the sacrifice stone. Not a man was hurt. Then Landolf called out aloud: "'O Lord God, gracious and merciful, long-suffering and abundant in goodness and truth, that forgiveth iniquity and will by no means clear the guilty!' Brothers, the Lord has spoken from heaven. It is not Thor that is God; surely else he would not have destroyed his own altar and borne witness against himself. The Lord, he is the God; He has shattered the altar and left you alive; give the glory to God."

"'The people dispersed. But Heinrich repaired to Hermannsburg with Hermann and Landolf, to the dwelling of the former, and remained there eight days; during which time he was instructed by Landolf in the Christian faith. This teaching took deep hold of him; yet more did the utter revolution in Hermann's domestic life. After the eight days, he went back with the two to the little island, and was baptized in the Oerze. And on the spot where the round stone had been, there was a little chapel built, with an altar, and on the altar stood the image of the crucified Christ. This was the second great victory that Landolf fought for and gained. From that time forward Heinrich was his faithful helper. All the great influence which until then he had enjoyed as the much reverenced priest of Thor, he used now only for the glory of Christ. It seemed as if the old, grey-haired man had become young again. With all the zeal of a first love, with all a young convert's ardour, he witnessed for the Lord Jesus Christ, the mighty Hero, the Conqueror of Satan and of Thor, who had offered himself a sacrifice for men and died a hero's death; and in crowds the Saxons came over to him, and by crowds they received baptism from Landolf. His own sons alone remained hard, and his daughter was unmoved. This last, Ikia the chronicle calls her, never entered her father's house again; and the three sons, Tyr, Freyr, and Schwerting, who had so tenderly loved their father and so deeply revered him, declared to him now that they were no longer sons of his, since he was no longer priest of Thor. So then the venerable old man, sometimes alone, sometimes with Landolf or Hermann for a companion, every week set out to pay a visit to his sons and his daughter and preach the Lord Jesus to them. In the winter he was not to be daunted by the snow, nor in summer by the burning sands; leaning on his staff he pressed on through it all. The love of Christ fired him, and love to his children urged him forward; he would so fain take them with him to heaven. He had brought them up in the idolatrous worship of Thor; if they were lost, it seemed to him it would be by

his own fault. Therefore he made his weekly pil-
grimages to them, since they avoided his house as
though it were spotted with the plague. And then,
when he had preached Christ to them, he went back
to pray for them. Yes, he even made it a persis-
tent petition that the Lord Christ would not let
him die until he had seen his children walking in
the Lord's way.

"'A year and a half went by in this manner, and
still the hearts of his children seemed unimpres-
sible and hard as stone. But Heinrich walked,
preached, and prayed indefatigably, until at last
he gave way before the strain and the burden of
years. Eight days he lay on his bed, and yet
wrestled with God that he would not let him die
before he had seen the conversion of his children.
He sent messages to them, telling them that he was
sick; they never came near him. He sent to en-
treat them to come and receive his fatherly blessing; they answered, they did not want it. And so
all hope seemed to melt away. But the Scripture
says with truth, that Love is stronger than Death.
And if human love upon earth is so strong, how
great and strong must not the love of Jesus be!

"'One morning, Landolf was sitting beside his
friend's couch, trying to comfort him, and as he
thought, to prepare him for death, when in came
Schwerting, the youngest of Heinrich's sons, and
spoke: "Father, Ikia wants you. She is sick unto
death, and wishes to ask you to forgive her; she
sent me to you. But you cannot come," he went

on; "you are sick unto death yourself, and it may be will die now before Ikia, your child; and O she is so troubled! for she has never seen you again since that day on the island, and that is her fault!" At this, something like the glow of the sunlight swept over Heinrich's pale face, and leaning over to Landolf's ear, he whispered to him: "Pray to Christ with me, that I may go to Ikia, my daughter; and you will go along, that I may see her baptized." And Landolf kneels down by his friend's couch and prays, and Heinrich on his bed joins in the prayer, and they hold up to the Lord the word that he had given—"If two of you shall agree on earth as touching anything that ye shall ask, it shall be done for them of my Father which is in heaven;" and they doubt not that he is the Almighty and living God; therefore they ask that He will give strength and grace, that Heinrich may come to his daughter Ikia and see her baptism. And when they had finished praying, Heinrich rose up from his couch; bade them bring his horse; begged his friend and his son to help him to mount; and when he was seated on the beast's back he went forward, up the Oerze, towards the sanctuary of Freija, where Ikia was priestess. Landolf on one side, Schwerting on the other side, led the horse, and supported the tottering old man. Whoever met the procession joined it, for God's hand was plainly there; and after three hours of travelling Heinrich reached Ikia. He found her dying, but still in full possession of her senses. A happy smile flowed over her death-white features. "Father," said she, "the Christian's God is the true God. His hand has been too strong for me. I have been a godless child towards you; will you forgive me?" "My child," said her father, "I have forgiven you; and I have prayed to my God that he would not let me die till I have seen your conversion and that of your brothers, till I have seen you turn from false gods to the living God who has made heaven and earth, who has died for sinners and made intercession for the transgressors. I forgive thee, my daughter, and Christ also forgives thee, if thou wilt be baptized for the remission of sins. See here," pointing to Landolf, "here is the priest of the Lord. Let Landolf baptize my child, before she dies. Ikia, wilt thou be baptized?" She said, "Father, will Christ take me?" "My child, I have received you and not been angry with you, and I am a sinful man. And Christ, my Lord, is the Son of God; he died for sinners; and now he lives, and has the keys of hell and of death. He will receive thee, only believe." She turned her eyes inquiringly upon Landolf, and he spoke; "Ikia, it is written in the word of my God, 'this is a faithful saying and worthy of all acceptation, that Christ Jesus came into the world to save sinners, of whom I am chief.' So says the holy apostle Paul. And Jesus spoke to the thief on the cross, who had just been reviling him, but now had bethought himself, turned, and said, 'Lord, remember me when thou comest into thy kingdom'—He said to him, 'Verily, I say unto thee, this day shalt thou be with me in paradise!'" "Then baptize me, father, before I die. I believe that Christ is the Son of God." And Schwerting went out and fetched water in a bowl, and handed the bowl to Landolf. But when Landolf had spoken the prayer over the water and was about to baptize Ikia in the name of the Triune God, then down kneeled Schwerting at the side of his sister's couch; and from the crowd of people collected before the open door hurriedly broke forth two tall men and kneeled down by Schwerting's side; and all three cried out, "Father, baptize us with our sister!" The baptism was performed. And when it was done, and over the four newly baptized had been spoken the word—"The God of all grace by whom you have been born again in the washing of regeneration and renewing of the Holy Ghost, strengthen you and uphold you firm in the faith unto the end. Peace be with you,"—then the voice of old Heinrich who had sunk on his knees, came out in a shout of joy. "Lord, now lettest thou thy servant depart in peace, for my eyes have seen the salvation which I prayed the Lord for; that he would not suffer me to die before I had seen the conversion of my children." And when he had said that, he bowed his head and departed; and Landolf caught the dying man in his faithful arms. Ikia however did not die; the Lord, who had quickened her spiritually, gave her also her bodily life again. She recovered, and her recovery was a new salvation. For soon after, Freija's altar was broken to pieces, and an altar was dedicated to Christ on the same spot by the staunch Landolf, who founded a cloister there, *monasterium*, as it was called, from which the place took the name of Munster.　Heinrich's body was laid to rest in the churchyard at Hermannsburg.　So were the hearts of the children turned to the fathers; and it was not long before heathenism had disappeared from the valley of the Oerze, and the Lord Jesus was become the King to whom every knee in the country was bowed.'"

CHAPTER XI.

"Uncle Eden," said Maggie, "do you like Meredith's story?"

"Yes."

"Do you feel like talking now, Uncle Eden?"

"What about?"

"But I mean—do you feel like *talking*—about anything?"

"Depends on the subject, Maggie. Hark to that woodpecker!"

"Mr. Murray does *not* feel like talking, I know," remarked Flora. "He feels—if he ever feels!—lazy."

"No, Miss Flora, not exactly. And yet, how delicious this quiet is!"

"And the smell of the pines!"

"And the warm, luxurious air!"

"And the light through the pine branches, and upon the coloured leaves yonder."

"Yes, and the blue of the sky," said Mr. Murray, who lying upon his back had a good view. "Blue, through the pine needles. Such an ethereal, clear blue; not like summer's intensity."

"I like summer best," said Flora.

"I like this. But what did you want to talk about, children?"

"O Uncle Eden, a great many things. You see, we do not all think alike."

"Naturally."

"And we want you to tell us how we ought to think."

" *You* do"—said Mr. Murray laughing. "That will answer for ten years old. I am sure the others are more independent."

"But we want to know what *you* think, Uncle Eden—about ever so many things. We have been saving them up till you came. Ditto wants to know what Christians ought to do, about some things."

"And I hope you will tell him, Mr. Murray," said Flora, what Christians ought *not* to do—about some things."

Mr. Murray raised himself up on his elbows and looked at the young people around him. It was a very pretty picture. Fair young faces, that life had not clouded, intelligent and honest; bright young figures in all the freshness of neat attire and excellent personal care; the setting of the green wood, the brown carpet of pine needles, the hazy October air, here and there the crimson of a Virginia creeper, here and there the tawny hues of a cat briar or a wild grape vine; stillness and softness over all, the chirrup of a cricket, the cawing of two crows flying over, the interrupted tap of the woodpecker, just making you notice how still and soft it was; and then the bright, living young faces raised or turned, and waiting upon him. Mr. Murray looked and smiled, and did not at once speak; then he asked what subject came first? So many answers were begun at once that all had to stop; then Maggie getting the field said,

"We want to know how much a Christian ought really to give, Uncle Eden."

"Say rather—how much he ought to do," put in Meredith.

"Yes," added Flora; "we do want instruction on that point. Some of us are rather wild."

"Too big a subject for the present time and place," responded the referee of the little company. "To-morrow is Sunday; let us keep it for to-morrow, and come out here, or to some other place and discuss it."

"That is delightful!" cried Maggie clapping her hands. "Now—what were some of the other things, Ditto?"

"About the Saxons? But Mr. Murray did not hear our first story."

"O I know. I guess he knows. You do know about the old Saxons, don't you, Uncle Eden?"

"I know there was such a people."

"And you know they were very good and very bad—both at once; and we wanted to know *how* they could be so much worse, and yet so much better, than people nowadays."

"How 'so much better'?"

"They told the truth, Uncle Eden."

"There were no cowards and no marriage-breakers among them," Meredith added.

"And then how 'so much worse'?"

"O they were cruel! they offered human sacrifices; they were frightfully cruel."

"Yes," said Mr. Murray thoughtfully, "the contrast seems strange. They were a noble people in many ways."

"But Pastor Harms says they are not half so good now that they are Christians," Maggie went on.

"If that is true, there must be a reason for it."

"Yes, Uncle Eden; of course."

"And that reason cannot be found in their Christianity."

"But how is it, Uncle Eden?"

"Human nature is very much alike at all times, my child."

"But the old Saxons were not like the old Romans, Uncle Eden?—the word of a Saxon was better than a Roman's oath."

"And the modern Saxons are not like their forefathers," said Meredith; "at least according to Pastor Harms."

"I have no doubt he is right."

"And Frenchmen are very different from Englishmen," added Flora.

"And both from Americans. And the Dutch from all three. We might go on indefinitely."

"Yet they are all descended from Noah's sons," Meredith remarked.

"It is a very curious subject, and rather deep for some of the present company. Many things go to make the differences between one nation and another. In the first place, the several families of Shem, Ham and Japheth are all strongly marked."

"Are they, sir?"

"Then, among the tribes of any one family differences grow up from many causes. From the sort of country they inhabit, the climate that prevails, the scenery their eyes rest on, the ease or difficulty of obtaining food and the means necessary to that end; from the religion they believe in, their situation with respect to commerce and intercourse with other nations; their habits of life superinduced upon all these."

"But the modern Saxons live where the old Saxons did, sir?"

"Barely. The country was at that time all one wild tract of forest and moor; where life had need be of the simplest, and where it was sustained in great measure by the chase and by a rude husbandry. No cities, no churches, no libraries, no merchants, no lawyers, no fine furniture, no delicate living. Nobody therefore wanted money; and nobody tried to get it. That makes all the difference in the world, children."

"Money, Uncle Eden?"

"Look at the map of Germany now; run your eye over the cities. Remember the treasures of art in this and that gallery; the beautiful old buildings almost everywhere; the great trading houses; the life of complicated interests, political, literary, scientific, social, critical, artistic, mercantile; think of the books, the pictures, the statuary, the jewellery, the carvings and engravings, the luxurious and magnificent living; everybody wants money now, and nearly everybody either has it, or is working hard for it."

"Does money make so much odds in national character?" Meredith asked.

"It is the root of all evil," Mr. Murray said smiling.

"But Mr. Murray, you do not seriously mean that?" said Flora.

"The Bible says it, Miss Flora; not I."

"But what can you have, or do, that is worth anything, without money?"

"Exactly. That is the general opinion. So everybody is striving to get money."

"Well, people would stagnate, if they did not strive for something."

"Quite true. Nevertheless, the Bible award proves itself. If you examine facts, you will find that the love of money is at the bottom of nearly all the crimes that are committed; and at the root of all the meannesses, speaking generally."

"Then you would make out money to be a bad thing, Mr. Murray!"

"Not money necessarily. But 'if any man *will be rich*, he shall fall into temptation and a snare, and into many foolish and hurtful lusts, which drown men in destruction and perdition.'"

"Then was that the reason, Uncle Eden, why those old Saxons were so noble, because they had no money?"

"One reason, I fancy. Along with trade and riches, don't you see, comes the temptation to underhand and false dealings, that money may be got faster; and so comes cringing for the sake of advantage, and flattery for the same. And then, with luxury comes dislike of hardships, and neglect of manly living, and people's moral sense gets weak along with their bodily powers. Self-indulgence drives out the noble uprightness that was maintained when people feared nothing."

"But religion — Christianity?" said Meredith. "That ought to have made more difference the other way."

"So it would if it prevailed. But a name is not Christianity; and the real thing is only here and there. The wheat in the midst of tares, as the Lord said it would be."

Maggie drew a long sigh.

"The wheat must shew itself for what it is," said her uncle smiling at her, "and bear a fine head of fruit, to rebuke the tares. Your old Saxons however, were a fine stock to begin with."

"I think I understand this question," said Meredith.

"I do, too," said Maggie.

"I am sorry Mr. Murray thinks so ill of money—" remarked Flora.

"Of the love of it, say."

"But how can one have it—or not have it, for that matter—and help loving it?"

"So the danger comes in.   And the difficulty of giving it all to Christ."

"O Uncle Eden, you are getting upon another of our questions now."

"And we have had enough serious talk for one time.   Leave it till to-morrow, Maggie."

"Shall I read some more?" said Meredith.   "Or have you heard enough?"

"By all means, read.   This is luxury."

And Mr. Murray stretched himself comfortably on the pine needles and clasped his hands under his head, repeating, "This is luxury!" while Meredith opened his book again.

"Another Saxon story, Ditto?" Flora asked.

"Out of the Saxon chronicles.   Yes.   'The story that I am going to tell you now, happened in ancient times and at a place called Dageförde.

"'Our forefathers, the old Saxons, were then divided into ediling or nobles, freiling or free peasants, and serfs.   A freiling, by name Henning, lived on this farm, in the days when Hermann Billing was duke of Saxony.   At that time, it is 900 years ago, our country was already a Christian country, but still had hard fights to go through with the heathenish Wends, who made inroads almost yearly into our Eastphalian land, plundering and killing, and showing a special rage against the churches and the priests.   The strong arm of the two excellent emperors, Heinrich and Otto, it is true, kept back these heathen and held them in awe; but notwithstanding, they availed themselves of every opportunity to renew their murderous on-slaughts.

"'Now when once Kaiser Otto was gone to Italy, and staying a long while away, they were minded to profit by his absence; for they supposed that now they could burn and lay waste to their heart's de-sire, and with no hindrance. So they came with a great host, burned down the churches, killed the priests, dragged off men, women and children and treasures of booty, and came as far as to this part of the country. It is told of their frightful rage against Christianity, that on one occasion they took more than twenty Christian priests, stripped off their clothes, cut bloody crosses on their faces, breasts, bodies and backs, and then tied them by their feet to the tails of their horses, which they drove round and round till their victims were dragged to death.'"

"It cost something in those days to be a Chris-tian!" said Meredith with something of a shudder.

"There have been many such days in the history of the church," said Mr. Murray. "And yet, it pays, to be a Christian! It did then."

"I do not see, for my part, how people stood it, there and in other places," said Flora. "I should think they would not have dared to confess they were Christians."

"They could not be Christians and not confess. Neither in those days nor in these days."

"Why, Uncle Eden?" said Esther, who seldom said anything.

"You know the Lord's declaration—he will own those publickly who own him publickly; *and nobody else.*"

"But why couldn't they own him privately?"

"Will you tell me how that is to be done my dear?"

"Why—by beautiful Christian living and acting," said Flora.

"Don't you see, if such living could be found among those who are in name and profession not the Lord's, it would fight all *against* his cause and him? What sort of confessing of *him* is that?"

Nobody answered and Meredith went on.

"'In the meanwhile the valiant Duke Hermann had gathered his faithful followers and moved forward to meet the enemy. All the ediling and freiling were called upon for such expeditions of war, none other having the right to bear arms. The ediling served on horseback and the freiling on foot, and each one brought his own weapons with him. And Henning, the freiling of Dageförde, was among the Christian warriors who accompanied the duke. Not far from here is the Hünenburg, an extent of heath, on which there are a number of burial mounds. There it came to a battle between the Christians and the heathen. The fight was long and bloody; Christ led the one host, Satan the other. The Christians fought for their faith, the heathen fought for their prey. Before the battle,

Hermann with his warriors had cast himself upon his knees and besought the Lord Christ that He would be their leader. Therewith came the storm of the heathen upon them, already certain of victory, for they were many and the Christian number was small; Hermann in his noble eagerness to protect his poor people, not having had patience to wait for further reinforcements. But the Christians stood immovable, like a wall, and the heathen fell in heaps under their swords and spears. In the Christian army there were twelve priests wearing white garments, who bore a white banner with a red cross; and wherever the fight raged most madly, thither they carried their banner, singing, "Kyrie Eleison, Christe Eleison, Kyrie Eleison;" the Christian warriors dashing after them, joining in the holy song, wielding their hacked swords, and with irresistible force driving the heathen back. In vain the heathen sought to slay the priests and to seize their white banner; every Christian presented his breast as its bulwark against the foe. Whichever way the banner turned, victory went with it. Louder and louder sounded the "Kyrie Eleison," with more and more valour and joy of victory the Christians pressed forward. Then one of the Wendish leaders, Zwentibold by name, gathered once more the bravest of his people to make a stormy effort for the banner of the cross. His rage of onset broke through some ranks of the Christians; already he had penetrated to the near neighbourhood of the priests; when a foot soldier from among the Christians manfully planted himself in his way and thrust his sharp spear against the heathen's broad breast so that the coat of chain armour he had on was broken, and the spear pierced through his heart. Now there was no stand made any longer; the heathen fled, and in terror they cried out, "Christ has conquered! Christ has conquered!"

"'Duke Hermann looked about him to see the brave freiling who had done such a deed of heroism; it was Henning, the freiling of Dageförde. For his reward, Hermann dubbed the brave man knight upon the field of battle; and Henning returned to his house as an ediling. Though but for a little while. For Hermann was minded to profit by his victory and compel his stubborn enemies to keep the peace in future. So he pushed on with his army, now greatly reinforced, into the country of the Wends, and Henning went with his duke.

"'Not far from the Elbe there was a temple of the heathenish idol Radegast; this temple stood within a strong fortress, called the fortress of Radegast; where now the village of Radegast lies. The heathen had collected and carried to this place all the treasures of the prey they had seized in their plundering incursions. Hermann resolved to storm this fortress, and therewith to destroy the bulwark of heathenism on this side the Elbe. The heathen defended themselves with the bravery of despair; many assaults were beaten back, and many a Christian fell in death before the ramparts of the fortress.

The tenth day of the siege, the Christians held divine service and on their knees prayed the Lord of hosts to give them victory. Then they rushed upon the place to take it by storm; and among the foremost of those who clambered up the ramparts of the fortress was Henning of Dageförde, who in order to inspirit the Christians and terrify the heathen set up the field song of the Hünenburg— "Kyrie Eleison, Christe Eleison, Kyrie Eleison!" Just as he had sung it through, an arrow from one of the enemy pierced his bold heart; he fell to the ground in death, but as a dying conqueror, who has gained the battle for Christ and with Christ. The fortress was won; those of the heathen who would not yield were put to death. Hermann dashed away a tear from his manly eye as he buried the brave Henning, and he said to Hilmer, Henning's oldest son, a boy of sixteen, who had come along to the war, "My son, you are early fledged. Your father was a true Christian and a true Saxon; follow in his steps, and so long as I live, I will be your father." Of all the enormous booty which Hermann found in the Wendenburg Radegast, this noble man kept nothing for himself. One half of the treasures he set apart, to rebuild with them all the churches which the Wends had burned down; the other half he distributed among his knights and warriors. Hilmer of Dageförde got his share too, and indeed a double portion, one for himself and one for his father. When he returned home, he took counsel with his mother what they should do with it; and they agreed together that it should be used for the glory of God. They erected a chapel in their own house, with an altar and all the fittings of a church. Part of the money was applied to this use, and with the remainder a chaplaincy was founded in the church at Hermannsburg, which at that time was the only church in the whole Oerze valley, with the stipulation that the chaplain should come every Sunday to Dageförde and hold divine service in the chapel there. A servant, with a led horse, must go to fetch him every time from Hermannsburg and bring him back thither again. This service at Dageförde lasted till the Reformation. But when the evangelical faith was preached in Hermannsburg by the valiant Pastor Grünhagen, who, as I told you awhile ago in Tiefenthal, was converted to the pure Lutheran doctrine by an artisan fellow who read him the little Lutheran catechism, then this service at Dageförde ceased, because the possessors of Dageförde held stiffly and firmly by the Catholic faith and obstinately rejected the pure doctrine. But now for a long time there have been lords of Dageförde no more. The race died out; and when one only of the family was left, he entered a Catholic cloister, where in the year 1616 he died. Then the reigning duke gave the manor of Dageförde to the lords of Lüneburg, and they again sold it to some peasants, after they had divided the farm into two. So these farms have again become what they were originally—peasant farms. God grant to the present owners that they may stand firm and true to the pure faith of our beloved church, that they may earnestly strive to be genuine Christians and genuine Saxon peasants; then will it go well with them and with those that come after them.'"

CHAPTER XII.

Meredith paused, half closed his book, was evidently pondering for a minute, and then exclaimed, "I have learned something!"

"Why so have we all," said his sister. "What now particularly?"

"I have got a hint."

"What about? There is no fortress for you to storm—and you do not want the treasure."

"I think I should like to have lived in those times," Meredith went on. "People were in earnest, Mr. Murray."

"Yes. So are some people in these times."

"But not the world generally; or only about making money. *Then* people were in earnest about things worth the while."

"It does seem so from these stories," said Mr. Murray; "but dear Meredith, you may be equally in earnest about the same things now, and with as good reason."

"Isn't it more difficult, sir, when nobody else, or only a few here and there, think and feel with you?"

"Yes—more difficult; or rather more easy to go to sleep; but so much the greater need of men who are not asleep. What is your hint? I am curious, with Miss Flora."

"The way that fellow spent his treasure, sir. I was thinking. Wouldn't a chapel—that is a little church, a little free church, at Meadow Park be a good thing? The nearest church is two miles off; we can drive to it, but the people who have no horses cannot, and the poor people—"

Meredith got a variety of answers to this suggestion. His sister opened her mouth for an outcry of dismay. Maggie clapped her hands with a burst of joy. Esther stared; and a smile, very sweet and wise, shewed itself on Mr. Murray's lips.

"Quixotic!—ridiculous!" said Flora. "Isn't it, Mr. Murray? Ditto has not money enough for everything either. A church!—and then, I suppose, a minister!"

"Is it a bad notion, Mr. Murray?" inquired Meredith.

"I should think not—very."

"Is it extravagant?"

"Miss Flora thinks so."

"Well, Mr. Murray, think what it would cost!" cried the young lady.

"Not so much as a large evening party—that is, it ought not. I suppose Meredith is not thinking of stone carvings and painted windows, but of a neat, pleasant, pretty, plain house where people can worship God and hear the words of life."

"That is it exactly," said Meredith.

"Then I should say that one very fine evening entertainment would build two."

"But the minister? he must be paid," said Flora.

"Yes, and I am not for starving a minister, either," said Mr. Murray. "But what is Meredith to do with his income, Miss Flora?"

"That's just what I want to know," remarked Meredith in an undertone; while Flora answered with some irritation—

"He can let it accumulate, till he has made up his mind."

"'Riches kept for the owners of them, to their hurt,'" said Mr. Murray. "Better not, Miss Flora. Remember, Meredith is only a steward. 'The silver is mine, and the gold is mine,' saith the Lord of hosts."

"Do you mean, Mr. Murray, that we cannot do what we like with our money?"

"You can do what you like with it, certainly."

"But I mean, isn't it *right* for us to do what we like with it?"

"I should like to do that,"—murmured Meredith.

"Miss Flora, the question is, rightly stated,—May a steward use his lord's money for his own or his lord's pleasure?"

Flora coloured, and pouted. "But that makes religion—Why, I never thought religion was strict like *that*. Then it isn't right to buy jewels, or dresses."

"Dresses—certainly."

"But I mean, rich dresses; dresses for company. And pictures—and horses—and books—and—"

"Stop, Miss Flora. The servant himself belongs to his lord; therefore he must make of himself the very best he can. For this, books will certainly be needed and to some degree all the other things you have named, except jewels and what you call *rich* dresses. The only question in each case is—'How can I do the Lord's work best? how can I spend this money to honour and please him most?' That will not always be by the cheapest dress that can be bought; nor by checking the cultivation of taste and the acquiring of knowledge, nor even by the foregoing of arts and accomplishments. Only the question comes back at every step, and must at every step be answered—'What does the Lord want me to do *here?* Does he wish me to spend this money—or time—on myself, or on somebody else?'"

"Why it would be *always* on somebody else," said Flora, looking ready to burst into tears; "and there would be no real living at all! no enjoying of life."

"A mistake"—said Mr. Murray quietly. "The Lord told us long ago—'He that will save his life shall lose it; and he that loseth his life for my sake, *the same shall find it.*'"

Flora put up her hand over her eyes, but Meredith's eyes sparkled.

"Then you think well of my plan, Mr. Murray?" he said.

"As far as I understand it."

"How would the Pavilion do, for a skeleton of the church?"

"O Ditto! the dear old Pavilion!" exclaimed Maggie.

"Why not? I do not want to shut myself off from everybody now—and I have the whole house; more than enough. And the Pavilion stands in a good-place, near the road."

Mr. Murray and Meredith went into a discussion of the plan, and Maggie listened, while Flora after a while resumed her work and went moodily on with it. At last Mr. Murray remarked,

"This is not so interesting to everybody, Meredith, and we have time enough to talk it over. Suppose you go on reading."

"Do you like these Saxon stories?" said Meredith, pleased.

"Very much."

"There is some more here about—not Dageförde exactly,—but that same fight, which I think you would like perhaps to hear."

"And Meredith, you did not read us about that minister who was converted by the catechism," said Maggie.

"No, that is another story—Pastor Grünhagen. I will read to you first about the fight at the Hünenburg.

"'The Hünenburg is situated in a deep dell in the midst of the heath about an hour from Hermannsburg; and I will relate to you what I have

found in the chronicle about it.   It is nine hundred
years now since a hard-fought and terrible battle
took place here, which was fought between the
Christians and the heathen.   At that time the pious and Christian kaiser, Otto the Great, ruled in
Germany (A. D. 936–973), who loved the Lord his
God with all his heart.   He had gone away out of
Germany into Italy, in order to free a captive queen
who was kept in prison there by some godless folk.
But he would not leave Germany without protection; therefore he made over this country to Duke
Hermann, to govern it and to take care of it.   In
like manner Adaldag, archbishop of Hamburg and
Bremen, who went with the kaiser, confided his
dominions to the same guardianship.   Now the
Wends, who lived on the other side of the Elbe,
especially in Mechlenburg, and had spread themselves abroad on this side the Elbe also, were at
that time still heathen.   And now when the kaiser
was absent, they thought the time was come for
marauding and plundering, hunting the Christians
out of their country, or utterly destroying them.
So they summoned up all their warriors, and that
so secretly that the Christians knew nothing of it
until they came breaking into the country.   As
there was nowhere any preparation for defence
against them, they robbed and plundered all that
came in their way, burned down the churches,
killed the priests, and dragged the rest into cap-
tivity for slaves.   Duke Hermann was just then in
the Bremen territory, from whence he had expelled

the piratical Northmen (the Danes). There the
terrible news found him. In the greatest haste he
collected his warriors to come and save his country. For the Wends had already penetrated to
Lüneburg, as far as this heath, and had laid everything waste with fire and sword; the Hermannsburg church was destroyed by them at that time.
Here upon this ground they had made a strong en-
campment, and surrounded it with ditches and forti-
fications like a fortress; they were from fifty to six-
ty thousand men strong, in horsemen and footmen,
and all of them alive with the same enraged hatred
of the Christians, and determined that every trace
of Christianity should be wiped away from the
land. In August of the year 945 Duke Hermann
marched hither out of the Bremen country, over
the northern heights of Liddernhausen and Dohn-
sen. When he saw himself with his eight thousand men on foot and two thousand horsemen con-
fronted by the great host of the Wends, he said to
his faithful followers—"We must fight; whether
God will give us the victory, we must leave with
him." Then stepped up one of his knights before
him, who is called in the chronicle "the brave
Conrad," of the now extinct race of them of Haselhorst, and spoke:—

"'"Let us get a token from God. I will go forward and challenge one of the enemy to single
combat; so will the Lord shew us to whom he has
allotted the victory."

"'Duke Hermann gave permission. The knight,

followed at some distance by a hundred men, who were to see that all was done in order, rode alone into the defile and challenged Mistewoi, the leader of the Wends, to send one of his people to meet him in single combat. Then stepped forward Zwentibold, a Wend of giant stature, clad in a dragon skin and with a shirt of link mail over it, and on the head of his helmet the black image of his god Zernebok; behind him also a hundred men to look on. The Christian knight first called upon God to be his helper and protection; "Lord remember how thou gavest strength to thy servant David against the giant Goliath who had reviled thy name; so now to-day establish thy glory among the heathen, and shew plainly that thou art the true God."

"'Upon that, with lances in rest they charged upon each other; and when the spears were splintered in that first shock, then it came to a fight with swords, man against man. Suddenly comes a traitor's arrow from the Wends flying through the air and kills the Christian's horse. But their wickedness turns to their own knight's ruin. For as the Wend gallops up to the fallen Christian, and is about to cut him down with a stroke from above, up springs the Christian knight and thrusts his sword in under the other's shoulder, so that he falls dead from his horse. The victory is won! But hereupon comes new treachery. For now those hundred Wends charge straight down upon the German knight. As his own attendants perceive this, they hasten to his help, nothing loath;

the armies on both sides close in, and the fight soon becomes general. It is fought with the utmost bitterness and bravery on both sides, till evening fall. But the Christians all the while press steadily forward.

"'While the men wielded the sword, the wives of the Christians came out to the field, drew away the wounded and sucked the blood from their wounds (because they believed that the arrows of the Wends were poisoned), bound them up, and encouraged their husbands and sons to make brave fight. A company of twelve priests carried a banner with a red cross on a white ground. The priests sang, "Kyrie Eleison!" ("Lord, have mercy upon us!") "Christe Eleison! Kyrie Eleison!" and the people chimed in. A terror of God went with them wherever they went and scattered the Wends from every place where the white banner came. As one of the heathen leaders with a company was making a determined rush upon the banner, the peasant of Dageförde drove his spear through the chieftain's coat of mail into his breast. Thereupon the heathen all fled. And all the Christians fell upon their knees and all cried out, "Lord God, we praise thee!" Then the priests spoke the benediction over the victorious host. And they left nothing remaining of the enemy's camp, but destroyed it entirely, because they would not suffer any heathen works upon their ground. But the name has remained; for Hühnen was the name our forefathers gave to all heathen; that came from the

Huns in the first place, who fell upon the Christians with such heathenish rage. So that place is called Hühnenburg until this day.

"'The church at Hermannsburg was rebuilt again after that time. And soon also Christianity came to the Wends, and the Lord Jesus was conqueror over them all.'"

"You read part of that before," said Maggie.

"Part of the story, but I thought you would like to have the whole."

"O I do. But I thought it was Zwentibold that Henning of Dageförde killed, when he was trying to get at the white banner?"

"Maybe there were two Zwentibolds. Or the story got a little confused among the old chroniclers."

"Then how is one to know which is true?"

"It is difficult very often, Maggie," her uncle said smiling. "Human testimony is a strange thing, and very susceptible of getting confused."

"What will you read next, Ditto? About the minister who was converted—"

"O no," said Flora. "Let the catechism alone. Haven't you got some more Saxon stories, Meredith?"

"Plenty. Which shall it be, Mr. Murray?"

"Saxon, for this time."

"'THE REMMIGA FARM.

"'As in my former narrations I have told of the glorious victory which with God's help Landolf

13

gained over the old priest Heinrich and his children, I will tell you now of a third victory which the Lord granted him. An hour from here was a farm which in the chronicle is called the Remmiga manor; it was inhabited by a free man, named Walo. His wife's name was Odela; sometimes the chronicle calls her Adela. The name is one, for the word Adel is often written and spoken as Odel in the old manuscripts. The pair had a son, who bore his father's name.

"'As owner of a head manor, Walo was at the same time priest of the community; which dignity always went along with the possession of a chief manor among the old Saxons. All the councils and courts of the community were held under his presidency; he brought the sacrifices thereto pertaining; and it is easy to imagine what consideration on all these accounts he enjoyed. This consideration was still further heightened by the fact of his knowledge of the old laws and customs, and by his incorruptible truth and uprightness. Like Heinrich, he too was at the beginning a determined enemy of the Christian religion. Landolf visited him frequently and told him about the Lord Jesus, but Walo's ear was deaf to the truth of the Gospel. He knew from old legends that once upon a time two brothers, the white and the black Ewald, who had preached Christianity among the Saxons, had been by them sacrificed to their idols. And so, with Saxon tenacity holding fast to the old traditions, he told Landolf to his face, that in justice he ought to

suffer the same fate which had fallen upon the two
Ewalds; and that it could not be carried out upon
him, simply because the decision of the people,
taken by the national assembly at the stone-houses,
once taken became a law, according to which the
free preaching of the Gospel was permitted. Landolf did not allow himself to be daunted by this,
but continued his visits and his teachings; for he
observed that Walo, in spite of all that, always listened with attention when he told about the Lord
Christ.

"'One day Landolf came again to Remmiga.
He found Walo sitting in front of his dwelling, by
the place of sacrifice, where the assemblies of the
district were wont to be held; still and sunk in his
own thoughts. Near him stood his wife Odela and
his little son, who was perhaps twelve years old.
The boy ran joyously to meet Landolf and said,
"It is nice that you have come. I have just been
asking father to let me go away with you; I would
like to hear a great deal about the Lord Jesus; I
want to be his disciple. Mother is glad; and"—
he whispered softly, "she loves the Son of God too;
but father feels very troubled, and don't like it;
he says he has lost his wife and his son to-day!"
Odela gave Landolf her hand and spoke aloud.
"Yes, I love Jesus; I want to be his disciple; but
Walo will have none of it; and so I too will go
with you, that I may hear about Jesus and be baptized."

"'Landolf hardly knew where he stood. Until

this time Odela and her son had listened in silence when he talked about Jesus, but never a word had they spoken. Now they told how, while he talked, the Lord Jesus had so grown into their hearts that they could not get loose from him again; and they did not wish to get loose; for they wanted to be saved and to come into the Christian's heaven where Jesus is and the holy angels.

" 'Then up rose Walo, turned a dark look upon Landolf and said to him, "Thou hast led astray my wife and my son with thy words, and now I have no wife and no son any more. Go out of my grounds; take my wife and my son with thee; they have no love for me any longer; their love is for Jesus."

" ' "O Walo," Landolf answered, "seest thou not yet that thy gods are dead idols?. Dost thou not see that Jesus is the true, the living God? Jesus has won their hearts; thine idols cannot win hearts; thou mayest see that by thy wife and thy son. Let Jesus gain thy heart too. You shall all three be saved."

" 'Walo shook his head. "He wins not my heart!"

" ' "Then," cried the servant of the Lord joyfully, "then shall thy wife and thy son win thy heart for Jesus. Thy wife and thy son desire to be baptized. Thou canst not hinder them; they are free; they are noble born. I am going to baptize them now, this day, in thy presence; for they believe in Jesus, that he is the Son of God. But I know that thy wife and thy son are dear to thee, and thou art very dear to them, only Jesus is dearer yet. Let them remain with thee after they are baptized; do not thrust them out from thy house. And if when they are baptized they love thee still better than formerly, if they are more dutiful to thee than formerly, wilt thou then believe that Jesus is mightier than thine idols? Thou hast often told me that Odela is proud and passionate, though in all else good and noble. Now if when she is baptized she becomes humble and gentle, wilt thou then believe that Jesus can give people new hearts?"

"'Walo looked at the glad Landolf with an astonished face. "Odela humble and gentle?" said he. "Yes, then I will believe that Jesus can make the heart new; I will believe that he is God, and I will worship him."

"'"Give me thy right hand, Walo," said Landolf; "I know a Saxon keeps his word and never tells a lie, and Walo before all others."

"'They shook hands. Landolf did not delay. He went immediately for Hermann and Heinrich and fetched them to share in his joy and to act as the sponsors. And O how gladly they came. That same evening Adela and her son were baptized in the name of the Triune God; and Landolf joyously reminded them that he had promised Walo his wife and his son should win his heart for Christ.

"'A year passed away, and on the very day on which Adela and her son had been baptized, Walo also received baptism; for the Christianized

Adela had become humble and gentle, because Jesus dwelt in her heart; and after their baptism she and her son had loved the husband and father still more ardently and had been more obedient to him than before. Walo confessed, "they are better than I." O the Christian walk, the Christian walk! how mighty it is to convert; the walk of Christians is the living preaching of the living God.

"'And now a Christian chapel was erected by Walo at Remmiga, on the place of sacrifice; and around the chapel there rose up a Christian village, which established itself upon his soil and territory; a brook ran through the new village, which was therefore called Bekedorf, and is called so at the present day; it lies in the parish of Hermannsburg. The chapel stood till the thirty years' war; it was burnt down then by Tilly's marauders and has never been built up again. But there is more of the story. Walo died old and full of days, in the arms of his wife and son. Landolf had gone home long before, and so had old Hermann and Heinrich. But the young Walo had grown to be the most faithful friend of Hermann's son, who was also named Hermann, and who by Kaiser Otto the Great was made duke of Saxony. So then, when Hermann Billing was made the kaiser's lieutenant of the kingdom in northern Germany, upon occasion of Otto's journey into Italy, Hermann made his faithful Walo a graf, that is, one of the chief judges of the country; and he travelled about and wrought justice and righteousness, and was, as the Scripture says of an upright judge, "for a terror to evil-doers and the praise of them that did well." He married Odelinde, a noble young lady; who also loved the Saviour, and had been brought up by the good cloister ladies at the Quänenburg. They led a happy and God-fearing life, but they had no children. When now both of them were old and advanced in years, Odelinde one day was reminding her husband of the blessing she had received from the pious training of the cloister ladies; and she asked him whether, as they had no children, and were rich, they might not found another cloister with' their money, in which noble young girls should be educated by good cloister sisters. Walo complied with her wish gladly; for he loved the kingdom of God, and at that time the cloisters were simply the abodes of piety; they were not yet places of idleness, but of diligence; not homes of lawlessness, but of modesty; not of superstition, but of faith.

"'About four miles from his place on the river Böhme lay a wide tract of meadow land, bordered by a magnificent thick wood of oaks and beeches. When Walo travelled through the country as graf, he had often been greatly pleased with this spot; and it had occurred to him that such beauty ought not to remain any longer given up to wild beasts, but should become a dwelling-place for men. This thought recurred now vividly to his mind. His wife desired to see the place too. So they went to view it, and decided to build a cloister there, around which then other human dwellings would grow up,

but the cloister itself should be the home of pious
ladies whose special business should be the bringing up of nobly born young girls. The wood was
rooted up' (*roden* is to root up); 'and on the *Rode*'
(that is, the space cleared) 'the cloister was built,
which thereupon was called *Walo's Rode;* about
which later the village *Walsrode* was settled, which
still later spread itself out into a little city, having
the cloister to thank for its origin. Walo not only
built the cloister at his own expense, but also endowed it for its support with the tithes of the Bekedorf village, which belonged to the manor. It is
but a little while since the Bekedorfers bought off
these tithes.

"'I must state, however, that in my extracts
from the chronicle there occurs a divergence from
the usual dates. That is, I have formerly read
under a picture of Graf Walo in the cloister church
at Walsrode the number of the year 986. In my
extracts on the other hand it is said that the cloister was founded by Walo in the year of grace 974,
and consecrated by Bishop Landward of Münden.
The last can be explained by the fact that the valley of the Oerze belonged to the see of Münden
and not to the nearer Verden, and therefore Walsrode also being founded from hence, must be consecrated by the Münden bishop. But as to the difference of the two dates, I can do nothing further
to clear that up; since I am no investigator of history, but have simply written down what I have
found.'"

CHAPTER XIII.

"I like that," said Maggie sedately.

"How curiously near it seems to bring the Middle ages," said Meredith. "The picture of Graf Walo! And Pastor Harms has seen it."

"Why couldn't Walo build a school-house, without making a cloister of it?" asked Maggie.

"There were really reasons, apart from religious ones," Mr. Murray replied. "You remember your views of old castles on the Rhine, perched up on inaccessible heights?"

"It must have been very inconvenient," said Flora. "Imagine it!"

"It would have been worse than inconvenient to live below in the valley. A rich noble could not have been sure of keeping any precious thing his house held—unless his retainers were very numerous and always on duty; and in that case the lands would have come by the worst. The only really secure places, Maggie, were the religious houses."

"What dreadful times!" said Flora.

"So these stories shew them."

"Uncle Eden," said Esther, "it is time to go in and get ready for dinner."

"Is it? O this pine wood is better than dinner! Look how the light is coming red through the boles of the trees! Feel this air that is playing about my face! Smell the pines!"

"But you will want dinner, Uncle Eden, all the same, and it will be ready."

"Well—" said Mr. Murray, rousing himself so far as to get upon one elbow.

"Where shall we go for our reading to-morrow afternoon?" said Maggie.

"The Lookout rock"—suggested Meredith.

"Do you like that, Uncle Eden?"

"I like it all, Maggie. If to-morrow is like to-day, I think the Lookout rock will be very enjoyable."

"And then you can look at the sky while you are talking to us," said Maggie comfortably.

"Why precisely at the sky?" Meredith asked laughing.

"O it's so beautiful up there!—sometimes."

They sauntered slowly back to the house, through the sweet pines, under the illuminating red rays which were coming level against the tree-stems. Then out of the wood and among the flower-beds and shrubbery surrounding the house; with the open view of sky and river, purple-brown and ruddy gold lights flowing upon the sides of the hills, reflecting the western brilliance, which yet was warm and rich rather than dazzling.

"I never saw such a place as this!" exclaimed Meredith for the fourth or fifth time.

"The world is a wonderful place generally," observed Mr. Murray thoughtfully. "Rich—rich! 'the riches of his grace,' and the riches of his wisdom."

They were a very happy party at dinner. Fenton, it is true, came out singularly in the conversation, and gave a number of details respecting life at school and his views of life in the world. Mr. Murray's answers however were so humourous and so wise and sweet at the same time, that it seemed Fenton only furnished a text for the most pleasant discourse. And after dinner Maggie got out stereoscopic views, and she and others delighted themselves with a new look at the Middle ages.

"What a strange thing it must be," said Meredith, "to live where every farm and every church has a history; of course every village."

"Haven't farms and villages in our country a history?" Maggie inquired.

"No," said Esther. "Of course not."

"A few," said Mr. Murray. "Such New England farms for instance as still bear the names 'Lonesome'—and 'Scrabblehard.' But the histories are not very old, and refer to nothing more picturesque than the struggles of the early settlers."

"What struggles?" Maggie wanted to know.

"Struggles for life. With the hard soil, with the hard climate, and with the wild Indians. But such struggles, Maggie, left an inheritance of strength, patience and daring, to their children."

"Why haven't we stories like those of the Saxons?"

"Why!" exclaimed Fenton impatiently, "are you such a simple? There was nothing here but red Indians till a little while ago."

"We have not been a nation for more than a hundred years, Maggie," said Meredith.

"And before that, were the Indians here at Mosswood?"

"No, no," said Fenton. "You had better study history."

"As *you* have," put in his uncle, "won't you tell Maggie when the first settlements of the English were made in America?"

However, Fenton could not.

"In the beginning of the seventeenth century, it was, Maggie, that the first colonies were established here. The Dutch came to New York, and the Puritans to New England, and a little earlier, the English colonists to Virginia. We are a young country."

"Is it better to be a young country, or to be an old one?"

"The young country has its life before it," said Mr. Murray smiling;—"like a young girl."

"How, Uncle Eden?"

"She has the chance still to make it noble and beautiful."

"We can't have these grand old castles, though," said Meredith, looking at the view of Sonneck.

"Those are the picturesque scars remaining of a

time which was not beautiful—except to the eye. I suppose it was that."

The conversation took a turn too historical to be reported here.

The next day was a worthy successor of the preceding. All the party went to church in the morning; on account of the distance nobody went in the afternoon. Mr. Candlish would not have his horses and servants called out in the latter half of the day. The dinner was early; and so then after dinner the party set out upon a slow progress to the Lookout rock; carrying Bibles, and Meredith with his little German volume in his pocket.

Another such afternoon as the yesterday's had been! Warm, still, fragrant, hazy; more hazy than ever. The outlines of the distant hills were partially veiled; the colours on the middle distance glowing, mellow and soft, all the sun's glitter being shielded off. Slowly and enjoyingly the little company wandered along, leaving the lawns and pleasure ground of flowers behind them; through the cedars, past the spot where a day or two ago they had sat and read and eaten their chicken pie. Past that, and then up a winding steep mountain road that led up to the height of the point above. Just before the top was reached they turned off from the way, towards the left whence glimpses of the river had been coming to them, and after a few steps over stones and under the trees which covered all the higher ground, emerged from both upon a broad, smooth top of a great outlying mass of granite rock which overhung the river. Not literally; a stone dropped from the edge would have rolled, not fallen, into the water; a stone thrown from the hand easily might have done the latter. The precipice was too sheer to let any but those sitting on the very edge of the rock look down its rugged, tree-bedecked side; however, Mr. Murray and Meredith at once placed themselves on that precise edge of the platform, while the girls and Fenton. sat down in what they considered a safer position. A hundred feet below, just below, rolled the broad river; Mosswood's projecting point to the right still shutting off all view of the upper stream, while the jutting forth of Gee's Point below on the other side, equally cut off the southern reach of the river. The trees at hand right and left, above and below, standing in autumn's gay colours; the hillsides and curves of the opposite shore shewing the same hues more mild under the veil of haze and the distance. Not a leaf fluttered on its stem, in the deep stillness; but far down below one could hear the soft lapping of the water as it flowed past the rocks. The stillness and the light filled up the measure of each other's beauty.

For a while everybody was silent. There was a spell of nature, which even the young people did not care to break. Flora drew a long breath, at last, and then Maggie spoke.

"Uncle Eden—we came here to talk."

"Did we?"

"I thought we did,—to talk and to read."

"Nature is doing some talking, and we are listening."

"What does Nature say?"

"Do you hear nothing?"

Maggie thought she *did*, and yet she could not have told what. "It is not very plain, Uncle Eden," she remarked.

"It becomes plainer and plainer the older you grow, Maggie,—that is, supposing you keep your ears open."

"But I would like to know what your ears hear, Uncle Eden."

"It will be more profitable to go into the subjects you wanted to discuss. What are they?"

"I made a list of them, Uncle Eden," said Maggie, foisting a crumpled bit of paper out of her pocket. "Uncle Eden, Ditto read to us some stories which you didn't hear,—it was just before you came,—about poor people who gave the only pennies they had to pay for sending missionaries, and went without their Sunday lunch to have a penny to give; and Flora said she thought it was wrong; and we couldn't decide how much it was right to do."

"It is a delicate question."

"Well how much *ought* one, Uncle Eden?"

"You do not want to go without your lunch?"

"No sir.—Ought I, Uncle Eden?"

"My dear, the Lord's rule is, 'Every man according as he purposeth in his heart, so let him give.' What you *want* to give, that is what the Lord likes to receive."

"Don't he like to receive anything but what we like to give?"

"He says,—'The Lord loveth a cheerful giver.'"
There was a pause.

"But Mr. Murray," said Flora, "isn't there such a thing as a duty of giving?"

"There is such a thing."

"That is what we want to know.   What is it? What is the duty, I mean."

"What does the Bible say it is, you mean?"

"Yes sir, certainly."

"I am afraid you will think the rule a sweeping one.   The Lord said, 'This is my commandment, that ye love one another as I have loved you.'"
Another pause.

"But we were talking of *giving*, Mr. Murray."

"Love will give, where it is needful."

"But will nothing but love give?"

"Not to the Lord."

"To what then?" said Flora hastily.

"To custom—to public opinion—to entreaty—to conscience—to fear—to kindness of heart."

"And isn't that right?"

"It is not giving to the Lord."

"Well, Mr. Murray—take it so; how much ought one to give, as you say, to the Lord?"

"All."

"And be a beggar!" said Flora quickly.

"No; only the Lord's steward."

"That is exactly what I thought Mr. Murray would say," said Meredith.

"Then it comes back to the first question, Mr. Murray. Suppose I am a steward; how much must I give away? out of my hand?"

"If you are a good steward, your question will be different. It will rather run thus—'What does my Master want me to do with this money?' and if you are a loving servant, naturally the things which are dear to your Master's heart will be dear to yours."

"You are speaking in generals, Mr. Murray," said Flora frettedly; "come to details, and then I shall know. What objects are dear to his heart?"

"Don't you know that, Miss Flora?"

"No, I don't think I do. Please to answer, Mr. Murray, What are the objects, as you say, dear to his heart?"

"All the people he died for."

Flora paused again.

"I can't reach all those people—" she said softly.

"No. Do good to all those who come within your reach."

"What sort of good?"

"Every sort they need," said Mr. Murray, smiling.

"Do you think it is wrong to wear diamonds, Mr. Murray?"

"Certainly not,—if you think the money will serve the Lord best in that way, and if your love to him can express itself best so."

A muttered growl from Fenton expressive of extreme disgust, was just not distinct enough to call for rebuke.

"Then I suppose, according to that, I am never to buy a silk dress that is at all expensive," said Flora, the colour mounting into her handsome face. "And costly furniture of course must be wrong, and everything else that is costly."

"*Your* conclusions — not mine, Miss Flora," remarked Mr. Murray good-humouredly. "It is a matter of loving stewardship; and love easily finds its way to its ends, always."

"And Meredith wants to know what he shall do with Meadow Park," said Maggie.

"Yes. Ah, Mr. Murray, do say something to stop him,". added Flora. "Do not let him spoil Meadow Park!"

"To turn the Pavilion into a pretty little church, would spoil nothing, Miss Flora, as it seems to me."

"No, but that is not all. Meredith is persuaded that he must make the place a home for old women, and a refuge for sick people, and fill it with loafers generally. Mamma and I will have to run away and be without any home at all; and don't you think he owes something to us?"

"I have not decided upon anything, Mr. Murray," said Meredith, smiling, though he was very earnest. "I just wish I knew what I had best do."

"Pray for direction. And then watch for the answer."

"How would the answer come, Mr. Murray?" asked Flora.

"He will know when he gets it. Come, Meredith,—read."

"About the man with the catechism?" said Maggie.

"If you like. It will be a change from the Saxon times," said Meredith. And he wheeled about a little and reclined upon the rock, so as to turn his face towards his hearers—"But what a delicious place to read and talk, Mr. Murray!"

"Nothing can be better."

"This story begins with Pastor Harms' account of part of one of the Mission festivals that used to be held at Hermannsburg every year."

"Will that be interesting?" said Flora.

"Listen, and see. I pass over the account of the first day."

CHAPTER XIV.

" 'The first day's celebration of our Mission festival was at an end. It was then not early, but still on until late in the night the sounds of the songs of praise and thankfulness were to be heard in the houses, from the parsonage out to the furthest outlying houses of the peasants, and so it was also in the surrounding villages; for the parish village could by no means accommodate all the guests who had come to the festival, albeit not only the chambers and dwelling-rooms but also the hay-lofts were made lodging places for the sleepers. And that was a blessed evening, when so many brethren and sisters from far and near could refresh themselves with one another's company and pour out their hearts together. I thank God that so many pastors and teachers were come too, and also our faithful superintendent was not wanting; it is right that the heads of the church should not be missing at such a festival.

" 'The next day, and we had prayed the Lord to give us good weather for it, we were to go to a place in the midst of the lonely heath, called Tiefenthal.'"

"What does that mean?" Maggie interrupted.

"*Tief* means deep. *Thal* means valley."

"'Deep valley,'" said Maggie. "But I do not understand what a *heath* is."

"Naturally. We do not have them in this country, that ever I heard of," said Meredith.

"Neither here nor in England," said Mr. Murray. "For miles and miles the Lüneburger heath is an ocean of purple bloom; that is, in the time when the heather is in blossom. But there are woods also in places, and in other places lovely valleys break the spread of the purple heather, where grass and trees and running water make lovely pictures. Sometimes one comes to a hill covered with trees. And here and there you find solitary houses and bits of farms; but scattered apart from each other, so that great tracts of the heath are perfectly lonely and still; you see nothing and hear nothing living, except perhaps some lapwings in the air, and a lizard now and then, and humming beetles, and maybe here and there some frogs where there happens to be a wet place, and perhaps a land-rail; elsewhere a general, soft, confused humming and buzzing of creatures that you cannot see, and the purple waves of heather only interrupted here and there by a group of firs or a growth of bushes along the edge of a ditch."

"O Uncle Eden," cried Maggie, "have you been there! And do you know the village, too?"

"*The* village? Pastor Harms' village, do you mean, Hermannsburg? Yes. It is like many others. Two long lines of cottages, the little river Oerze cutting it in two, beautiful old trees shading it,—that is the village. The cottages are not near each other; gardens and fields lie between; and at the gable of every house is a wooden horse or horse's head; from the old Saxon times, you know. No dirt and no squalor and no beggars nor misery to be seen in Hermannsburg. That, I suppose, is much owing to Pastor Harms' influence."

"Thank you, Uncle Eden," said Maggie with a sigh of intense interest;—"now you can go on, Ditto. They were going out into the heath. All the people?"

"I suppose so. 'To a place in the midst of the heath solitudes, called Tiefenthal. Why? I had not told them that; I wanted to tell it to them first of all on the spot. I had another reason besides, though; I wanted to have the sun beat a little in African fashion on the heads of the guests at our festival, so that our brethren in Africa might not be the only ones hot! So at nine o'clock the next morning the great crowd of those who were to make the pilgrimage with us from Hermannsburg, were assembled at the Mission house under the banner of the Cross, which fluttered joyously from the high flagstaff. It was hard for me not to be able to walk with the rest, but I was only just recovered from a severe illness. A pilgrimage is the pleasantest going on earth to me. One can sing by the way so joyfully with the hosts that are moving along; one can talk so cordially and so familiarly about the kingdom of God in the crowd of the brethren; and now and then one gets a chance by a shallow ditch to tumble one of one's fellow pilgrims over, especially one of the children; I had to do without all that and get into a waggon. When I came to the Mission house, the procession set itself in motion towards the high grounds of the heath. With sounding of trumpets and amid songs of praise the crowds travelled on, for nearly two hours long, all the while mounting higher and higher, and truly, for God had heard our prayer, under a burning sunshine. Many a one had to sweat for it soundly, even I in the waggon. It was a picturesque procession; a whole long row of carriages, and these crowds of people; the solitary heath had become all alive. At last a not inconsiderable height was reached, where the ground fell off suddenly into a steep, precipitous dell. This was Tiefenthal. It is a very narrow valley, or rather a cut between two hills, one of which is bare; the other covered with a luxuriant growth of evergreens. Below stands an empty bee enclosure, called the Pastor's Beefield, because it as well as the wood-covered hill belongs to the pastor of Hermannsburg. From all the farms round about hosts of pilgrims were coming at the same time with us, travelling along; and like the brooks which after a thunder-shower plunge down from the hills to the lower ground, even so the waves of humanity rolled towards Tiefenthal. At last then I took

my stand on the slope of the bare hill, surrounded by
the brethren who bore the trumpets in their hands,
the blast of which sounded mightily through the
dell and broke in a quivering echo upon the opposite hill. Countless hosts lay upon the two slopes
and in the bottom of the dell, and out of many
thousand throats the song of praise to the Lord rose
into the blue dome of the sky.

"'First was sung, with and without accompani-
ment of the trumpets, the lovely hymn,

> "Rejoice, ye Christians all,
> His Son by God is given," etc.

to the glorious melody, "Aus meines Herzens
Grund!" Then, when the mighty sounds died
away, followed the preaching, upon Hebrews xi,
32–40.'"

"Read that passage, Maggie," said her uncle.
Maggie read.

"'And what shall I more say? for the time
would fail me to tell of Gideon, and of Barak, and
of Samson, and of Jephthah; of David also, and
Samuel, and of the prophets: who through faith subdued kingdoms, wrought righteousness, obtained
promises, stopped the mouths of lions, quenched
the violence of fire, escaped the edge of the sword,
out of weakness were made strong, waxed valiant
in fight, turned to flight the armies of the aliens.
Women received their dead raised to life again:
and others were tortured, not accepting deliver-
ance ; that they might obtain a better resurrec-

tion: and others had trial of cruel mockings and scourgings, yea, moreover of bonds and imprisonment: they were stoned, they were sawn asunder, were tempted, were slain with the sword: they wandered about in sheepskins and goatskins; being destitute, afflicted, tormented; (of whom the world was not worthy;) they wandered in deserts, and in mountains, and in dens and caves of the earth.'—Uncle Eden, that was a great while ago, wasn't it?"

"*That* was."

"But I mean—people don't do so now, do they?"

"Not here, just now, in America. But nothing is changed in human nature or the relations of the two parties, since the Lord said to the serpent, 'I will put enmity between thee and the woman, and between thy seed and her seed.'"

"But does that mean *that*, Uncle Eden? I thought the seed of the woman was Christ?"

"It is. But the devil fights against Christ in the persons of his people; and the 'seed of the serpent,' the children of the devil, hate the children of God, from Cain's time down. 'If they have persecuted me they will also persecute you,' the Lord said."

"There is no persecution here, though, in this country, Mr. Murray?" said Flora.

"Not persecution with fire and sword. But nothing is changed, Miss Flora. It will be fire and sword again, just so soon as the devil sees his opportunity. So all history assures us. Go on Meredith; let us see what Pastor Harms made of his text—or doesn't he tell?"

"I'll go on, sir; and you'll see. 'As you have just heard out of the holy Scriptures, so it has been, my dear friends, with the faithful witnesses and martyrs of the truth; hacked to pieces, run through the body, slain with the sword, or left to wander in the deserts, on the mountains, in dens and caves of the earth, of whom the world was not worthy. Even in the New Testament we read how Peter and Paul had to suffer imprisonment, how Stephen was stoned, James beheaded with the sword; how the Jews persecuted all the confessors of the most blessed Saviour, dragged them out of their houses, threw them into prisons, and took joy in stoning them. And even as the Jews began it, the heathen have carried it on; and not hundreds or thousands, but many hundred thousands of Christians in the ten great Christian persecutions sealed their belief in the Lord Jesus and their faithful confession of his holy name with their blood. In our last year's mission festival in Müden, I told you how the holy apostles Peter and Paul met their death like heroes and martyrs; our beloved Hermannsburg church is named after them; and I told you about Saint Lawrence, after whom the church in Müden is called. "And to-day," you are questioning, "to-day are you going to tell us about martyrs again? We conclude so, from the text you have chosen! But wherefore always about martyrs?"—My beloved, I have a special love to the martyrs; and I do not know how it happens, at every mission festival they come with special vividness before my mind. I believe it arises from this; that I am persuaded the ever-growing zeal for missions among all earnest Christians is a token that before long the church of Christ will have to take her flight out of Europe; and so the unconscious effort of Christians is towards preparing a place for the church among the wilds of heathenism. And therefore I believe that the times of martyrdom will cease to be far-off times for us any longer; that the kingdom of Antichrist is drawing near with speedier and speedier steps, is becoming daily more powerful; the apostasy from Christ is becoming constantly greater and more decided; Christianity is growing more and more like a putrid carcass, and where the carcass is, there the eagles are gathered together. And therefore missions are becoming more evidently the banner around which all living Christians rally; for what is written in the Revelation xii, 14–17, will soon receive its fulfilment. And when I see such great crowds of Christians singing praise and keeping holy day, then the thought always comes to me, How would it be, if persecution were to break loose now? would all these be true witnesses and martyrs, and rather bear suffering and yield up the last drop of their blood and endure any torments, than fall away and deny Christ? O, and when I reflect how mightily in those times of bloody persecution the Christian church gave her testimony and fought and suffered;

what a power of Faith, Hope and Love made itself known, that could shout for joy at the stake; and when I think how cold, how lukewarm, how loveless Christianity is now—I could almost wish for a mighty persecution to come, to break up the rotten peace of Christians who have grown easy and luxurious and to arouse again the right heroism of the soldiers of God.

"'It is not only in the times of the Jews and the Romans, at the first founding of the Christian church, that such mighty battles of heroes have been fought; the dear and blessed time of the Reformation has had its martyrs, who for the pure word and true sacrament of our beloved Lutheran church staked their persons and lives. Who does not know those two faithful disciples, who amid songs of praise were burned at the stake at Cologne on the Rhine? that Heinrich von Zutphen, who had to give up his life in Ditmarsh? those thousands who were murdered or burned by the Catholic Inquisition? those thousands who had to pine away in the prisons and cloisters of the Catholics? without reckoning the hundreds of thousands in the religious wars stirred up by the Catholics who made the battle-fields fat with their blood and have died for the faith of their church? And now I will tell you why I have brought you here to-day to this Tiefenthal. We stand upon holy ground here; upon ground of the martyrs. Hear what your fathers suffered for the sake of the pure, true word and sacrament.

"'The story that I am going to tell to you must have been acted out somewhere between 1521 and 1530. For in the chronicle where I have read the story, mention is made of the Diet at Speier; but nothing is said of the Diet at Augsburg.'"

"Stop, Ditto, please," said Maggie. "What's a diet?"

"The supreme council of the German empire, composed of princes and representatives of independent cities of the empire. The famous Diet of Augsburg was held in 1530."

"What was it famous for?"

"Famous for an open, bold confession and declaration of the Protestant faith, by a few Protestant princes, in the midst of the crowd of Catholics assembled at the Diet. Well, Meredith—"

"'Nothing is said of the Diet at Augsburg. And certainly some mention would have been made of it, if it had already taken place, since our beloved princes, the dukes Ernst and Francis of Lüneburg, had their share in the precious confession of faith. At that time there was in Hermannsburg a young Catholic pastor, descended from a noble patrician family; he was called Christopher Grünhagen, and was a kind-hearted man. One day—'"

"Stop a minute, Ditto. Some people were Catholics then, and some were Protestants?"

"Why that is how they are now, Maggie," said her sister.

"But I mean, there—in Germany."

"It is so still in Germany," said Meredith. "But

then was just the beginning of the Reformation, Maggie. Luther was preaching, and the world was in a stir generally."

"'One day there comes to Pastor Grünhagen a sort of artisan fellow, who asked for a bit of bread. It was in winter time, and the poor man was quite benumbed with cold. Pastor Grünhagen took pity on him, had him served with food and drink, and made him sit down in the *Flett* (that is, the open hall of the house with its low fireplace) that he might also warm his cold limbs. After the man had eaten, not forgetting to pray either, he stretched his legs comfortably down by the warm hearth, and then drew a small MS. book out of his pocket, in which he began to read with eager and devout attention. Grünhagen wondered that the man could read, and more especially, that he could read writing. Now, indeed, an artisan would take it ill if anybody were surprised to find him able to read. But the fact that all of us, even the poorest and the smallest, can read now, is just one of the blessings of the Reformation, under which the first schools for the people were established. In those days only scholars and priests could read, and the laity, even the nobles, knew nothing about it. So Grünhagen steps up curiously to the remarkable artisan who knows so much as to read, and asks him, " Pray what have you there ? " For all answer, the man hands him the book. Grünhagen takes it and reads and reads, and the more he reads the more eagerly and attentively he devours what he finds there. It was a copy of Luther's smaller catechism. Like a lightning flash, darts through his soul the thought, "What stands in this book is THE TRUTH." He asks his guest now, where he has come from? The answer is, "From Wittenberg; I have heard Luther preach there, and I brought away this catechism with me."

" ' Why he had a written copy of the catechism and not a printed one, I cannot tell you; perhaps he had not been able to buy a printed copy and had been at the pains of writing it out; but that is not said in the chronicle. And now, while I am speaking of the catechism, I will shew you also that I am a scholar. Therefore know, that Luther printed his smaller catechism in the year of grace 1529; because in the two years previous he had been travelling about all through Saxony, examining the churches; and had found, that the pastors were so stupid that they did not know even the principal things. Therefore, and surely with the assistance of the Holy Spirit, he wrote the small catechism, which I hold to be the best of all human books. Before that, however, he had already written some similar works; for example, a short exposition on the ten commandments, the Creed, and the Pater noster; from which, on account of its remarkable quality, I will quote a little. So in it Luther says—"The first commandment is transgressed by every one who in his difficulties turns to sorcery, the black art of the devil's allies; every one who makes that use of letters,

signs, words, herbs, charms and the like; whoever uses divining rods, treasure-conjurings, clair-
voyance and the like; whoever orders his work
and his life according to lucky days, sky tokens,
and the sayings of soothsayers. The third commandment is transgressed by those who eat, drink,
play, dance and carry on unholy doings; by those
who in indolence sleep away the time of divine
service, or miss it, or spend it in pleasure drives,
or walks, or in useless chatter; by whoever works
or does business without special need; by whoever does not pray, does not think on Christ's suf-
ferings, does not repent of his sins and long for
mercy; and who therefore only in outward things,
as dressing, eating, and posture-taking, keeps the
day holy."

" 'I have brought forward this proof of learning
only to shew you that good people are not quite so
simple as perhaps they look; and now I will go on
with my story.

" 'Grünhagen was so delighted with the dear
catechism that he says to the workman, " Friend,
you must stay with me long enough to let me
make a copy of your MS., for you won't get the
book again before I have done that." The friend
was very willing to have it so; and now they
made an honest exchange one with the other.
For the pastor ministered to the poor starved and
frozen body of the artisan, and the artisan ministered to the poor, starved and frozen soul of the
pastor. Day by day his accounts grew more and

more fiery and spirited about Luther's powerful preaching, about the many thousands who were streaming to Wittenberg to hear the man of God, about the German Bible which Luther had translated, about the glorious songs of praise which the Lutherans sung, about the pure Sacrament in both kinds; that is, that in Wittenberg both the bread and the wine were given to the communicants, and not the bread merely, as is done by the Papists against the Lord's commandment. He told how, amidst all the rage of his foes, Luther was so joyful and brave, that on one occasion he said to the electoral prince of Saxony, who he saw had become anxious, " I do not ask your princely grace to protect me; for I am under much higher protection, which will take good care of what concerns me." Grünhagen's whole soul was moved by these narrations.

" 'After a good many days he let the workman go, laden with gifts, and with tears in his eyes dismissed him! for through him he had learned to know the truth. And now he goes to studying. Soon the little catechism is fixed in his heart and his head; and now he procures Luther's other works, and first of all, the New Testament. And then he can conceal it from himself no longer, that the word of God and the Sacrament are basely falsified in the Romish church, and that he himself, without knowing it, has been all this while misleading the people; he who in his office as pastor should have been a servant of God. This thought

15

burns into his inmost soul, so that he almost
falls into despondency. But soon he finds grace
through faith in the dear blood of Jesus Christ.
And now in him also that word goes into fulfilment—"I believed, therefore have I spoken." He
begins to preach the pure word of God, in demon-
stration of the Spirit and of power; he begins to
give to communicants the whole, entire supper, the
emblems of Christ's body and blood; and he teaches
the children the catechism. And how could he fail
of fruit! The parish of Hermannsburg stirs with
life, the whole region is waked up, and thousands
come to hear God's word. O that must have been
a blessed time, when the Holy Ghost breathed thus
upon the dry bones, and the Light shined in the
darkness. But then, too, the cross could not fail;
for on the baptism of the Spirit follows always the
baptism of fire; and David in the very psalm quoted
above says, "I believed, therefore have I spoken.
I was greatly afflicted."

"'There was at that time in Hermannsburg a
warden, that is a steward and judge in one person,
who was called Andreas Ludwig von Feuershütz
(from whom the neighbouring property still keeps
the name of Feuershützenbostel), a rash, determined
man, and very zealous for the old popish church.
Writing in those days did not amount to much;
the warden's scribes were his soldiers. So he went
to the pastor and without any circumlocution for-
bade him to preach the Lutheran heresy, adding,
"If you don't stop it, I'll shut the door before your

nose." When Grünhagen rejected this demand as an improper one, and told him to attend to his office, but leave the church to the pastor, the warden grew wrathful and called Grünhagen a renegate heretic; and the next Sunday he actually did set his soldiers to keep the church doors and closed the entrance to pastor and congregation both. The thousands who followed their pastor were not unwilling to use violence against the doer of violence; but Grünhagen prevented that, and tried to hold divine service in his house, and when that also was interfered with, in the houses of the peasants. But wherever they might be, the warden would come with his soldiers and break up the service.

"'And this went on for many a week, and yet so great was the power of Grünhagen's good influence over the believers that no act of violence was attempted against their tyrants. At last one day the following peasants, Hans von Hiester, Michel Behrens, and Albrecht Lutterloh of Lutterloh, Karsten Lange of Ollendorf, and the great Meyer from Weesen, came to Grünhagen and told him they knew a spot in the heath, still and solitary and remote, which neither high road nor footpath came near; the warden could not easily find it out; "let us go there on Sundays and hear God's word from your mouth!" And so it was arranged. Quietly one tells it to another, and no one betrays it. The next Sunday, while it is still night, the house doors everywhere open, the indwellers come out one by one, and travel in mist and darkness, by distant paths, through moor, heather and thicket, hither to Tiefenthal. Grünhagen is there, and with him is his clerk, Gottlob; a believer, converted by his pastor's means; and he carries the sweet burden of the church service: O my beloved, here stood Grünhagen, here were your fathers who had renounced false idols and worshipped their Saviour according to the pure word and ordinance he has given; their songs of praise echoed here, here they bent the knee; for a long while your fathers' house of God was here under the blue heaven; here were the new-born children baptized in the name of the triune God and the grown men and women were fed with the bread and wine which mean the body and blood of the Lord, and so received new strength to mount up with wings as eagles. In this place your fathers grew to a strength of faith which would waver no more. But more trials were coming upon them. The warden was struck by the sudden quietness; he had expected that new attempts would be made to get into the church. He guessed that something was going on, and could not find out what it was. So he set his soldiers on to serve as sleuth-hounds, and they scented the game so well that they discovered the whole. Then one Sunday morning he got up early and watched with bitter rage to see how the people came out of all the houses, men, women, young men and girls, old men and children, all quiet and yet so joyous, dressed in their Sunday clothes, and hastening to Tiefenthal. Stealthily he followed after them; and at their place of refuge heard them preach and sing and pray. Suddenly he heard his own name spoken; it gave him a great shock; he heard the pastor praying for his conversion and the congregation saying Amen. Then a great surging and conflict of feelings arose in his brazen heart. But the time was not yet come. He dashed down the tears that would come into his eyes, and let his supposed duty get the victory. Resolved to suppress the hated heresy that had almost made him soft, but too weak to do it with the force at his command, he made known the affair to the justiciary of Zelle and asked for help. The Zelle justiciary nothing loath, next Sunday dispatched two hundred of his soldiers, who lay hid in the wood till the congregation had assembled. Then they broke forth, surrounded our fathers, just as they were gathered around their beloved pastor for the holding of divine service, fell first of all upon Grünhagen himself and the crowd which pressed round him, laid hold of him and dragged him off, and a hundred others with him, to Zelle; with brutal ill-treatment. There the captives were obliged to pass three days and three nights in the court-yard of the official's house, in snow and ice (it was in November), and it was only with difficulty that they could get a bit of bread to eat. Then they were thrown into prison; and there for a long time our fathers had to share the bonds and imprisonment of God's faithful servant; but no threats, no contumely, no distress could move them to apostasy from the faith they had confessed.

"'How long they lay there I do not know. At last, when the dukes came back from Augsburg, the hour of their freedom struck; they were let go, and returned to their homes shedding thankful tears; the church was again opened to them too, and the heroic Grünhagen preached the Gospel to his people anew with fresh power. Then also struck the warden's hour of grace; he grew tender, and was overcome by the might of the blessed Gospel; and whereas he had formerly been a zealot for the mistaken service of God, now he became one of the strongest friends of the pure Lutheran doctrine in all the community. Out of gratitude the parish gave to its beloved watcher for souls this Tiefenthal, with the wooded hill here, to be for all time the property of the Parsonage, which it still is to the present day. My beloved, we have come here to-day for pleasure; are we to come here again perhaps some day in distress? You answer possibly, "No, that is not to be apprehended; our times are too humane." Yes! they are humane towards all that is *human; i. e.*, towards banqueting and drinking, dissolute living and deceit. But that our times are not too humane towards what is *godly*, is testified by the persecutions directed against the Lutherans in Baden and Nassau, where various Lutheran preachers have had to pay fine after fine, and lie in the common prison, because they preach and baptize and observe the communion in the Lutheran manner, and where too the preaching must often be held in mountains and clefts of the rocks, to be had in peace. And besides, the kingdom of Antichrist is advancing with constantly quicker and more decided steps. Even now it everywhere rains words of abuse upon the saints, the praying people, the hypocrites, the enthusiasts, the mad folk, and by whatever other names beside they may call them. And who knows how soon the time may come when the word will again be true,—"they will put you out of their synagogues," and "whosoever killeth you will think that he doeth God service." I could if I would read you letters that have come from many cities and villages, filled with such threatenings and cursings and coarse words against me that they would fill you with astonishment. Therefore ask yourselves again seriously the question,—would you also be ready to give money and blood, body and life, for the Lord Jesus and for your faith? would you also be ready to suffer bonds and imprisonment for the Lord's sake? If it be so, that you could not or would not do that, then you are not worthy to bear the name of Jesus Christ; for whoever hateth not father and mother, wife and child, farm and farming stock, and his own life also, for Jesus' sake, he is not worthy of me, the Lord says. To confess Christ in peace and in pleasant times, that is easy enough; but to do it through distress and death, to stand fast in the baptism of fire, that is another thing, Christians of nowadays are accustomed to easy liv-

ing; how would the cup of suffering taste to them?
They are drowned in delicate and luxurious habits;
how would they bear privation? They have cor-
rupted themselves in cowardice and indolence; how
should they be strong and brave under persecution?
And listen to me now, you who are gathered here
together in such numbers; what do you think? If
the soldiers all of a sudden came upon you, to
run you through, or to carry you off somewhere
where there are no feather beds, would you stand
it? would you cheerfully give yourselves up to
be dragged off? Or would you make long legs,
keep a whole skin, and deny your Saviour? O
God grant that all of us may be able to cry with
the Apostle Paul, "I count all things but loss, that
I may win Christ." "I am persuaded, that neither
death, nor life, nor angels, nor principalities, nor
powers, nor things present, nor things to come, nor
height, nor depth, shall be able to separate me from
the love of God, which is in Christ Jesus our Lord!"
Let us now sing with the sound of the trumpets
our Luther's hero song—

" ' "Ein' feste Burg ist unser Gott."' "

"What does that mean?" said Maggie.

"It means, 'The Lord is my strength and my
fortress;' or more literally, Maggie, 'Our God is a
sure stronghold.'"

"'When this hymn had been sung, it was time
for our noonday meal. So after we had prayed the
prayer before eating, the people arranged them-

selves everywhere in larger and smaller groups, on the green grass or the brown heather, and with giving of thanks enjoyed the food they had brought along with them. Those who had nothing took gladly the spare bits of those who had too much. And all were filled; and beer, and water, and even sugar water, were on hand too to quench the burning thirst. I had myself a further particular pleasure. A few of our festival companions had brought with them some mighty pieces of honey-cake, as a gift for me. That suited me exactly, and I had it packed in with other things in my basket of provisions. Now you should have seen the glee, when I called the children to me and snapped off the sweet bits for them. There came even a pretty good number of larger people, who wanted to be children too and have their bits after the children had had enough. When we had eaten we had the prayer of thanks, and then the beautiful song,

"Now let us thank God and praise him," etc.

A blast of the trumpets proclaimed the renewal of divine service; and again the people arranged themselves in their former places and order for a new and last refreshing of their spirits.'"

CHAPTER XV.

"Is that all?" said Maggie.

"All of that story," Meredith answered.

There was a long silence. On hill and rock and river, there was a stillness and peace as if nowhere in the world could blood ever have flowed, or wrangling been heard, or men been cruel one to another. So soft and warm the sunlight brooded, and the dry leaves hung still on the trees and not a breath moved them, and the liquid lap of the water against the rocks far down below just came to the ear with a murmur of content. There was nothing else to hear; and the silence was so exquisite that it laid a sort of spell on everybody's tongue; while the mild sunlight on the warm, hazy hills seemed to find out everybody's very heart and spread itself there. A spell of stillness and a spell of peace. All the party were hushed for a good while; and what broke the charm at last was a long-drawn breath of little Maggie, which came from somewhere much deeper than she knew. Mr. Murray looked up at her and smiled.

"What is it, Maggie?"

"I don't know, Uncle Eden.   I think, something makes me feel bad."

" Feel bad !" echoed Esther.

" I don't mean feel *bad* exactly—I can't explain it."

" I suppose she has been thinking, as I have been," said Meredith, "that it does not seem as if this day and my story could both belong to the same world."

" Ah !" said Mr. Murray—"this is a little bit of God's part, and the other is a little bit of man's part in the world; that is all."

" But Uncle Eden, in those dreadful times it don't seem as if there could ever have been pleasant days."

" I fancy there were.   Don't you think the people of Hermannsburg must have enjoyed Tiefenthal, sometimes in the early starlight dawn and sometimes in the fresh sunrise?"

" Uncle Eden, I should always have been afraid the soldiers were coming."

" On the other hand, those people always knew that God was there.   And there is a wonderful sweetness in living in his hand."

" But yet, Uncle Eden—he did let the soldiers come?"

" *He* did not go away, Maggie."

" No,—but those must have been dreadful times."

" Well, yes.   They were no doubt hard times. And yet, Maggie, it remains true—'When *he* giveth quietness, then who can make trouble?'   Think of Paul and Silas, beaten and bleeding, stiff and sore, stretched uncomfortably in the wooden framework which left them no power to rest themselves or change their position; in the noisome inner dungeon of a Roman prison; and yet singing for gladness. People cannot sing when they are faint-hearted, Maggie. The Lord keeps his promises."

"I wonder how many people would stand Pastor Harms' test?" Meredith remarked.

"They are not obliged to stand it," Flora rejoined. "There are no persecutions now; not here, at any rate. People are not called upon to be martyrs."

"Do you think the terms of service have changed?" said Mr. Murray looking at her.

"Why, sir, we are *not* called upon to be martyrs?"

"No, but are you not called to have the same spirit the martyrs had?"

"How can we?"

"What is the martyr spirit?"

"I don't know," said Flora. "I suppose it is a wonderful power of bearing pain, which is given people at such times."

"Given to everybody?" said Meredith.

"Of course, not given to everybody."

"To whom, then?"

"Why, to Christians."

"And what is a Christian?" said Mr. Murray. "Are there two kinds, one for peace and the other for war?"

"No, I suppose not," said Flora somewhat mystified.

"'Whosoever shall confess me before men, him will I also confess before my Father which is in heaven.' So the Lord said. Now in times of persecution, you know what confessing Christ meant. What does it mean in these days?"

"I do not think I understand the question, Mr. Murray."

"In the Roman days, for instance, how did people confess Christ?"

"I don't know. They owned that they were Christians."

"How did they own that? They refused to do anything that could be construed into paying honour to the gods of the people. They might have said in word that they were Christians—but nobody would have meddled with them if they would have hung garlands of flowers upon Jupiter's altar."

"No—" said Flora.

"How is it in these days?"

"What do you mean, sir?"

"I mean, how is Christ to be confessed in these days?"

"I don't know," said Flora; "except by making what is called a profession of religion,—joining some church, I suppose."

"Does that do it?"

"I do not know how else."

"Why Uncle Eden," said Maggie, "how can one do it any other way?"

"One cannot do it in that way, my pet."

"*Not?*" said Flora.   "How then, Mr. Murray?"

"What do people join the church for, then, Uncle Eden?" Esther inquired.

"Those who enlist in Christ's army must certainly put on his uniform.   But who shall say that the uniform does not cover a traitor?"

"A traitor, Mr. Murray?"   Flora looked puzzled.

"Yes.   There are many traitors.   There were even in Paul's time."

"Traitors among the Christians?"

"So he wrote.   'Many walk, of whom I have told you often and tell you now again even weeping, that they are *enemies of the cross of Christ.*' They were professors of his name, nevertheless, Miss Flora; but confess him before men, except in word, they did not.   So my question stands, you perceive."

"How to confess Christ nowadays so that there shall be no mistake about it?" Meredith added. Flora and Esther and Maggie sat looking at Mr. Murray, as at the propounder of a riddle.   Fenton pricked up his ears and stared at the whole group.

"What did those people do, Mr. Murray?" Flora asked.

"Paul tells.   He says of them that their 'glory is in their shame'; they 'mind earthly things.'"

"How can one help minding earthly things? as long as one lives in this world?"

"One cannot, Miss Flora.   But the characteristic of a Christian is, that he seeks *first* the kingdom of God."

"How?"

"First, to have the Lord's will done in his own heart; next, to have it done in other people's hearts."

"But you were talking of doing something to show to the world that you are certainly a Christian, Mr. Murray?"

"Yes, Miss Flora. Shall I tell you some of the ways in which this may be accomplished?"

"Yes, if you please. I am completely in a fog."

"I never like to leave anybody in a fog. Now listen, and I will give you some of the Bible marks of a real Christian.

"'*Whosoever he be of you that forsaketh not all that he hath, he can not be my disciple.*'"

"But Mr. Murray!—"

"Yes, that is just it exactly!" said Meredith delighted.

"How can one forsake all he has? Be a beggar?"

"Not at all. Give it all to Christ, and be his steward."

"Not to please yourself in anything!" cried Flora.

"I did not say so. And the Bible does not mean so. For another Bible mark of a Christian is, in the Lord's words—

"'*My meat is to do the will of him that sent me.*'"

"But can't one do anything that one wants to do?" cried Flora in dismay.

"Many things. But a Christian has no pleasure in what does not please God."

"How is one always to know?"

"I am going on to tell you in part. *'Whatsoever ye do, do all to the glory of God.'*"

"That don't tell *me*," said Flora. 'How can I tell what will do that? And how can one do *everything* so? Little things—and life is very much made up of little things. Dressing, and studying, and reading, and playing, and amusing one's self."

"O Flora?"—Maggie cried; and "Why Flora!" Meredith said, looking at her; but neither added anything more.

"The Bible says, '*whether ye eat or drink, or whatsoever ye do,*'" Mr. Murray answered. "In another place, '*whatsoever ye do, in word or deed.*'"

"Well, Mr. Murray, I don't understand it; take eating and drinking—how can that be done to the glory of God?"

"You can easily see how it can be done *not* to his glory. Any way that is not becoming his servant, is not to his glory. Therefore, in excess—of things that do not agree with you and therefore unfit you for duty—of costly dishes, which take the money that might feed starving people."

"But I can't feed all the starving people!" said Flora.

"It is something to feed one. But I will give you another Bible mark, Miss Flora, '*He that saith he abideth in him,*' that is, in Christ, '*ought himself also so to walk even as he walked.*' Now remember how Christ walked. He was here, '*as one that serveth.*' He '*went about doing good.*' He '*pleased not himself.'* He *'did always those things that please'* God."

" But one can't be like *him*," said Esther.

" That depends entirely upon whether you choose to be like him."

" Oh Uncle Eden ! He was—"

" Yes, I know, and I know what you are, and I, and all of us. It remains true,—' God is faithful, by whom ye were called unto the fellowship of his Son Jesus Christ our Lord; '— ' chosen, that we should be holy and without blame before him in love.' "

There was a pause of some length. Flora was silenced, but her eyes had filled and her face wore a pained and bitter expression. Meredith had glanced at her and thought it better not to speak. Maggie was in a depth of meditation. Fenton had gone scrambling down the rocks. Esther looked somewhat bored.

" Have you got your book there, Meredith ?" Mr. Murray asked.

" Yes, sir."

" Read us something more. And after that you may all bring your questions. We came here on purpose to talk, as I understood."

" There are different sorts of things here, sir. Shall I give you a change ? "

" What you will—

  " ' O day most calm, most bright,
   The fruit of this, the next world's bud—
  Th' indorsement of supreme delight,
   Writ by a friend, and with his blood;

16

> The couch of time; care's balm and bay;
>   The week were dark but for thy light;
>   Thy torch doth shew the way.' "

"That's better than anything I have got, sir,' said Meredith.

"No. But it is good. And just here and to-day the Sabbath seems dressed in royal robes. I could not but think of those lines."

"I confess, Mr. Murray, Sunday is nothing like that to me," said Flora.

"You are honest, Miss Flora. That gives me some hope of you. No, naturally the Sabbath does not seem like that to you yet.—Well, Meredith?"

"Is there more of it, sir?" Meredith's sister asked.

"More than you would care for, Miss Flora.—

> "'Sundays the pillars are
>   On which heav'n's palace archéd lies;
>   The other days fill up the spare
>   And hollow room with vanities.—'"

"And yet that need not be true, either. Go on, Meredith. What will you give us?"·

"'Two stories, sir, on the words, 'Hold that fast which thou hast, that no man take thy crown.'

"'On the twenty-fifth of June, 1530, therefore three hundred and forty years ago, as is well known, our Lutheran Confession of Faith was delivered before the Diet at Augsburg. There was the powerful emperor Charles the Fifth, and his brother, King Ferdinand, besides a number of electoral princes, dukes and bishops. Before this crowd of some three to four hundred nobles, stood a little company of seven princes and two represented cities; that is, the Elector John the Constant and his son John Frederick of Saxony, Margrave George of Brandenburg, Duke Ernst the Confessor and his brother Francis of Lüneburg, Landgrave Philip of Hesse, Prince Wolfgang of Anhalt, and the two burgermasters of Nürnberg and Reutlingen. These nine stood forth with the spirit of heroes, and confessed, under signature of their names, that in this faith they would live and die, and that no power of earth or hell should make them turn from it. For the Lutherans were wickedly slandered, as men who no longer believed in any thing, and who therefore deserved no other than to be rooted out from the earth. That was why the Lutheran princes had requested that it might be granted them to declare their faith publicly before the Diet; to the end that everybody might know how their belief rested upon the Scriptures and stood in harmony with the universal ancient Christian church; and indeed had flung away only the false human teachings which had found their way into the church. For this purpose the twenty-fifth of June was fixed. The electoral chancellor Beyer stepped into the middle of the hall with the written Confession of Faith in his hand. The evangelical princes rose and stood listening while it was read, and testified that this was the faith they held, to which by God's help they would stand unmoved. Then did all that were present hear what the faith of the Lutherans was; there stood the doctrine of the triune God, of original sin, of the eternal Godhead of Jesus Christ; of justification before God through grace alone by faith in Jesus Christ, etc., though I hope I do not need to tell you any more about it; I think you all know the Augsburg Confession and have read it, for surely you are all of you Lutheran Christians, and all Lutheran Christians know the Augsburg Confession. But if there be one among you who does not yet know this act of confession, let him be ashamed of himself, and get a copy with all speed, and read it, and read it again. When it was read aloud at Augsburg, the impression it made was very great; people saw that the Lutherans had been shamefully slandered. Duke William of Bavaria reproached De Eck with having represented the Lutheran doctrine to him in entirely false colours. The doctor answered, he would undertake to refute this writing from the Christian fathers, but not from the Scripture. Then the duke returned, "So, if I hear aright, the Lutherans are *in* the Scriptures, and we near by!"

"'There did the steadfast Lutherans keep that saying in their hearts—"Hold that fast which thou hast, that no man take thy crown." Ay, when before the beginning of the Diet the Lutheran ministers earnestly besought the Elector of Saxony that he would not for their sakes run into danger, but graciously permit them to appear alone and give in their declaration before the emperor, the undaunted prince made them answer—"God forbid that I should be shut out from your company; I will confess my Lord Jesus Christ with you."

"'This is one story about those words; now I will give you another—'"

"Stop one minute, Ditto. Uncle Eden, I do not exactly understand all that?"

"What do you not understand?"

"Who were all those people?"

"The Catholic nobles of the German empire, with Charles the Fifth, a very powerful emperor, at their head, and the chief Catholic church doctors and dignitaries,—all that on one side; representing the powers of this world. On the other side, a little handful of men whom Luther's teaching had wakened out of the darkness of the Middle ages, confessing Christ before men; representing the feeble flock of his followers."

"Yes," said Maggie thoughtfully. "Was there danger?"

"There was great danger to whoever got into the power of the Catholic lords."

"Do you think the world is always against the truth, Mr. Murray?" Flora asked.

Mr. Murray answered in the words of the psalm —"'How do the heathen rage, and the people imagine a vain thing! The kings of the earth set themselves, and their rulers take counsel together against the Lord and against his Anointed, saying, Let us break their bonds asunder, and cast away their cords from us!'"

"But all times are not like those times of the Reformation?"

"Not just. The world power strives against the church in a variety of ways, sometimes with force and sometimes with guile. The beast in the vision, who has his power from the devil, sometimes makes war with the saints; and sometimes 'he causeth all, both small and great, rich and poor, free and bond, to receive a mark in their right hand or in their foreheads; and that no man might buy or sell save he that has the mark.'—Miss Flora, I believe the war times are the less evil and dangerous. Well, Meredith, you bear interruptions philosophically. Go on with your new story."

"'This new story 'happened more than two hundred years ago, at the place called Galgenberg' (that is, Gallowshill, Maggie), 'in the neighbourhood of Hermannsburg. In old times a gallows used to stand there, on which thieves and oath-breakers were hung.'"

"Oath-breakers!" said Mr. Murray. "It seems the Saxons kept their hatred of untruth. But I beg your pardon, Meredith."

"It's half the fun, to stop and talk, sir. 'At that time the criminal jurisdiction was located in Hermannsburg; and four times in the year, at quarter-day, court was held here and the judgment carried into effect as soon as delivered. To this end the justiciaries of Hermannsburg, Bergen and Fallingbostel came together here and held the court, after they had first attended the weekly service in the church at Hermannsburg to prepare them for their vocation; for quarter-day always fell upon a Wednesday. However in those days perjury and theft were so rare, that once it happened that twenty years passed away, with court held every quarter-day, and nobody was sentenced. The justice of Hermannsburg had two staves, one all white and one parti-coloured. If he found no one guilty, he broke the coloured staff; if, however, anybody was convicted, then he broke the white staff, with the words,

> " ' "The staff is broken,
> The judgment is spoken,
> Man, thou must hang."

" ' And then, after the pastor had prayed with the criminal, the sentence was executed.' "

" Fearful times, sir," said Meredith pausing.

" Horrible ! " echoed Flora.

" Two sides to the question," said Mr. Murray. " I am musing over the novelty of the combination. Twenty years without one man convicted of theft or a false oath ! Think of that, and you will comprehend the horror of the crime which made such sudden work with the criminal."

" I will go on," said Meredith.—" ' Some old people are yet living who have seen the gallows which stood on the Galgenberg. Now I will tell you my story about the words, " Hold that fast which thou hast, that no man take thy crown." It was in the thirty years' war, which from 1618 to 1648 raged between the Catholics and the Protestants. Through all this miserable time the parish of Hermannsburg enjoyed the rare good fortune of having a faithful shepherd over it; his name was Andreas Kruse; he became pastor in 1617, and died in 1652. His successor, Paulus Boccatius, gives him this testimony in the church register—"True as gold, pure as silver. Ah, thou faithful and good servant, thou hast been faithful over a few things; I will make thee ruler over many things." For years at a time the church at Hermannsburg was closed to him. At those times he went with his people into the wilds and held divine service there. Furthermore, the whole of the neighbouring pastors were either dead of the plague, or killed, or driven away; so that he took care of all their parishes beside his own; and this he did for twenty-five years. One good supporter he had in a bailiff called Andreas Schlüter, who died in the year 1643 and lies buried in the church-yard at. Hermannsburg; a man after God's heart, who faithfully stood by his pastor and often hid him away in his house for weeks at a time. The pastor did not merely celebrate divine service; he had also preserved the silver church vessels from the plundering hands of the enemy. These silver vessels were used in the service of the Lord's supper; and after it was over the sacristan or clerk set tin ones in their place upon the altar. They did not mean to act any lie by the means, however, for the tin vessels were not made for the purposes of deception, but had been there beforetime. Things went on in this way until the year 1633. At that time Duke George assembled an army and marched against the imperial forces. His men were burning with an eagerness for the fight, which delighted the duke. The enemy were stationed at Nienburg and Hameln. Seeing that the duke was approaching them they drew back to Oldendorf in the Hesse country, and there the duke got hold of them in the month of June, 1633. When his faithful followers asked him, " What shall the battle-cry be ? "—" God with us ! " answered the duke; and therewith they went at the enemy bravely. And soon the foe was so fearfully beaten that they scattered and fled in every direction; fifty imperial standards and twenty cannon remaining in the duke's hands.

" 'Among the fugitives were the two imperial generals Merode and Gronsfeld. The former was wounded to death and died at Nienburg. Gronsfeld fled in such haste, that he lost his sword and plumed hat. The duke kept these for himself; to be his share of the spoils. In their flight the imperialists came through the Lüneburg country, with the most frightful outrages which they committed by the way. Among these, the record tells of a lieutenant captain, named Altringer, who came to the village of Hermannsburg and plundered the inhabitants; he pushed his way even into the parsonage, and asked the pastor " what he had to give him ? " " I am a poor man," the latter replied; " you may open all my boxes." They did so, and

—ten shillings was all they found. In a rage at this, they beat the doors and windows to pieces, and summoned him—"You must have some church furniture too—here, out with it!" The pastor answered, "Have you been in the church yet?" "Those are tin vessels," said the enemy; "you are bound to have silver ones as well. Where are they? give them up." "No," said the faithful pastor, "that is what I will not do." "Where have you hidden them?" "You are not going to find out."

"'Upon this they condemned the brave man to the "Swedish drink." This frightful punishment consisted in the following: The victim was brought to the dung-pit, his mouth was forced open, a gag put between his teeth, and then dung water poured down his throat; after which men stamped with their feet upon his bloated body, until either he confessed or gave up the ghost. Now they had already brought Pastor Kruse to the dung-pit. There, before they began, he prayed with a loud voice, "Lord Jesus, have mercy on me." The lieutenant captain was moved with pity. "No," he said, "this man shall not die by the 'Swedish drink.' To the gallows with him! he shall hang." Arrived at the gallows he was there asked again, "Where is the church service?" He answered, "I shall not tell you where." Thereupon order was given to execute the sentence. But in the first place he kneeled down and prayed, for his enemies also, that God would not lay this sin to their charge, but give them grace to repent. Then he mounted the ladder, and the noose was already round his neck; meanwhile a tall man coming from Celle stepped up behind a tree, where, himself unseen, he could observe everything. At the same instant people were seen on the other side coming from Hermannsburg and making signals with a white cloth to signify that they had got the church vessels. Where had they found them? They considered, that surely the pastor would have buried them in the deepest part of his house, that is in the cellar. But in what spot? This they discovered in the following manner. They poured five or six pailfuls of water on the cellar floor. At first for a while, it stood there; then all of a sudden it began to run together towards one place and there sink in. "Ha, ha," said they; "here is a hole in the ground; the things must be buried there." So they dug it up and found the church vessels. When the pastor saw the communion service in the hands of the enemy, then the tears rose to his eyes. But as for the effect those people had hoped for, that is, that his life might be saved, they found it would not do; the hard lieutenant captain would not change his order; the man must hang.

"'Then stepped out yonder tall man from behind the tree; it was General Gronsfield; and he spoke. "Will you put to death this man who in dying prays for his enemies, and who weeps for his church service and not for his own life? Set him at liberty!" The pastor stretched out his hands to the general and implored, "Ah, my lord general, the church vessels!" But he answered, "I cannot give you those back; they are the booty of my soldiers; but your life is granted you."

"'The parish people of Hermannsburg used the tin service for a long while after that, till towards the end of the war silver vessels were again provided. Kruse remained pastor here until 1652. He too kept that saying in his heart—"Hold that fast which thou hast, that no man take thy crown."'"

"What awful times!" was Flora's comment when Meredith stopped reading.

"The world has moved a little since then," Mr. Murray observed. "Let us be thankful, such barbarous cruelties are no longer practised by the civilized part of the world; and civilization is spreading."

"But I don't think much of that story," Esther went on. "The man made a great deal more fuss about the soldiers having his church service than was at all necessary. That wasn't a thing to die for."

"By his lights, and his love for the sacred vessels, it was. You must take his point of view; and then you will find him, as I do, very noble."

"But it is very difficult to take other people's point of view, Mr. Murray; especially when it is unreasonable."

"Who shall judge?" said Mr. Murray smiling.

"You mean, *I* might be the one who was unreasonable."

"Anybody might, occasionally. And it is of the very essence of charity, Miss Flora, to take other people's point of view. Only so can you possibly come to a right estimate of their action."

"I don't like that story much, Ditto! I mean, not so much. I wish you would read another," said Maggie.

"I will read you another," said Meredith; "and it shall be very different.

"'The story that I am now about to tell you is such a one as certainly nobody expects to hear from me; it is namely, the story of a night-watch-man. But there is no sort of reason why you should laugh at this word, for indeed the story is a pretty one; and I wish all the night-watchmen in city and country would take after this man and do as he did; that is, provided they could do it from the bottom of their hearts. A poor cottager in one of our country villages, some years ago, out of curiosity, came to one of our mission festivals. There to his astonishment he heard that the Lord Jesus will have all men to be saved, that are in the whole earth, even the poor heathen; and that accordingly he has commanded his servants, the Christians, to cast the net of the Gospel into the sea of the heathen world. He heard how the heathen are to be saved, because Jesus died for all men; how they can nevertheless no otherwise be saved than through faith in him; because there is salvation for sinners in no other but only in the name of him, who was crucified for sinners and is risen again. Meanwhile

however, by means of this mission festival the dear
man himself is taken in the net of the Gospel; for
he sees that he also is a sinner, and therefore for
him also there is no salvation, except in him who
forgives sins because he has made reconciliation
for sinners with God. And now, finding himself
salvation in Christ, this experience of his convinces
him that nobody but Jesus can really help the poor
heathen. But then since Jesus can come to the
poor heathen in no way but by his word and sacrament, and his word and sacrament the heathen
have not, it becomes very clear to his mind that
the word and sacrament must be carried to them.
This moreover can be done only by messengers to
the heathen, who must be sent to them, because
they have not got wings to fly thither. Then he
begins to ponder the question, how he can do something to help. So he buys himself a mission box,
that he may always be putting something in there
when he has anything to spare. As nevertheless
what goes in is only the mites of poverty, it looks
to him a great deal too little. He makes the resolve now that every quarter of a year he will go
round the village with his box to collect for the
mission. But this is a resolve he cannot perform;
for inasmuch as the mission is not known to the
people of his village, he reflects, that where there
is no heart for the mission naturally there are no
gifts for it. And there he was quite right, and did
a wise thing to let his collecting project alone.
So about that he gives in, and quietly hangs up

his mission box in his room, on a nail opposite the door, so that every one who comes into the room can see it. And people do observe it, and many a one asks what sort of a thing that can be? He makes answer, it is for this purpose; that whatever goes into it will be applied to the converting of the heathen. And so in this way some few mites do actually get in; which however at the end of each year bring but a small sum. Now as this sum is still far too small to content him, he turns simply to the dear Lord Jesus, and says to him—"Dear Lord, as for going to the heathen myself, that I cannot do: I am too old, and I have not learned enough. But because thou hast done so much for me and in me, I would like greatly to do something for thee, and truly a little more than I have done hitherto. So give me thy Holy Spirit, that I may know how to manage it; for without him, man's knowledge is nought." Following upon such a prayer then, the Lord appointed him to be night-watcher. For without his having in the least anticipated such a thing, the village community invited him to undertake the service of the night-watch in the village. He made answer, he must take the matter into consideration before God and with his wife. The latter was not at first disposed to be pleased that he should wake while others slept; and his own flesh also takes to it not kindly, to have to wander about in the village in snow and rain, when it is cold and when it is stormy, while everybody else is lying upon his ear. But his for

mer prayer recurs to him, the Lord is certainly
now giving him something to do; and so he says
to the Lord Jesus—"My dear Saviour, if thou canst
use me in this way, keeping watch in the village
with thy holy angels, who are about us at all times,
then give me strength and joy to do it!" And as
the Lord grants him both, the thing is settled, and
in the name of Jesus he accepts the office of night-
watch. The custom in that place makes it a rule,
that on New Year's night the night-watch should
sing under people's windows a couple of pretty
Christian verses, as it were a New Year's greeting;
to one this verse, to the next the other verse, and
so round at all the houses. New Year's day then,
or the day after, he may go round again visiting
house by house, and wish happy New Year; and
the people give him according to their means and
according to their inclination a gift, smaller or
larger, and these gifts belong to his service earn-
ings; it is no begging either, for the stipulation is
made at the time he is put in office. With true
gladness of heart now in the New Year's night he
sings under all the windows in the village; and as
he does this, he seems to himself just the same as a
priest of God; his office seems to him a right holy
one. And particularly where he knows that a sick
person is lying in a house he sings the loveliest
verses of faith and comfort, so that tears run down
over his own cheeks in the doing of it. That night
is verily a night of triumph in his work; and he
begins to bear a cordial love to his calling, as one

the Lord has given him and has sanctified. To go
round on New Year's day however and wish the people joy, that is what he can not make up his mind
to; it is a festival and a holiday; it belongs to the
Lord; and it must be spent in the church and with
the Bible. But the next day he has time, and then
he will go; and then his mission box occurs to him,
which is still hanging there on its nail. Now he
knows what he is to do. He takes the box in his
hand and goes the rounds, house after house, and
gives his good wishes. Everywhere the people receive his hearty congratulations kindly, and every
one puts his hand in his pocket with alacrity to
fetch out a little present for him; the faithful man
has indeed done his work so honestly, and but just
now has sung for them so heartily and such beautiful verses! But he holds forth his box to his benefactors, and begs them to put whatever they de-
sign for him in there, for what they give is to go
to the conversion of the heathen. So upon that
one asks him a question, and another asks him a
question, and he has opportunity to open his mouth
with gladness and testify of the misery of the poor
heathen, and of the sacred duty of helping them,
that so they may be converted. And God gives
his blessing both to deeds and words; and now the
man finds himself able to send in not a little, but a
good deal, for the conversion of the heathen, who
lie so heavily on his heart.

"'Do you ask, where this happened? and who
did it? It happened in our country, and six night-
17

watchers have done it. Who are they?—Go along and ask the Lord in the last day; he has got all their names written down. I shall not tell them to you, for I will not rob them of their blessing. It might happen however that one or the other of them may read these lines. If that be the case, then I say to him, "Keep still and do not betray thyself, that thou lose not thy humility."""

CHAPTER XVI.

"I must say, Ditto, you read us the most extraordinary variety of stories!"

That was Flora's utterance. Meredith however sat looking very gravely into the water, which was rolling its little waves along at his feet far below. The sun had got lower while he had been reading; the lights and colours were changing; shadows fell from the hill-tops and began to lie broad on the river, cast from the western shore; but all softened in the haze, which now was getting in a strange way transfused with light; and a few little flecks of cloud were taking on the most delicate hues.

"Mr. Murray," Meredith broke out, "that story is not exaggerated! I mean, the doing of the people in the story is not; is it?"

"Miss Flora thinks so."

"Don't you, Mr. Murray?" said the young lady.

"Let us hear your reasons, please."

"Well, Mr. Murray, surely life is given to us for something besides bare work. We are meant to be happy and enjoy ourselves a little—aren't we?"

"Most certainly."

"Those good men,—I dare say they were good men,—seem to me to have been mistaken."

"You think, for instance, they might have kept some of their New Year's money to buy their wives new dresses?"

"Yes; or to get a good dinner, which I suppose they never had; or a carpet, suppose, for the bit of a room they lived in."

"What do you say, Esther?"

"O I think just as Flora does, Uncle Eden. I think those people were very extravagant."

"Maggie?"

"Uncle Eden, I do not know if they were extravagant; but it seems to me they might have kept *a little* for their own New Year."

"You all overlook one thing."

"What is that, sir?" several voices asked eagerly.

"Those good men were not acting so very contrary to your principle. They were doing, every one of them, what gave him the most pleasure with his money. That is what I understand you to advocate. The only difference is, that they found their pleasure in one thing, and you would find yours in another."

"But, Mr. Murray,—" Meredith began.

"Yes, Mr. Murray," said Flora eagerly taking the words out of her brother's mouth, "you have really not said anything. The question comes round,— *ought* we to find our pleasure in what they did? and in nothing else?"

"That is not the right way of putting it. The

Lord does not demand that, nor desire it; but that we should seek *first* the kingdom of God. You may remember too that the spirit of our life, if we are Christians, must be the same as Christ's; for 'if any man have not the spirit of Christ, he is none of his.' Now the motto of his life was, 'My meat is to do the will of him that sent me.' And that, Miss Flora, must make pleasing God the great pleasure of a child of God."

"That is what I think," said Meredith.

"Then are we to have no pleasure?" Flora repeated. "I mean, no pleasure of our own?"

"I have been trying to explain that. I do not know any pleasure much sweeter than pleasing some one that we dearly love; do you?"

Flora looked very gloomy.

"Put out of your head any notion of bondage or hard lines of action. 'I *delight* to do thy will, O God!'—is the true way of stating it. And that is the only sort of service, I think, that the Lord really is pleased with."

"Well, does he want us to do like those people, and give literally all we have got, for the heathen, or the poor?"

"The Bible rule is, 'Every man *according as he purposeth in his heart*, so let him give.' If his heart will be satisfied with nothing less than all, you would not forbid him?"

Meredith's eyes sparkled and he looked at Flora, but she would not meet him.

"It may be and often is the case, that the Lord's

best service requires some of a man's money to be spent on things that seem personal; still, if he loves God best, all will be really for God. Education, accomplishments, knowledge, arts, sciences, recreation, travel, books—provided only that in everything and everywhere the man is doing the very best he can for the service of his Master and the stewardship of his goods. That does not shut out but increases his delight in these things."

"That is enough!" exclaimed Meredith. "You have answered all my questions, sir. I see my way now."

"It will be a way apart from mamma and me, then, I suppose," said Flora, her eyes filling and her cheeks reddening.

"No," said Mr. Murray gently, "perhaps not. Meredith, we have had a sufficient interval of talk; suppose you read again. I am selfish in saying so; for while my ears listen, my eyes can revel in this wealth of colour. What will you give us next?"

"May I choose, sir? It touches what we have been talking about, another little story. It is a story by the bedside of a sick day-labourer."

"I don't believe we shall like it, Ditto," said his sister.

"It will not hold us long. Let me try.—

"'It is a long while ago, that I was once standing by the bedside of a sick day-labourer, who had a wife and four children. The man had been ill for weeks, and the sickness had swallowed up all his money. Death was near, and he was glad of it; he had only one remaining wish, that he might receive the symbols of the body and blood of the Lord Jesus in the holy Communion. I administered them to him.

" ' We sang with a number of friends and neighbours who were gathered together, the song,

" ' " Who knows how near my end may be!"

" ' He sang the words correctly along with us, for he knew the hymn by heart. His wife and children sang too. As we stopped at the fifth verse, I saw great tears in his eyes; but I said nothing at the time. The sick man spoke his confession devoutly and afterwards received the bread and the wine which are in figure the body and blood of our Lord Jesus Christ. His eye beamed with joy. Then after the blessing was said we sang the most glorious verse of the same hymn,— "I have fed on Jesus' blood," etc. The neighbours and friends went away, after they had cordially pressed his hand and said to him, "In the Lord's presence we'll be together again." I remained alone with the sick man and his family. Then I asked, why he had wept when we were singing? whether perhaps it was a trouble to him that he must go away from his wife and children? He looked at me with open eyes, almost reproachfully, when I said that; and answered, "Does not Jesus stay with them then? Has not the Lord said he would be 'the father of the fatherless and a judge of the widow?' No; they will be well looked after ; I have prayed the Lord that he would be a guardian to them. Isn't it so, mother, that thou art not worried either, and thy heart is not anxious? Thou too, hast faith in Jesus!" "Surely," said the woman, "I believe in Jesus; and I am glad thou art going to Jesus. In good time I will come after thee with the children. Jesus will help me by his Holy Spirit to bring them up." "Well —why did you shed tears then?" "For joy. I was thinking, if the singing goes so lovely even down here, how beautiful it will be when the angels sing with us. That was what made me weep, for joy, because such blessedness is so near before me." And now he made a sign to his wife. She understood the sign, went to the cupboard, and fetched out a little sort of a cup dish, which was her husband's money-box. Six groschen were in it, all that was left over of his possessions. He took them out with trembling fingers, laid them in my hand, and said, "The heathen are to have those, that they too may learn how to die happy." I looked at the wife; she nodded her head pleasantly and said, "We have agreed upon that. When all is paid that will be needed for the funeral, it will leave just these six groschen over." "And what will you keep?" "The Lord Jesus," said she. "And what are you going to leave to your wife and children?" I asked the man again. "The Lord Jesus," said he; and with that whispered me in the ear, "He is very good and very rich." So I took the six groschen for the heathen, and put them, as a great treasure, in the mission money-box; and it was hard for me to give them out again; only if I had not paid them out, I should not have fulfilled the dying man's wish. In the following night he fell asleep. We buried him as a Christian should be buried, that is, publicly, with the ringing of the bell, with preaching, singing and prayer; and there was no weeping done, neither by his wife nor by his three oldest children, neither in the church nor by the grave. But the youngest child, a boy of five years old, who followed the bier along with the rest, wept bitterly. I asked him afterwards, why he had wept so bitterly at his father's grave? The child answered me, "I was so troubled because father didn't take me with him to the Lord Jesus; I had begged him so hard to take me." "My child," said I, "your father could not take you along with him; only the Saviour could do that; you ought to have asked *him*." "Shall I ask him now then?" he questioned. "No, my child. See—when the Saviour wants you, he will call you himself. But if he chooses that you shall grow to be a man first, then you must help your mother and let her live with you. Will you?" He said, "I would like to go to Jesus; and I would like to be big too, so that mother can live with me." "Well, then say to the Lord Jesus that he shall choose." "That is what I will do," said the boy; and was quite contented and pleased.

"'The faithful Lord and Saviour Jesus Christ give us all a happy end. Amen.'"

There was the usual pause after Meredith had done reading. Flora however could not keep back long her expression of opinion.

"I protest!" she said. "Those people were utterly fanatical! Mr. Murray isn't it true?"

"O Uncle Eden, do you think so?" cried Maggie. "I think it is beautiful."

"Maggie is too young to understand," remarked Esther. "Those people were very unnatural, I think."

"How?" said Meredith.

"Yes, how?" Mr. Murray echoed. "I should like to hear the arguments on both sides."

"A man who is dying, and has a wife and four children," said Flora solemnly, "has no *right* to give his last six groschen away. I don't know how much a groschen is, but that don't make any difference. He has no right to do it!"

"You emphasize, 'a man who is dying,'" said Meredith. "Would the case be different if he were a man living and going to live?"

"Why of course."

"How?"

"He could work then, and earn more. How stupid to ask, Meredith!"

"But an accident might happen to him; or he might fail to get work; or he might miss his pay."

"Yes, of course. I think it would be fanatical even then. But when he was dying, and couldn't do anything!—"

"But if in any case he must trust for a day—

what does it signify? God can send help in a day."

" I should not think he would, when people throw away wantonly what they have got already."

" What is given to Jesus isn't thrown away,"— said Maggie.

" And he always pays it back, with interest," said Mr. Murray. " And what is entrusted to him is never neglected. I think that old German peasant was very safe in his proceeding."

" But so unnatural!" cried Esther. " Not to be sorry to leave his wife and children!"

" I have no doubt he was very sorry to leave them. The only thing is, he was more glad to go to Jesus."

" I cannot understand that."

" Not till you know the Lord yourself; and I do not deny that one must know him well, to be so eager to go to him. One does not easily leave the known for the unknown."

" Let me read another bit of a story, or history," said Meredith. " We cannot come to an agreement by talking; these things must be *lived in*—must they not, Mr. Murray?"

" Yes, read. But see the sky!" said Mr. Murray. " And the colours along the shore! Wonderful, wonderful! What a Sunday evening this is."

Meredith sat silently looking for a few minutes. With every quarter of an hour of the descending sun, the world was growing now more like a fairy-tale world. The lights and the shadows and the colours were making such exquisite work, that the bit of earth the gazers were looking upon seemed not to belong to the earth of history or the life of experience, but to be something unearthly, and glorified. With all that, the Sabbath stillness! There was the lap of the water at the foot of the rocks; the rustle of the dry leaves down below where Fenton was prowling about; the call of the bugle sounding out some order for the dragoons on the other side at the post; between whiles the absolute repose of nature.

"I wonder if the new heavens and the new earth will be anything like this!" said Mr. Murray with a long breath. "This is not like our common world. Well, Meredith—it is hard upon you, but it is better than too much talking."

"It is not hard upon me, sir. I am getting all my ideas cleared up.

"'Holy Scripture saith, that the hearts of the children shall be turned to the parents, and the hearts of the parents to the children. I will tell you a story about that, which, I hope, may be of use; so much the more, that in this regard one sees so much that is senseless.

"'I knew a man once, who was the very ideal of a just living, upright, honourable man; but Jesus he knew not. Among his fellow-men he was held in general, well-deserved esteem; for he was pleasant and winning in intercourse with them, and in his whole character there was something naturally noble. No prayer was ever heard in his house, neither at table, nor mornings and evenings, nor was ever the morning and evening blessing read. But love and peace reigned in the house, between parents and children, and master and mistress and servants; and nothing dishonourable was tolerated. In other things however, the way of the house was the way of the world; card-playing was had there, now and then dancing, and sometimes it might happen that an oath came out, when the angry vein was swollen; nevertheless, worldly gaiety was never permitted to go beyond bounds; the man would not suffer that. Nobody read the Bible; though the man had a Bible which he had inherited from his pious mother and held in high honour; it had the chief place on his bookshelf; but it was made no use of, only now and then taken down to have the dust brushed off it. This man had a whole flock of children; and a wife who clung to him with such inmost affection, that many a time when she heard his step on the floor she would call him into the room where she was, and when he came in and asked what she wanted, would answer him, "O, I only just wanted to see you, and now you may go off again." In outward things he was pretty comfortable; made a living, but also had a good deal of a burden to carry; was a diligent worker, however, and by little and little got on in the world. He was not often seen at church or the Lord's Supper; yet did not absolutely neglect them. Nevertheless, the man had a special spite against *pious people*, of whom in his life he had known a few. Those pious people of his acquaintance can indeed not have been of the right sort; for from their example he had come to the firm persuasion that pious people, all and sundry, were no better than hypocrites. He used often to tell of a pious man he had known, who used to read a great deal in the Bible and in religious books, and used also to hold meetings for prayer in his house, while at the same time he was a miser and put out his money to usury. Another one he had known, who in externals made as fair pretences; but with that was of such ungovernable temper and such unmeasured brutality that on more than one occasion he had beaten a man nearly to death. Therefore, as I said, he held all pious people to be a humbug.'"

Meredith paused a moment, and Flora spoke up.

"There!" she said, "*I* know such people. Don't you think, Mr. Murray, that sort of good people do more harm than good?"

"What sort of good people are they, Miss Flora?"

"Why sir, I mean, like these Meredith was reading about. I know such people. They are selfish, and envious, and get angry, care for nobody in the world but themselves, and are not at all particular about telling the truth."

"Therefore *not* good people."

"But they are members of the church, sir, and they go to the Communion."

"Don't you know, the Lord forewarned his disciples that a large portion of his so-called church

would be none of his? You need not be surprised
at it. It is just what he told us would be."

"Then how are we to know?"

"You can know with certainty about yourself," said Mr. Murray with a smile. "It is not
difficult to find out in your own heart, whether
Christ or self comes first. For other people, you
can afford to wait till the judge comes, cannot
you?"

"You are thinking, Flo, are you not, that this
man and his family were just about the right pat-
tern?" said her brother.

"I think such people are pleasant," Flora confessed. "They make no pretences. That man
seems to have been just and kind and nice."

"Ah, you make a mistake," said Mr. Murray
again. "We all make pretences, of one sort or
another, true or false. Such people as you are
speaking of pretend *not* to be Christians; and no
doubt with perfect truth."

"But is not God pleased with justice and kindness and benevolence?"

"*With* disobedience?"

"Surely he commands us to love one another?"

"He commands first, that we love *him*."

"Isn't that loving him?"

"Love always shews itself towards the beloved
one; *afterwards* towards the objects the beloved
one cares for."

"May I go on?" said Meredith, as Flora paused.
"I think my story will illustrate this."

"Go on, by all means. Perhaps an illustration will make it clear to everybody."

" 'This man was a scholar in the law; and was already pretty well on in years, when one of his sons, a special favourite with him on account of his fine parts and who was just studying law at the time, at the University, learned to know his 'Saviour, and turned to him with all his heart. The instrument of his conversion was a faithful minister, whose preaching he had attended diligently, and with whom he afterwards came into very intimate terms of intercourse. Now when this son's heart was filled with intense love to his Saviour, such as I have seen equalled in few men, nothing was more natural than that he should send longing wishes towards the parents and brothers and sisters whom he loved so tenderly; wishes that they too might learn to know the Saviour; and so, in his letters, he poured his whole heart out, told them without reserve what had gone on in his own heart, and how he was now rejoicing in the certainty that his sins were forgiven and in the sure hope of everlasting life. "O that all men were as happy as I!" he cried out in his letters. For a long time he was left without an answer. At last came a letter from his father; it ran thus. "My son, your letters were wont always formerly to be a refreshment and a delight to me; now on the contrary they are a vexation and a bitter grief. I see that you are exactly in the way to become like those hypocrites of whom you used to hear me tell. I beg that you will either write as you have been accustomed to do, or not write at all."

" 'The son answered, "Father, you have always enjoined it upon me to tell the truth; you always impressed it upon me that there is no more contemptible and cowardly being than a liar, for he has not even the spirit to be honest; and now do you want to compel me to be untrue? Either I must write you what is according to my heart; for lie I cannot and will not, neither will I make believe; or I must indeed do as you say and not write at all." This startled the father, for he had in former times said to his friends,—"The lad will not tell a falsehood; he would sooner let his head be taken off;"—and he was honest enough to write to his son, "Well, write what you like; if you are not a hypocrite, you are a fanatic; but you shall tell no lies; there you are right, and I was wrong."

" 'Soon after this the time of the holidays came about, and the son took his journey to his parents, to spend the holidays with them as it was his wont to do; for it has been already remarked that love and peace reigned in that house. As he came in, his mother met him with tears, and looked at him in a very critical way, as if she feared he were not right in his head; but he caught her heartily round the neck and kissed her and hugged her, whispering at the same time, "Mother, don't look at me with such a doubtful face; I have got all my five senses yet." Then he went to his father in the sitting-room, and would have fallen on his neck too,

18

but the father at first kept him off with all his
strength; till his son asked him, "Thou art my dear
good father always, and always wilt be so; am I
thy son no longer? and why not? what have I
done that is wrong? is reading the Bible and praying, anything wrong?" Then the father kissed his
son and spoke—"I must honour the truth—thou
hast done nothing wrong, my son!" For an hour
or so they talked together about the professors at
the University, and about the lectures the son had
been attending there; and in the meantime the
mother had got supper ready, and they went to
table. The son stood up, folded his hands, and
prayed. With that, the father thrust his chair
back till it cracked, and ran out of the room, and
the mother full of anxiety, ran after him. The son
however did not follow them, but after he had
heartily prayed for his father and his mother, he
sat down, and with tears eat his supper. When he
found his parents did not come back, he sought his
own room, and once more poured out his heart
before his faithful God and Saviour; then he slept
quietly until morning. Next morning, naturally
the first thing was to go at his prayers again; then
he read a chapter in his beloved Bible; and went
afterwards to the dwelling-room, as he was accustomed. His father was there, sitting in his arm-
chair, and turned pale one minute and red the next.
The son gave him his hand cordially and bade him
good morning, and to his mother as well. "My
son," his father then asked him, "are you master in

the house? or am I?" The son answered, "Who but you, father?" "Why do you take upon you then to introduce prayer at meals, seeing you know that it is not our habit here?" "Father," the son answered, "did I then say that you and my mother were to pray? I asked expressly only, 'Come, Lord Jesus, be *my* guest'—whereas elsewhere usually the prayer is, 'be *our* guest.' I knew it was not your custom to pray; therefore it would have been an untruth to say, 'our guest,' and that would have been assuming, too, for it would have been trying to draw you in." "But why did you not let the whole thing entirely alone? you knew very well we have no such regulation here." "Not for you, father; for me, however, there is such a regulation; and if I had taken my supper without praying, I should have been false to my God; and it is certainly not your pleasure that I should be false towards God, since you cannot endure any falsehood towards men." "No," said his father, "you are not to be false; well, pray away, for all I care; but only when we are alone, not when strangers are by, else we should become a laughing-stock." "Father, I could not be untrue to God for my own dear father's sake; should I for the sake of strangers? I am not ashamed of my God and Saviour before any man, neither before strangers nor before the king himself; and I will be faithful and true to my God. If it is not your pleasure to have this thing done when strangers are present, then do not call me to table." The father said, "Boy, where did you get your pluck?" "I love the Lord," the son answered, "who has redeemed me; I would go into death a thousand times for him." "You are no hypocrite, my boy," said the father; "well, for all I care you may be pious, if you only will not be a hypocrite.'"

"'From that time the ice was broken; and I have myself seen it with my own eyes, how father and mother and son used to read together in the Bible, pray and sing together, and how the brothers and sisters one after the other turned to the Lord. Rarely have I known a house in which the Lord Jesus was so fearlessly acknowledged as in that house. And do you know what of this history I would like to inscribe in your hearts, yea, would like to burn into your hearts with letters of fire? It is this. Let your Christianity be no lip-work; let your religion not consist in words; lip-work Christianity is hypocritical Christianity. True religion is a fact. The genuine believer is upright and makes no pretence, neither to God nor man. The heartfelt conviction—"Boy, you are no hypo-crite"—ought to be forced upon the beholder by the walk and behaviour of every real believer; if that had been the case, the world would present a differ-ent aspect from what it offers now. But most peo-ple's Christianity is a fashion of speech; and so it is lying and hypocrisy; therefore it can at one and the same time, like Pilate, chastise and set free, pray and neglect prayer, confess and not confess, just as happens to be convenient in the circumstances. It is not required that you should preach to everybody you fall in with, as if it were your vocation to set up lights for everybody's guidance; much more would often be spoiled than mended in that way. But to be a Christian, to walk as a Christian, and thus to confess one's Christianity honestly in action, just because it is so and you are not going to be false either towards God or towards men; that is the way in which the hearts of the parents are turned to the children and the hearts of the children turned to the parents.'"

CHAPTER XVII.

The sun had got low, in fact he was dipping behind the dark line of Eagle hill; and everybody looked and watched. The bright ball of fiery gold disappeared, leaving a trail of glory; lights glowed against shadows on the hazy hill shore; little flecks of cloud in the west grew gorgeous, and a low-lying rack of vapour in the southeast took on the loveliest changes of warm browns and purples and greys. And as the sun got further below the horizon the cloud scenery became but the more resplendent.

"Mr. Murray," Flora began, "you will think I am always taking objections."

"Well, Miss Flora—what now?"

"Please to criticise this story Ditto has been reading. I would rather you did it than I."

"By 'criticise' you mean, find fault?"

"If you see reason."

"Suppose I do not see reason?"

"But do you not, really?"

"Wherein?"

"Mr. Murray, I like things kept to their proper places."

"We are agreed there."

"And I think it is a pity to make religious observances, or what are meant for them, repelling and disgusting to other people."

"Certainly. As how, for instance, Miss Flora?"

"Well, I never like to see people—I *have* seen it—make a show of praying at table, where no general blessing has been asked by the person at the head of the table or a minister. It just makes them conspicuous, and as good as says that they are the only right people there."

"That is not a pleasant impression to receive."

"No, and I did not receive it. I thought it was a mistake. And quite ill-bred."

"But perhaps those people felt that they wanted a particular blessing, where there was no general blessing asked, as you say."

"They might ask for it quietly, secretly."

"Yes. Would they get it?"

"Why Mr. Murray! Doesn't the Lord always hear prayer?"

"No. It is written—'He that turneth away his ear from hearing the law, even his prayer shall be abomination.'"

"But what law is there about saying grace at meals, in public?"

"There is this, Miss Flora. 'Whosoever shall confess me before men, him will I also confess'—"

"But everywhere, Mr. Murray? Must we be confessing *everywhere?*"

"What places would you make the exception?"

Flora was silent.

"Public places in general?"

Still Flora was silent.

"Allow me to ask—Do you approve of the custom anywhere of asking a blessing upon our meat?"

"Certainly—in one's own house.   Papa did it always.   Meredith does it."

"Then, Miss Flora, if it is a right thing to do at home, how is it not a right thing to do abroad?"

"Everywhere, Mr. Murray?   Would you do it in a restaurant?"

"If it is a right thing to do, Miss Flora?—why not in a restaurant?"

"Or in somebody else's house perhaps, where it is not the custom?"

"Why not?"

"Why it seems to me like a sort of preaching to people; like saying to them that you are better than they are; setting one's self up."

"Pardon me—how can it be setting myself up, to thank my Father in heaven for what he has given me, and to ask him to let me have also a blessing with it?"

"Why couldn't you do it quietly?"

"I should always in such places do it quietly; not aloud."

"But I mean,—without letting anybody know it?"

"Why should not people know it?"

"Excuse me, Mr. Murray; but I always think it is making a show—making a pretence."

"If it is a pretence, the worse for me, whether at home or abroad. But a *show* I want it to be, Miss Flora; a show that I am a child of God, and love to own my Father's hand everywhere."

"You are very good to let me talk just what I think, without being offended," said Flora. "You will not think me rude, Mr. Murray? I really want to know your opinions. Don't you think that in such things there is a tacit implied reproof of the other persons present who do not as you do?"

"How can I help that?"

"But is that polite?"

"That question sinks before the other—Is it duty?"

"I cannot see it to be duty," said Flora.

"I have always been a little confused about it," said Meredith; "in such cases and places, I mean."

"It makes one very disagreeably singular," Flora added.

"It is impossible to follow Christ fully, Miss Flora, and not be that, more or less."

"*Disagreeably* singular, Mr. Murray?"

"I agree with you, I am sure, in thinking that it is disagreeable to be singular."

"But must one? I always thought it was such bad taste."

"You perceive it is not a question of taste."

"Why then of necessity?"

"Because whoever follows the Lord fully will live in a way the very opposite of that which is followed

by the world. He will be marked out from it—
even as the Lord was himself."

"Still, one is not to make one's self unnecessarily
odd," said Meredith; "and I have until now been
in doubt whether people did not do it in this very
matter of asking a blessing at tables where nobody
else followed the practice."

"I am sure it is not unnecessary," said Mr. Murray. "I am sure that thought is a temptation of
the enemy. I am sure that the simple fact of having, though in so small a matter, shewn one's colours and confessed Christ, is a help all through
the day to go on confessing him, as occasion may
serve."

Silence fell after this, and some of the party no-
ticed how the sky and clouds were changing. The
sun had sunk below the actual horizon now; long
since he had dipped behind Eagle hill; and the
gold and the purple were fading from the racks of
vapour which had caught and given the colours so
brilliantly. Pale purple, pale fawn, ashes of roses,
then soft greys succeeded one another. The eastern hills had lost their light; the shadows were
gone; night was softly letting her mantle fall on
the world. Still the little party sat on the rock,
and looked, and felt the soft breath of the air,
and watched the fading glory. Nobody wanted
to move, and twilight would last long enough to
let them get home; and so they waited. Fenton,
I suppose had gone home, for they heard the rustle
of his footsteps no longer. By and by, as they

watched the grey strips of vapour which had been so brilliant a little while ago, they began to change again. The greys took on a purplish warm hue, which brightened and brightened, and then pure carmine began to touch the soft under folds and edges of the clouds, increasing in vividness, until over all the sky every speck and mass of vapour was glowing in brilliant crimson. For a few minutes this; and then it too faded, and rapidly the crimson sank to purple and the purple back to grey, and all knew that the reign of night and shades would be broken no more till the sun rising. Slowly the little party got up from the rock; unwillingly they turned their backs upon it; lingeringly they left the place which had been so pleasant, and took their way down the hill through the gathering dusk. The walk was still very pretty; Maggie held her uncle's hand, the others clustered round, and they went running and skipping till the level land was reached, then slowly again, as if loath to have the evening quite come to an end.

It was pleasure of another sort to gather round the tea-table, bright with lights and covered with good things.

"I do not think," Meredith observed, "that I ever enjoyed more in one day."

"Lucky for you!" said Fenton. "I don't see the use of having Sundays, for my part."

"How can you help having them?" said Maggie. "They must come, just like Saturdays, or Mondays."

"That's deep!" said Fenton. "But if they must

come, as you have originally discovered, why can't one use them reasonably."

"As how?" said Mr. Murray, preventing an eager outbreak of Maggie's.

"Like other days. Why shouldn't I fish, for instance? or shoot partridges? The fish don't know the difference. Why should one mope on one particular day?"

"I never do," said his uncle. "I am sorry you have such a bad taste."

"As what, sir?" (fiercely).

"As to mope."

"How's a fellow to do anything else?"

"Depends on himself."

"Well, what's the use of my not fishing? Why shouldn't I fish on Sunday?"

"Don't you know?"

"No, I don't," said Fenton. "That's just it. If I knew any good reason, of course it would be different." And he sagely muttered something about "priestcraft."

"There are two reasons," said Mr. Murray calmly, while Maggie flushed up and even Esther stared at her brother.

"I never knew any," responded Fenton.

"Do you care to know them?"

"If they *are* reasons," Fenton rejoined impudently, "it would be unreasonable not to care."

"Very true," said Mr. Murray smiling. "I will begin with the lesser of the two. It is found in the nature of man, Fenton. Man is so constituted that he cannot, year in and year out, stand a seven days' strain. Neither brain nor muscle will bear it. That has been tested and proved. In the long run, man cannot do as much, working seven days, as he can do working only six days."

Fenton knew that what his uncle gave as a fact was likely to be a fact; he had no answer ready at first. Then he said, "I spoke of fishing, sir; that is play, not work."

"As you do it, I suppose it is. But we are talking of the fact of one day in seven being set apart from the rest, and the reasons. You see one reason."

"What's the other?"

"The other is still more difficult to deal with. It consists in this—that God says the day is his. As Ruler and King of the world, he lays his hand upon that seventh day and says, This is mine."

"I don't see any reason in that," said Fenton.

"No. But you see the claim and the command. Those must be met, or disobeyed at our peril."

"What's the use?"

"One great use is, to remember and acknowledge that God *is* Ruler and Owner of all. So when we cross the boundary between Saturday and Sunday, we step over on ground that is not ours."

"There is no good in being stiff and pokey," said Fenton.

"No. It is only a stranger on the ground who can be that. One who knows the Lord and loves him, is specially at home and free on the Lord's day."

"But I thought the Jewish Sabbath was done away?" said Flora.

"The formal Jewish Sabbath. But not the spiritual. If you study the matter, you will see that Christ made careful exceptions to the literal rule in only three cases—where mercy, or necessity, or God's service demand that it shall be broken."

"Don't you think a farmer ought to get in his hay on Sunday, sir, if he saw a storm coming up?" Fenton asked.

"I dare not make any other exceptions than the Lord made," his uncle answered.

"Don't you think trains ought to run on Sunday, Mr. Murray?" said Flora.

"I must say the same thing to you, Miss Flora."

"But in cases of sickness and accident, sir?"

"Have you the notion that Sunday trains are filled with persons who have been summoned somewhere by telegraph?"

"No—but there are such cases."

"Yes; well. Do you think, honestly, that thousands of people ought to break the Lord's rule every Sunday, in order to give relief here and there to the anxiety of one?"

"I can tell you," Fenton broke out, "your doctrine is furiously unfashionable. There is not a fellow in our school that doesn't do as he has a mind to on Sunday."

"Other days too, I suppose."

"Of course."

"That is just what, in your sense, a Christian

gives up; not on Sunday more than on other days. That is the difference between a Christian and another man; one does his own will and the other the will of God, which is also his own."

Fenton muttered something to Esther, who sat next him, about an "old fogy," but the subject of conversation was carried no further. Mr. Murray purposely changed it, and the evening passed in very pleasant talk, alternating with some Bible reading. Only, towards the close of the evening Fenton started the question, "where they would go the next day?"

"Suppose we leave that for Monday to take care of," Mr. Murray answered.

"But, sir, there might be some arrangements to make."

"To-night?"

"Perhaps; but at any rate I might want to give some orders in the morning."

"I don't think we should have a good time, if we consulted about it now."

"Why not, sir?"

"You forget. It is the Lord's time. And if we want him to give us his favour on our expedition, it seems to me we had better not offend him about it beforehand."

"But, sir!—"

"But, Mr. Murray!"—put in Flora. "Just to *speak* about things?"

"Time enough to-morrow, Miss Flora. And this is the Lord's time, you know."

"But just *talking*—not doing anything?"

"Doing a good deal in imagination. What's the difference? Study the fifty-eighth chapter of Isaiah, the last two verses. Sir Matthew Hale gave it as his testimony, that he found business concocted on Sunday did not run off well in the week. No, we will leave the question till to-morrow at breakfast if you please."

"I can't understand it!" said Flora as she went upstairs.

"Study those verses in Isaiah," said Meredith, who overheard her.

CHAPTER XVIII.

A bright little party gathered round the breakfast table Monday morning.

"Now, Uncle Eden," cried Maggie, "where shall we go to-day? It is Monday now."

"What is proposed?"

Several plans were ready.

"Down in the cove of the bay," said Fenton, "where the lower brook comes in—then I can fish off Old Woman's rock till lunch is ready."

"I propose the Indian falls," said Esther. "Flora and Meredith have never seen them."

"*I* say, Fort Montgomery," said Maggie.

"Fort Montgomery!" There was a general exclamation.

"Where is that?" Meredith asked.

"Seven miles down the river. O it is just lovely!" Maggie explained. "We go down with the tide and come back with the tide, and spend the day down on the hill there, opposite Anthony's Nose. I shewed you from the front door which Anthony's Nose is, Ditto."

19

"That would be delightful. The day is going to be perfectly quiet and warm and sunny—just the thing."

"Seven miles," Fenton grunted. " Who's going to do the rowing?"

" I," said Meredith.

" And I," said Mr. Murray.

" And we can take Fairbairn," said Maggie; "and we had better, for there will be the baskets to carry."

"Nonsense—I can carry baskets," said Meredith; "and get wood, and all that."

"I think we can do without Fairbairn," said Mr. Murray. "I like the plan. It is just the day for it. If it only turn out to be just the time of tide also!—"

"We'll soon see about that," cried the boys. There was a rush and a whoop and a race to the boat-house, and then a more leisurely return.

"It's all right," said Meredith. "Couldn't be better. It is half past eight now, and the tide just beginning to turn. It will be running down till two o'clock—and just give us a nice current home."

"And a good pull too," said Fenton.

" *That's* all right, old boy. Come! don't you pull backwards. Now, how soon can we be ready?"

"Just as soon as we can get our lunch ready, and the things," said Maggie. " You might pack the things, Ditto, and get them into the boat, while we see about lunch."

" What are 'things'?"

" Why, cups and saucers, and tea-kettle, and

matches, and plates, and paper to light the fire, and everything, you know."

"Go off," said Mr. Murray, "and see about victualling the ship. I can manage the cups and saucers."

So Maggie and Esther ran to consult Betsey, who now held a nondescript position of usefulness in the family and was acting cook while Mrs. Candlish was away; cook proper being absent on leave.

"O Betsey, we are going out, to be gone all day; and now, what can we have for lunch?"

"Lunch, Miss Maggie!—"

"Yes, and you know we want a good deal. There are six of us."

"You know, it's Monday."

"Well, what of it?"

"There h'aint so much as if t'was any other day. You see, yesterday it was Sunday."

"O well! what have we got, Betsey? I know you have got something."

"There's bread, Miss h'Esther."

"We want more than bread. And butter, and tea and coffee and all that. We must have something more, Betsey. What *have* you got?"

"The chickens is nothing left of 'em; and that 'am bone h'aint got much on it. I do think, Miss Maggie, ye consume a great deal in the woods!"

"Of course we do. And we want a good, hearty lunch to-day, because the boys and Uncle Eden will have a long way to row. Come, Betsey, make haste."

"There h'aint a living thing in the 'ouse, but h'oysters, and h'eggs, and potatoes. That is, nothing cooked. And ye want dressed meat."

"Oysters?" said Maggie doubtfully.

"Capital," said Esther. "And sweet potatoes. We can bake them in the ashes. And eggs are good. Meredith will make us another friar's omelet."

"There's nothing else for ye," said Betsey summing up.

So Fairbairn carried a great bag of oysters down to the boat, and a basket with the potatoes and eggs, and the kettle, and a pail to fetch water in. And into other baskets went everything else that everybody could think of as possibly wanting from the house. Affghan and worsted, finally, and the merry party themselves.

Ten o'clock, and a soft, fair, mild day as could ever have been wished for. Not much haze to-day, yet a tempered sunlight, such as October rejoices in. No wind, and a blue sky far more tender in hue and less intense than that of summer. Little racks of cloud scattered along the horizon were, like everything else in nature, quiet and at rest; no hurry, no driving; no storms, no ripening sun-heat; earth's harvests gathered in and done for that year, and nature at rest and at play. And with slow leisurely strokes of the oar the little boat fell down with the tide; she was at play too. Sunshades were not opened; shawls were not unfolded; in the perfection of atmosphere and temperature there was nothing to do but to breathe and enjoy. At first even talking was checked by the calm beauty, the grand hush, of earth and sky. The boat crossed over to Gee's Point, and from there coasted down under the shore. There the colours of the woods shewed plainly in their variety; dark red oaks, olive green cedars, dusky chestnut oaks and purple ashes; with now and then a hickory in clear gold, or a maple flaunting in red and yellow. They all succeeded one another in turn, with ever fresh combinations; on the opposite shore the same thing softened by distance; overhead that clear, pale blue of October.

"I do not realize that I am living in the common world!" said Flora at last. "I seem to be floating somewhere in fairy-land."

"It's October—that is all," said Mr. Murray.

"Then I never saw October before."

"Aren't you glad to make his acquaintance!" said her brother.

"But how can one come down to November after it?"

"Oh, November is *lovely*!" cried Maggie. "It is lovely here."

"At Mosswood? Well, I can believe it. But at Leeds November comes with a scowl and a bluster and takes one by the shoulders and gives one a shake—to put one in order for winter, I suppose."

"I don't think shaking puts anything in order," remarked Esther.

"No. Now *this*—" said Flora wistfully looking

around her—"this comes as near making me feel good, as anything can."

"Take a lesson—" said Mr. Murray.

"But after all, the months must be according to their nature," said Flora.

"Certainly. The difference is, that *you* may choose what manner of nature you will be of. It all depends, you know," Mr. Murray went on smiling, "on how much of the sun the months get. And on how much of the Sun you get."

"How can I choose?" said Flora.

"How? Why, you may be in the full sunshine all the time if you like."

Again the boat dropped down stream silently. The way was long; seven miles is a good deal in a row-boat; so they took it leisurely and enjoyed to the full the consciousness that it *was* a long way, and they should have a great deal of it. By and by they came to a little rocky island or promontory, connected with the main land by marsh meadows at least if by nothing more, to get round which they had to make quite a wide sweep. When they had passed it and drew in to the shore again, they were already nearing the southern hills which from Mosswood looked so distant and seemed to lock into one another. They had the same seeming still, though standing out now in brighter tints and new and detailed beauty. On and on the little boat went, coasting along. No further break in the line of shore for a good while; only they were nearing and nearing that nest of hills. At last they came abreast of one or two houses, where a well-defined road came down to the river.

"Do we land here?" asked Flora.

"Not yet. Round on the other side of that bluff we shall come to a creek, with a mill; that is the place. Are you in a hurry?"

"I should like to sail so all day!"

They floated down with the tide and a little movement of the oars; there was absolutely no wind. The sloops and schooners in the river drifted or swung at anchor. Hardly a leaf moved on a stem. The tide ran fast however, and the little boat slipped easily past the gay banks, with their kaleidoscope changes of colour. This piece of the way nevertheless seemed long, just because the inexperienced were constantly expecting it to come to an end; but on and on the boat glided and there was never a creek or a mill to be seen.

"Uncle Eden," said Maggie, "there *used* to be a creek here somewhere."

"Certainly."

"There is none here now," said Flora.

"That you see."

"I can look along the shore for a good way, Mr. Murray. Are we going quite down to those mountains?"

"No. You will see the creek presently."

"The banks seem without the least break in them."

"It will not do to trust appearances. Have you not found that out yet?"

"I tell you what; I'm getting hungry," said Fenton, who was taking his turn at the oars.

"Eleven o'clock. You will have to control your impatience for some time yet," said Meredith.

"I can tell you, this boat is awfully heavy," said Fenton. He had meant to use a stronger word, but changed it. "Can't we get lunch by twelve?"

"O no! we shall have some reading first, I guess," said Maggie. "Lunch at twelve? Why you never have it till one, Fenton."

"Makes a difference whether you are pulling a dozen people and forty baskets along," rejoined her brother. "It's an awful bore, to have to do things."

There was a general merry burst at that.

"What sort of things, Fenton? Do you want to live like a South Sea Island savage?" his uncle asked.

"Uncommonly jolly, *I* should think," responded Fenton. "Dive into the surf and get a lobster, climb into a tree and fetch down a cocoanut— there's your dinner."

"A very queer dinner," remarked Maggie, amid renewed merriment.

"I never heard that lobsters were fished out of breakers, either," said Flora.

"You seem to think it is no work to fight the breakers and climb the cocoanut trees," remarked Mr. Murray. "However, I grant you, it would not occupy a great deal of time. Is your idea of life, that it is useful only for eating purposes?"

"It comes to that, pretty much," said the boy. "What do people work for, if it isn't to live? I don't care how they work."

"Some people's aim is to get where they will do nothing," said Mr. Murray. "Do you see a bit of a break yonder in the lines of the shore, Miss Flora?"

"Is it?—yes, it is the creek!" cried Maggie joyously. "It is the creek. Now you can see it, Flora."

It opened fast upon them now as they came near, quite a wide-mouthed little creek, setting in among wooded banks which soon narrowed upon it. Just before they narrowed, an old mill stood by the side of the water, and there were some steps by which one could land. There the boat was made fast, and the little party disembarked, glad after all to feel their feet again; and baskets one after another were handed out.

"What is all this cargo?" said Fenton grumbling; "and who's going to carry it to the top of the hill? Suppose we stay down here?"

"And lose all the view?" said Maggie.

"And the walk? and the fun?" said Esther.

"Fun!" echoed Fenton. "Just take that sack along with you, if you want fun. What ever have you got in it? cannon balls?"

"Oysters."

"Oysters! In the shell! Why didn't you have them taken out? What's in this basket? this is as bad."

"Cups and saucers, and spoons and plates, and such things."

"We could have done without them."

"How?"

"Eat with our fingers."

"You had better go to the South Sea Islands, and done with it," said Esther. "Come—you take hold of one side of the basket and I of the other."

"No, Essie," said her uncle; "that would be very unchivalrous. Do not ask Fenton such a thing. In the South Sea Islands men may make women do the work for them; but not here. Come, my boy, here are three of us and only a basket apiece; take up your burden and be thankful, and be brave."

I am afraid Fenton was neither; but he shouldered his basket; and being an athletic fellow, managed to reach the top of the hill without more muscular distress than the others showed. Of the state of his mind I say nothing further; but the truth is, the way was rather long. Nobody knew the shortest cut to the place they desired to reach; so they wound about among thickets of low cedar, sprinkled here and there with taller pines, going up and down and round about for some time. At last they found their way to the top of the ridge, and wandering along in search of a suitable place for their rest and pleasure, came out upon an open bit of turf and moss on the highest ground, over which a group of white pines stretched their sheltering branches. The view was clear over a very long stretch of the river with its eastern shore;

indeed they could look up quite to the turn of the river at Gee's Point; Gee's Point itself hid Moss-wood from them.

With acclamations the party deposited their baskets and threw themselves down on the bank. The gentle warmth of the sun was not shorn of its effect by the least stir of wind; the moss and grass were perfectly dry; and the lookout over river and shores was lovely. Sugarloaf shewed now true to its name, an elegant little cone. The sails of the two or three vessels the party had passed in coming down the river were so still that they served to emphasize the general stillness; they hung lazily waiting for a breeze and could not carry their hulls fast or far.

For a while the pleasure party could do nothing but rest and look. But after a while Meredith roused himself to further action. He began wandering about; what he was searching for did not appear, until he came back with an armful of green, soft, pine branches.

"Now if you will just get up for a few minutes," said he, "I will give you a couch to rest upon." And he went on to lay the branches thick together, so as to form a very yielding comfortable layer of cushions, on which the party stretched themselves with new pleasure and strong appreciation. Meredith had to bring a good many armfuls of pine branches to accommodate them all; at last he had done, and flung himself down like the rest.

"When do you want your fire made?" said he.

"Somebody else is hungry, I am afraid," said Flora.

"I cannot deny it. But I can wait as long as you can!"

"I am *very* hungry," said Flora.

"I believe I shall be," said Mr. Murray, by the time our luncheon can be ready. Here's for a fire!"

They all went about it. To find a place and to arrange stones for the kettle, and to collect fuel and to build and kindle the fire. Stones for the chimney-place were not at hand in manageable size; so Mr. Murray planted three strong sticks on the ground with their bases a couple of feet or so apart and their heads tied together; and slung the kettle to them, over the fire. This was very pretty, and drew forth great expressions of admiration. Then, while waiting for the kettle to boil, they all threw themselves on their pine branches again and called for a story; only Fenton sat by the fire to keep it up. Meredith took his book from his pocket and laid it on the pine branches, open before him.

"You could not attend to anything very deep till you have had something to eat," he said. "I will give you something easy."

"Most of your stories are so profound," added Flora.

"Never mind; listen."

CHAPTER XIX.

"'The story that I am going to tell now, happened here in Hermannsburg.'"

"A great many things seem to have happened in Hermannsburg," Flora remarked.

"Yes. Just think what it must be to live in a village with a history.—

"'It is, for one thing, a beautiful story for Passion week; and then it gives a lovely picture of the relation in which princes and their vassals at that time stood to one another. The thirty years' war had brought frightful misery over our country. Havoc and devastation had come even into the churches. So, for example, in this place; the imperial troops had not only plundered the church and carried away everything that was of value; for to be sure the people here were Lutheran heretics; but they had even broken to pieces all the bells in the tower, and driven off no less than five baggage waggons full of brass metal, to be recast for cannon. And the last one, the big bell, was broken up and about to be carried away by the Croats; the horses were even put to the waggon;

when suddenly the blast of trumpets and the battle-cry, " *God with us !* " announced the coming of Lutheran troops, and scared the Croats away. So the metal was left behind. After the thirty years' war, gradually the people gathered together again; but the number of them was very small, and many a farm had to lie waste, for want of both farmer and farming stock. There are said to have been at first only ten families come back to our parish village, with four oxen and two cows. Besides all that, towards the end of the war epidemics were constantly prevailing, so that for example, in this parish, in the thirty years from 1650 to 1680, three pastors died one after another of contagious epidemics; namely, Andreas Kruse'" (that was the fellow who stood out so for his church vessels), "'Paulus Boccatius, Johannes Buchholz; and the fourth Justus Theodor Breyhan, who died in 1686, was three times at death's door. Those were troubled times!

"'This Breyhan was a childlike good man, whom his parish held in great love and honour, for both in spiritual and in material things there was no better counsellor for them. Like a true father he stood by the bedside of the sick and the dying, to shew them how to die happy, and like a good father he comforted the survivors, and by the live and powerful words of his preaching, poured new strength and fresh courage of faith into all hearts. With all that, this man was a singular lover of the *sound of the bell.* In his opinion it was a remarkable thing, that the heavenly King would allow his bells to be cast of the same metal in which earthly princes cast their guns; and his highest wish was, to get a great church bell again. The metal indeed was still on hand; but who would have it cast? There was only a little bell still hanging up in the tower, which was called the Bingel bell, and dated back to the year 1495; (it is there still) and had been too insignificant to tempt the Croats. With that on Sundays people must be rung to church, and with that the tolling for the dead must be done at funerals. It did, it is true, give out a fine, lovely, clear note; but the good dear Breyhan often wept great tears when he heard the sound of it; it seemed to him that it was too disrespectful to the great King in heaven, that he should have no better bell than that. He could hardly sleep at last for thinking of it. Especially at the high festival days and in Passion week, and on occasion of funerals, he was in great uneasiness. Then, it was in the fast season of the year 1680, he was again sick unto death, and in his fevered fancies he was continually praying to the dear Lord that he would not let him die before he could have the bell properly tolled at his burying. He recovered, and on Good Friday was again able to preach. The congregation wept for joy at having their beloved pastor among them again, and never perhaps have more ardent thanks gone up to God from the parish than did that day. The time of the Easter festival passed by, and they rejoiced with one another over the glorious resurrection of the Lord Jesus. The third day of the

Easter festival (at that time there were still always three feast days) he told the congregation that they must pray for him faithfully; for the next day he was going on a journey after a bell, which in his illness he had promised to the Lord.

"'The next morning his honest old parish farmer Ebel was at the door with a little farm waggon, and asked him where they were to go? and whether it was to be a long or a short journey? You must know the man was under obligation to take several long journeys for his pastor, lasting some days, and several short expeditions of a day only each. "It shall be a short one for to-day," the pastor answered. "I think with God's help to ride to Zelle." So after Ebel had attended morning worship in the parsonage, for he would not willingly have missed that, Breyhan mounted into the waggon, set himself down upon a spread of straw, took his hat off and said reverently—"In God's name!"—and then they went forward, step by step, as the manner was then; for in those days people were not in such a hurry as they are now. Before the city they stopped, and with prayer and thanksgiving eat the breakfast they had brought along with them. Then Breyhan took his vestments out of a clean linen cloth and put them on, and one could see by his lips that he was speaking to himself or praying. Good Ebel felt himself growing quite devotional at the sight, and he drove into the city with twice the spirit he had had before, because now everybody might see that he had a pastor in his waggon.'"

Meredith paused a moment to glance up at the river and hills opposite, and Maggie broke forth,

"The people in that country seem to be very unlike the people in this country!"

"You mean, nobody here would care so much about carrying a minister in his waggon," said Meredith laughing.

"Well—he wouldn't, would he?"

"I am afraid not. More's the pity."

"Why, Ditto?" said his sister. "What are ministers so much more than other people?"

"They are the King's ambassadors," said Mr. Murray, taking the answer upon himself. "And you know, Miss Flora, the ambassador of a king is always treated as something more than other people."

Flora looked at him. "Mr. Murray," she said, "ministers do not seem like that?"

"When they are the true thing, they do."

"But then besides," Maggie went on,—"how could anybody, how could that good man care so much about a *bell*? What difference did it make whether the bell was big or little?"

"Superstition"—said Flora.

"No, not exactly," responded Mr. Murray.

"That other man cared so much about his silver service, and this one about his bell—they were both alike, but I don't understand it," said Maggie.

"How would you like your father to have his table set with pewter instead of silver?"

"O Uncle Eden! but that—"

20

"Or to drive a lame horse in his carriage?"

"But Uncle Eden—"

"Or to wear a fustian coat?"

"But that's different, Uncle Eden?"

"Yes, it is different. This concerns our own things; those matters of the vessels and the bell concerned God's things."

"Then you approve of building very costly churches, sir?" asked Meredith, whose head was running on churches lately.

"No, I do not."

"How then, Mr. Murray?" said Flora curiously.

"Because *the* temple of the Lord, the only one he cares much about, is not built yet. I hold it false stewardship to turn aside the Lord's money into brick and mortar and marble channels, while his poor have no comfortable shelter, his waifs want bread, and a community anywhere in the world are going without the light of life and the word of salvation."

"What do you mean by *the* temple of the Lord, Uncle Eden?" said Maggie. "I thought there was no temple of the Lord now?"

Mr. Murray pulled out his Bible from his pocket, opened and found a place.

"'Now therefore ye are no more strangers and foreigners, but fellow-citizens with the saints, and of the household of God; and are built upon the foundation of the apostles and prophets, Jesus Christ himself being the chief corner-stone; in whom all the building, fitly framed together, groweth unto an holy temple in the Lord; in whom ye also are builded together, for an habitation of God through the Spirit.'"

"How lovely!—" said Meredith.

"I didn't know that was in the Bible," said Flora.

"The literal Jewish temple was in part a type of this spiritual one. And as in Solomon's building, 'the house was built of stone made ready before it was brought thither; so that there was neither hammer, nor axe, nor any tool of iron heard in the house while it was in building,' but the walls rose silently,—so it is in this temple. The stones are silently preparing, 'polished after the similitude of a palace;' silently put in place; 'lively stones built up a spiritual house;' so the Lord says, 'He that overcometh, will I make a pillar in the temple of my God.'"

There was silence for a few moments, when Mr. Murray added, "*That* is the temple, Meredith, that I think the Lord wants us to build and help build. I think any diversion of the money or strength needed for this, a sad, sad waste; and no honour to the Lord of the temple, though it may be meant so. Come, go on with Pastor Breyhan; I like him. His was a true-souled care for God's honour. I hope he got his bell."

Meredith went on.

"'To Ebel's question, "where he should drive to?" the answer was, "to the Stechbahn;" that was a road which lay opposite the ducal castle.

Ebel's wonderment grew greater and greater, but Breyhan kept still, slowly dismounted, gave orders to Ebel that he should drive to the inn, but he himself went straight on to the ducal castle. As he had expected, for it was just eleven o'clock, he found the duke sitting in front of the entrance to the castle. For about this hour the duke was wont to sit there and allow everybody, even the lowest of his vassals, to have free access and speech of him. If there were no petitions, or complaints, or the like on hand, he would converse in the kindest and most affable way with everybody, and many a peasant could boast that in all simple-heartedness he had shaken hands with his liege lord. Breyhan found the duke (it was George William) surrounded by a number of people. However there can have been nothing of consequence going on, for when the duke saw the pastor approaching, he signed him immediately to come near. Breyhan presented himself; and related simply and in childlike wise how things stood in Hermannsburg, and how the people had not yet been able to get their affairs rightly under way since the terrible war. George William listened kindly, and many a tear came into his mild eyes as Breyhan told him of the sick beds and the dying beds.

" ' " You want to ask some help in your need?" demanded the duke.

" ' " No," was the answer; "we can manage as yet to get along with these earthly troubles. But we have a spiritual trouble, that we feel more keenly, and which we cannot deal with by ourselves, and in that you must help us, my lord duke; this is what I have come for to-day." He told him now all that he had on his heart respecting the bell; how that the beautiful metal was there yet, but no means to get it cast, and that that was for the duke to do. The duke was delighted with the childlike, honest nature of the man and his hearty confidence that the duke's help was certain; and he could not help putting Breyhan's faith a little to the test.

"'"Dear pastor," said he, "you are suffering in a small way from the after effects of the thirty years' war; on the other hand I am suffering the same thing on a great scale. Your village treasury is empty, my castle treasury is empty, and the country's treasury to boot. So I cannot shake down the money for you out of my sleeves. If all the people in the land came to me to get their bells cast for them, what would be the end of it?"

"'Breyhan was of opinion that the case was somewhat different with Hermannsburg. Since one of the duke's ancestors had founded the church there, one of the descendants might well have a bell cast for it. The duke however would not yet give in, but teased the petitioner with all sorts of objections, just to see what he would answer; he loved clever and witty speeches. Breyhan did what he could to satisfy the duke's objections. At last it got to be too much of a good thing, and he said; "My lord duke, I have now been a good while asking a boon

of you, as a humble vassal may ask his prince; but
as asking does no good, I will now *order* you to
have the bell cast. Perhaps you are not aware
that I am lord of the manor to you, and that
you are my liegeman. A liegeman must stand
by his feudal lord with his goods and with his
blood, with life and honour. The bell we must
have; it is needful for our holding of divine service.
You are not obliged to give us the whole bell; you
are only to have it cast. Now it does not indeed
stand in your title-deed that you must have a bell
cast for us; therefore I cannot put you out of your
farm for not doing it. But it does stand therein
written that you must make hay for me three days
in every year, and do a day's work for me in every
week, for which service each time you are to get a
half gallon of beer. Hitherto your bailiff has put
a man to do it, and I have consented; but if you
do not have the bell cast, then you must come
yourself and make hay and cut wood."

"'You should have seen the duke then. "My
dear pastor," said he, "that is something I did not
know before, that you are my lord of the manor;
in that case, I must take shame to myself that
I have let you stand here all this while. Come
into the castle with me." He seized his hand and
led him into the house, sent for his wife, and said
in a solemn voice, "See here, my dear wife, until
now I have supposed that I was the first man in
the country; and now to-day I have come to know
that the Hermannsburg pastor stands highest, for

he is lord of the manor to me. Let preparation be made for his dining with us." While the servants made ready, the duke sought better information, and learned now that he actually held a farm in Hermannsburg from the Hermannsburg benefice, the contract for which on every occasion of the coming of a new pastor, or of a new duke's assuming the government, must be ratified over a cup of wine, and upon which, besides the yearly service money, the above obligations rested. The duke was so delighted at this, that he not only promised Breyhan to yield obedience and have the bell cast, but he begged him in the humblest manner that he would spare him in the matter of the hay-making and wood-cutting, for he was not exactly in practice in the matter of those two exercises; then jestingly he begged his wife to apply to the pastor herself for him, to let grace take the place of right. And as he was not slow to do this, all was soon settled. At table Breyhan was requested to make the prayer, and the conversation went on most charmingly about things of God's word.

The faithful carter Ebel meanwhile did not know at all where his pastor could be staying so long; and as he certainly understood so much as that the duke had taken him into the castle, he got into such trouble, because he thought something evil had befallen him, that he ran into the castle and demanded to have his pastor back; not a little wondering when he found him sitting at table with the duke. Still more was he comforted, when from the duke's table itself a draught of beer was given him.

"'After the meal was over, Breyhan drove joyfully back to Hermannsburg. The duke had not only granted his petition, but also declared that he would come to the consecration of the bell, and would be a guest with his lord of the manor. Breyhan promised him a friendly reception, but made the stipulation that he should bring only his lady duchess along with him, for his house was not prepared for entertaining guests. And now the business went forward according to his wish. The bell was cast in Hannover, and was, as Breyhan had desired that it might be, ready by the fast time of 1689. It was adorned with a threefold inscription. At the top stood:

"'"PRAISE HIM UPON THE LOUD CYMBALS; PRAISE HIM UPON THE HIGH-SOUNDING CYMBALS. LET EVERYTHING THAT HATH BREATH PRAISE THE LORD."—Ps. cl.

"'In the middle of the side stood:

"'"George William, by the grace of God duke of Brunswick and Lüneberg, patron of our churches."

"'And below (this is a verse—I will translate it as well as I can):

"'"*Through the grace of God I am alive again, and give you the call to church by my voice. Come willingly, be brisk and ready, then will I also speak out gloriously when you are going to the grave.*"

"'"*Anno* 1681, *Nicholas Greue in Hannover cast me.*"

"'Our ringing is still done with this bell, which

has a very fine tone, and whoever likes can still at the present day read on it the above inscription.

"'The Friday before Palm Sunday was fixed for the consecration of the bell; the duke arrived the day before with his wife; spent the night with his lord of the manor, attended the evening and morning worship and the preaching on Friday the fast day, and was present at the consecration of the bell, which took place immediately after divine service. When the bell was drawn up into the tower, and hung upon its scaffolding, ready for its first ringing, and when the first stroke softly sounded, then Breyhan and the duke and duchess beside him, the nobleman of Hermannsburg, who was called von Haselhorst, and the bailiff, whose name was Pingeling, together with the whole congregation fell upon their knees in the churchyard; and while the bell continued to be softly rung, the prayer of consecration was spoken. After the Pater noster, the full, sonorous notes of the bell pealed out, and there was not an eye but had tears in it as the long-missed tones floated off so gloriously through the air. The dear Breyhan's heart was bounding, and full of joy he spoke out—"'Lord, now lettest thou thy servant depart in peace.'" The afternoon they spent at home, only the duke could not refrain from making a trial at the wood-cutting, which however did not succeed very well; whereupon then the pastor magnanimously promised that he would content himself with the observance hitherto rendered, and never demand of the duke personally that he should make hay or do days' works. Then the duke requested that for his sake the evening worship might be held earlier to-day, for he wished to get back again to Zelle.

"'From that time he came again once every year, either for Good Friday or for Easter; and in the year 1686 he followed to the grave the remains of Pastor Breyhan, who died in the thirty-fourth year of his age. The evening of Wednesday before the sixth Sunday after Trinity (the date is not given in the church book), when he felt his end drawing near, he had the great bell rung once more ; and while it was ringing, at which time the greater portion of the parish either in their homes or standing in front of the house, were in prayer, with a glad gesture he fell asleep. His dying lips prayed, "Christ, thou Lamb of God, who takest away the sin of the world, have mercy on me, and give me thy peace, O Jesus. Amen."

"'The funeral was on Saturday. And as often as I hear the bell ring, I cannot help thinking of the dear, good Breyhan and the kindly duke George William, and the saying recurs to me—"The memory of the just is blessed."

"'Finally, I remark once more, that from this story I have taken up a thorough disgust for the new-fashioned *law of redemptions*. By this law the above-mentioned farm has lately been detached from the benefice. Before that, I was the most distinguished man in the kingdom of Hannover, for the king was my parochial tenant and I was lord of the manor to him; *now* I am an insignificant country pastor, and such, it is well known, have neither form nor beauty.'"

CHAPTER XX.

Fenton had been crying out that the kettle was boiling; and yet, when Meredith stopped reading nobody was in a hurry to move. The little group lying there upon the pine branches was as quiet as the day; and there is no describing the beauty of that rest in which nature for the moment seemed to be still. The delicate clear blue overhead; the still racks of white cloud here and there upon it, doing nothing and going nowhere, only lying fair on the blue; the breathless atmosphere in which an aspen leaf would have hung motionless; the broad river below moving its strong current so silently and so unobtrusively; there was no token of motion, unless in a vessel which was slowly drifting down while her sails hung windless by the mast; the profound quiet had something imposing. I cannot tell how, some grave, sweet influence seemed to press upon every heart in the company; and for a few minutes after the reader's voice ceased, the stillness was significant.

"We seem to be out of the world!" Flora remarked at last in an undertone.

"Why?" Mr. Murray asked.

"I don't know. Confusions and disturbance are nowhere in sight. It is all peace."

"And purity—" added Meredith.

"How nice if one could live so!" Flora went on.

"You may, to a great degree, live so," said Mr. Murray. "It will not be always October, and your couch may not always be such a feathery one; and yet, Miss Flora—I fancy that Pastor Breyhan lived in very much such an atmosphere all his life."

"The story is just in harmony with the day and the place; isn't it?" said Meredith.

"It is odd that one can be interested in such a story," said Flora. "And yet I have been interested."

"For that very reason, I suppose," said Mr. Murray. "There is something breathing out, both from the story and the day, which we all know we want, —unless we have got it already."

"But, Mr. Murray, one can not live in the world and be quiet," said Flora.

"There is a promise or two, however, to that effect. 'When He giveth quietness, then who can make trouble?' And the Master said to his disciples, 'Peace I leave with you.' 'He that cometh to me shall never hunger.'"

"I wish I knew what it means!" said Flora, furtively getting rid of a tear which had somehow found its way into her eye.

"I'll tell you what," cried Fenton, "if you don't come, the water will all boil away. Don't you mean ever to have luncheon? I don't know what you are thinking of, with your old stories!"

This brought the party to their feet. And now some went at unpacking and arranging the things which had been brought along in bag and basket; Flora lit the spirit lamp and set the coffee a-going; while Meredith and Fenton put the potatoes in the ashes and took care of the process of roasting the oysters. It was not so warm to-day that the fire was disagreeable, which was lucky, as the oysters demanded a good bed of coals; the potatoes likewise. Finally, Meredith set about making a friar's omelet. When all was ready and the tea drawn, they sat round the fire on the grass and made a most miscellaneous, and most enjoyable meal.

"Coffee! how good the coffee is!" said Meredith.

"And did you *ever* see such good roast oysters?" cried Maggie.

"They ought to be good," Fenton growled; "they cost a precious sight of work to get 'em up here."

"And Ditto's omelet is so nice!"—Maggie went on.

"If one could live in the open air!" said Meredith,—"how good it would be. I do not mean the omelet! but everything else. It's a great loss to live in houses."

"Lots of convenience, though," said Fenton.

"Look at the heap of oyster-shells Fenton is throwing behind him!" cried Maggie presently.

"What's that to you?" said Fenton. "There are

oysters enough. Don't meddle. If anything is a nuisance it is a meddling girl."

"How about a meddling boy?" Mr. Murray asked.

"Boys don't meddle," said Fenton. "It is girls."

"I suppose that is because the boys do the things that have to be meddled with," said Maggie sagely.

Fenton scowled, but the others laughed, and the meal went merrily forward.

"How much time have we?" Flora asked.

"For what?"

"For staying here, and reading. How long before we must break up and go home?"

"We can take our own time," said Meredith. "The tide will be good. Indeed it will be only getting better and better. It will turn about two o'clock."

"We must get home in time for dinner," observed Fenton however.

"I really should think you might wait a while for that," said Esther. "Uncle Eden, if anybody else comes here this fall, they will see exactly what we had for lunch."

"How so?"

"There are the egg-shells, and potatoe-skins, and Fenton's heap of oyster-shells."

"You do not think we will leave them here? Besides, there are several heaps of oyster-shells, I think; they are not all Fenton's."

"Fenton's is the biggest. But what will you do with all these things, Uncle Eden?"

"Carry them away."

"Where to, sir?" asked Fenton.

"Down the hill."

"Why, sir?"

"How would you like such a quantity of rubbish left in the woods at Mosswood, by some happy picnic party?"

"This isn't Mosswood, sir."

"No; it is some other wood."

"But it is nobody's ground."

"How can you venture to affirm that?"

"Well, I mean, it is nobody's ground in particular."

"That is more than you or I know, my boy, and is moreover highly improbable. We are certainly not intruding on anybody's privacy; but we have no right even here to leave things worse than we found them?"

"And we have got to lug all this trash down to the river again?"

"What do you think?"

Fenton thought it was "no end of a bore"; nobody else however did anything but laugh at him. After the oysters were all disposed of, the oyster-shells went back into the bag, ready for transportation; Fenton remarking with great disgust that they were just as heavy and took up more room than before. Egg-shells and potatoe-skins were swept up; cups packed away; coffee and teapot restored to the basket; hands washed; and finally the group gathered again on their couch of pine branches to enjoy every minute. They had a good space of time left them still, and the day promised to finish its fair course without change, except change of beauty. Fenton joined the group now, having nothing to do, and hopeless of inducing them to break up before the last possible minute.

"What are you going to give us this afternoon, Meredith?" Mr. Murray asked.

"I have been keeping it, sir; one of my best; a story out of the thirty years' war. Shall I read?"

"By all means."

"'In the parish of Hermannsburg there is a forest-house, situated about an hour and a half from the church village; the place is called QUELOH, and it lies in the midst of the forest. On the other side, about a quarter of an hour further on, is a beautiful beech wood, which goes by the name of BUCHHORST. In old times this place was inhabited by two peasants who belonged to the wide-spread peasant family of WEESEN. The name of the one was DREWES, and of the other HINZ. They were both good and God-fearing men, and with their whole hearts devoted to the dear Lutheran church. Those were the times of the thirty years' war in which they lived, and they had to bear their share in all the distresses which that miserable war brought with it; they bore it also willingly, for the Lord's sake.

"'Although they had been stripped of their goods a number of times by the Catholic soldiers, they had nevertheless preserved their most precious things, that is, their books; their Bibles, singing books and catechisms. These were, you must

21

know, very necessary to them, for in those days
there were as yet no village schools. In the entire
parish of Hermannsburg there was but a single
school, and that was in the church village; and
this school was attended by the children only for
one year, or it might be only half a year, previous
to their confirmation. For all the rest, every house-
father must himself play the school-master. And
in many respects, those must have been glorious
times. Every evening when the fire was kindled
on the hearth of the so-called Flett' (a sort of hall
or common room between the barn and the house),
'and the women were busy on the hearth with
their cooking, the house-father with the whole of the
household assembled around the fire; children, servants, and maids. Then the little ones were instructed in spelling and reading, in which business
the servants and maids were faithful helpers of the
house-father. After that, the catechism was taken
in hand; some spiritual songs were sung; a portion
was read aloud from the Bible and talked about,
in the course of which very lovely and profitable
words were often spoken; the old histories and
legends and stories of the country, handed down
from father to son, came in for their share of attention; the laws, manners and usages which custom
had made binding were discussed; and the "Flett"
hour was one so full of enjoyment and so full of
instruction that it was looked forward to during
the whole day by both old and young. And this
"Flett" hour was a strong fortress against the in-

trusion of innovations; and it can be shewn, that the new ways, that is, the godless new ways, never came until the " Flett" hours were given up. This Flett' (or great middle hall of the house) 'with its hearth was as it were the home sanctuary, in a certain degree the domestic altar. From there too, the peasant could overlook his whole house and prevent any disorders. Usually there was only one dwelling-room in the house, called the " Dönz," which however was for the most part used merely for eating and spinning, and served for the whole, for grandparents and father and mother and children and men and maids; for the meals were also in common; and that old people should be portioned off and take what was called their part, was a thing unheard of; it would have brought unending disgrace upon the peasant's head. It was just as little thought possible that the peasant should take his meals separate from his men and maid-servants; they all formed one great family.

" 'I said awhile ago, that in the ravages of the war these people had saved what they held dearest, namely, their books. They had managed it in this way. In every " Dönz" the furniture consisted only of a large table, a table with folding leaves'" (a Klapptisch—I don't know whether that is a table that folds together, or a table shelf that folds up against the wall) "'a cupboard, and some wooden chairs and stools; but by the side of the stove there stood a "grandfather's chair" of more pretension, covered with leather, in which indeed the peasant himself when he came home from the field in the evening, was wont to rest himself for a while. The seat, also covered with leather, they had made movable, so . that it could be lifted up and shut down; and beneath this seat the books were placed in security; nothing was to be seen of them when the seat was shut down, and nobody would look for them there. And it was quite needful that they should preserve their books so carefully; for the Catholic soldiers in the thirty years' war waged a regular war of extermination against Lutheran books.

"'One evening, Drewes the father, that is, the farmer, was sitting in his house, with his people around the hearth in the "Flett," and they were just speaking of the great victory which the Lutherans under General Torstensohn had fought for and gained at Leipzig; and the house-father was giving his opinion that soon now surely enough blood would have flowed, and that peace must be near. Upon that came his neighbour hastily in and said,—"Neighbour, hurry and loose your cattle, and let us flee to the wood; the emperor's forces are only half an hour off." Quick everybody sprang up; the cattle were muzzled to prevent their bellowing; the few bits of clothing and some victuals were caught up; and away they went plunging into the thickest part of the forest, as fast and as noiselessly as they could. Hinz closed the procession, and when the cattle were got out of sight he took post behind a tree, that he might see

what the soldiers would do. He had not long to
watch; for it was scarcely a quarter of an hour
later that bright flames went crackling up into the
sky; both houses together with the outbuildings
were in a blaze. The soldiers were enraged that
they had found no booty, and had set fire to everything. Hinz hastened now into the thick of the
wood after the others, and when he caught up with
them he told them of their misfortune. With that,
they all fell upon their knees and thanked God that
he had saved their lives and their cattle; and it
never came into any one's head to weep so much
as a single tear; they could build huts for themselves in the wood; and their hearts did not hang
upon things of this world. But what is this? what
could all of a sudden force such a deep sigh from
Father Drewes that it absolutely startled them all?
what could bring great tears into the eyes of that
strong man, whom nobody had ever seen weep before? "Godfather Hinz," he said with his voice
half stifled with pain,—"our books! our books!
Ah, they are burnt up by now! our own and
our children's only treasure and comfort!" And
behold, they all then fell to weeping, men and
women and children, men and maids, as if their
hearts would break. At last spoke out the old
Father Hinz, an eighty-years-old grey-headed man,
—"Hush, children! if our books are burned, our
God and Saviour is not gone with them; we have
him in our hearts; and his word we have too, not
only in the Bible but in our memories. I will say

out a chapter for you every morning and every evening, out of my heart." Then they grew quiet, and he folded his hands and began at once, and prayed first the twenty-third psalm, and then the seventy-third psalm, and finally the eighth chapter of the epistle to the Romans; all verse for verse from the beginning to the end.'"

"The twenty-third and the seventy-third?" said Maggie interrupting. "Which are they?"

"Don't you know? The twenty-third begins, —'The Lord is my Shepherd; I shall not want.'"

"And it goes on,—" said Mr. Murray,—"'He prepareth a table before me in the presence of mine enemies; he anointeth my head with oil; my cup runneth over.'"

"Not very appropriate," said Flora.

"I thought, very appropriate."

"Why they were just in great want, sir; even of the most ordinary comforts."

"A good time to remind themselves of their extraordinary comforts."

"What had they, to justify them in talking of their 'cup running over'?"

"Something which they know who know, Miss Flora, and other people would try in vain to comprehend."

"Well, the other word, 'I shall not want;'—they were in want already."

"No," said Meredith, "excuse me. I have read what comes after."

"They were in want, Ditto, certainly."

"Only such want—Never mind, I will not fore-stall my story."

"What is the other psalm?" Flora asked.

"Very beautiful in this connection," said Mr. Murray, who had got out his Bible. "It begins, —'Truly God is good to Israel, even to such as are of a clean heart.'"

"There again!" said Flora, "What reason had they just then to think that he was good?"

"That is faith, Miss Flora."

"Faith?" the young lady repeated.

"Yes. Faith takes on trust, when it cannot see." Flora looked at the speaker.

"The psalm goes on to describe the temptations to doubt which had beset the psalmist on observing the prosperity of wicked people and the hard times the Lord's people often had; and then how he saw his mistake; and then he breaks out, 'Whom have I in heaven but thee? and there is none upon earth that I desire beside thee. My flesh and my heart faileth, but God is the strength of my heart, and my portion forever.'"

"That is beautiful, and appropriate," said Flora.

"As soon as a man gets where he can say—'Thou shalt guide me with thy counsel, and afterward receive me to glory,'—he can stand a few ups and downs in this life. The choice of passages made by that old man was beautiful in the extreme; and proved not only that he knew the Bible, but that it was part of his life."

"And the chapter of Romans?"

"A worthy third in the trio. That is a chapter of triumph in the Christian's privilege and hopes, ending—'Who shall separate us from the love of Christ? shall tribulation, or distress, or persecution, or famine, or nakedness, or peril, or sword? . . . Nay, in all these things we are more than conquerors, through him that loved us. For I am persuaded, that neither death nor life, nor angels, nor principalities, nor powers, nor things present, nor things to come, nor height, nor depth, nor any other creature, shall be able to separate us from the love of God, which is in Christ Jesus our Lord.'"

Flora's eyes filled, and she said nothing; and Meredith took up his book again.

"There is another word in that chapter that fits, sir;—'All things shall work together for good to them that love God.'"

"It would certainly take faith to believe *that*," said Flora. "I can imagine a little that other things and hopes might console people suffering trouble in their persons and goods; but now, for instance, what possible benefit could it be to those people to have their houses burned, and to be driven into the wild wood with no shelter and nothing or very little to eat, and likewise very little to put on?"

"Well, I had better read," said Meredith. "Pastor Harms stops there, after telling how old Drewes recited Scripture, and asks, 'Could my dear readers all of them have done as much? just ask yourselves once quietly; and whoever is forced to say, "I could not do it," let him be ashamed from the bottom of his heart!

"'A special impression was made by the words, "Though I walk through the valley of the shadow of death," etc., and those others, "my heart and my flesh faileth," etc., and again, "I am persuaded, that neither death nor life," etc., and after they had all sat still a while, they raised their heads up cheerfully, took each other's hands, and broke out with one voice in the words—

"'"Dennoch bleibe ich stets an Dir," etc.'"

"What does that mean, Ditto?"

"'Nevertheless, I am continually with thee.' 'Then they went quietly to sleep in the wood, and lodged there beautifully, warm and safe under the wings of their God, and beneath the sheltering arms of the fir-trees; so that the sun was already shining through the branches when they waked up. Then they milked the cows, to get some breakfast for the children, and after that they all gathered round the old father to remind him of his promise. And the old man did not delay, but prayed first the twenty-seventh, and then the forty-second and forty-third psalms, and for the last, the twelfth chapter of the Epistle to the Hebrews; so devoutly and so confidingly and so unhesitatingly, that they all could not have supposed but that he was reading to them out of the big Bible that had been under the arm-chair; and in most of the parts they prayed with him word for word. Then they looked gratefully to the old man, and after they had first asked the blessing, then drunk the milk, and at last said grace, the others remained in the wood; but the two peasants, Drewes and Hinz with their two servants set out to go back to the place where their houses had stood. As they went off, the old father Hinz called after them, as if he were in a dream,—"Children, see about the books too!" Slowly they drew near the place of the conflagration; carefully listening and looking around them; but nothing was to be seen or heard, all was as still as death, only the birds were hopping and singing in the branches. At last they came within view of the place where the fire had been; but just as they were about to run thither, a low moaning came to their ears from the corner of the wood, near the place of the fire. They were Christians, therefore they did not do like the priest and the Levite, but like the kind-hearted Samaritan; they went off towards the quarter from which the moans came; and what did they see? Two badly wounded soldiers, sitting in the two grandfather's chairs at the corner of the wood. How came they there? The troops on their march through had had these wounded fellows with them; who for their weakness proved unable to go any further; so their comrades determined to leave them behind. But to let the houses stand for the sake of affording them shelter, was more than the inflamed rage of the soldiers, disappointed at finding everything empty, could see their way to. However, to shew some sort of humanity to their comrades, they had dragged the two old chairs out of the houses to the corner of the wood, placed the wounded men in them, and then completed their work of destruction; following which they had all marched off. And now, when the wounded soldiers saw standing before them the four men whose houses their comrades had laid in ashes, they looked for nothing else but death. But not anger nor revenge, but peace, yes, blessed joy, beamed from the faces of those four men; God had certainly saved their beloved books for them. Now they did not care that their houses were gone. The soldiers were treated, not as foes, but as benefactors. They carried them away into the wood where the rest of the people were; and when the chairs were seen, and the seats were lifted up, and the books found uninjured, then there was a thanksgiving and praising and glorifying so loud and so glad, that the angels in heaven must have joined in; the very little children ran to the books and kissed them devoutly and gleefully. The two soldiers were tended as if they had been blood kindred; milk was given them to drink; and now also, since the host of incendiaries had marched away, the way was open to fetch food again out of the villages. It was proposed to bring the wounded men to the nearest hamlet; but they were too weak for it; and they begged that they might be kept in the huts in the wood. And now it came to pass that nothing refreshed those two soldiers, more than old Father Hinz's talk from the word of God, and his prayers.

Even at the eleventh hour, they turned to the Lord Jesus; and the pastor in Hermannsburg gave them the holy Communion after they had confessed their sins, had received the assurance of forgiveness, and had declared that they believed in Jesus Christ, the only-begotten Son of God, and were persuaded that his body and blood were truly represented to them in the bread and the wine. This Communion was a right blessed day of joy for the inhabitants of the wood. But God was preparing for them yet another special rejoicing. For when the last hour of the two soldiers was drawing near, they summoned the old father and the two peasants to their dying bed, thanked them anew with tears in their eyes for the salvation which they had found for their souls, and made over to them the legacy of their military doublets; with the intimation, that after they were dead, they should rip out the seams of them. This was done, when the men had first been honourably buried; and now were discovered, sewed into the doublets, such a stock of gold pieces, that not only the burned-down houses and stables could be built again, but also the men and maids might receive a handsome reward, and a new altar cloth could be given to the church at Hermannsburg.

"'The lord of the manor of Hermannsburg had assigned to the two soldiers a place in his portion of the church-yard, where, at the northeast corner of the church-yard wall, their graves were covered with a stone. This stone lay there until, after the

male line of the lord of the manor had died out, the
so-called Allodium was sold, and along with it this
stone. It bore the following inscription:

"'"ANNO 1642 DOMINI NOSTRI JESU CHRISTI MORTEM
OBIERUNT ET HOC LOCO SEPULTI SUNT FRIEDERICUS WEN-
CESLAUS BOHEMUS ET MARTINUS JURISCHITZ LUSACIUS, QUI
BIBLIA INSCII SERVAVERANT ET PER BIBLIA IN ÆTERNUM SER-
VATI SUNT:" that is,

"'"In the year of our Lord Jesus Christ 1642 died
and are here buried Friedrich Wenzel of Bohemia,
and Martin Jurischitz of Lusatia; who without
knowing it had saved the Bible, and through the
Bible have been themselves saved unto everlasting
life."

"'On the other side of the stone stood the words
—"Hinnerk Hinz and Peter his son and Drewes
Johan have had this stone erected for two gold
gulden out of the Landsknecht's doublet."

"'Two years after the end of the thirty years'
war, those two peasants, of their own free will,
pulled down their houses in the Buchhorst and
built them up again in the village of Wesen; for
the reason, that after the devastations of those
years the wolves had so got the upper hand that it
was no longer possible to be secure from them.
Twice, with great difficulty, they had recovered
their children from the wolves, which already had
them in their grip and were dragging them off;
and then they thought, to stay there longer would
be to tempt God. Those two farms are still in
Wesen and are yet called Drewes' farm and Hinz's

farm, although the possessors in these latter days have long borne other names. May God give us from this old story the blessing, that we may be ever more as strong in the Bible and as firm in faith as the men of old were.'"

CHAPTER XXI.

"That is one of your very prettiest stories, Ditto," cried Maggie when he stopped.

"Yes," said Flora, "I think so."

"It must be a good story that can be listened to here," said Mr. Murray, — "and I have been listening with great attention. I have been thinking, while I was looking out over all this beauty and receiving so much by my ears of another kind of beauty, — I have been thinking and rejoicing to myself over the fact, how good our God is. 'Mountains, and all hills; fruitful trees, and all cedars; young men and maidens; old men and children: let them praise the name of the Lord.'"

"Uncle Eden," said Maggie meditatively, "how *can* hills praise the Lord? — or trees?"

"Don't they?"

"How, Uncle Eden?"

"*Don't* they, I ask?"

"But they could not hear anybody tell them to praise."

"You are a literalist. How can 'the trees of the field clap their hands'?"

" Does the Bible say they do ? "

" It says they will.   And it says ' Let the floods clap their hands; let the hills be joyful together before the Lord; for he cometh ! ' — "

" But that is very strange too," said Flora.   " ' He cometh to judge the earth; ' I know the chant; but it seems solemn and dreadful, and it is sung in the minor key."

" I know " — said Mr. Murray.   " The composer did not understand the rejoicing either."

" But how can any one, Mr. Murray ? "

" Those ' that love his appearing,' Miss Flora ? "

" I suppose I am very bad, Mr. Murray; but I tell you just how I feel.   That seems to me the most awful of times, and nothing but awful."

" Perfectly correct, Miss Flora, and just as it is described in the Bible.   When the kings and the great men and the rich men will say to the mountains and to the rocks, ' Fall on us, and hide us ! ' — "

" But you talk of being glad ? " said Flora looking a good deal troubled.

" Ay, but I was thinking of the other party," said Mr. Murray gravely, — " from whom will go up a very different cry, a shout of gladness — ' Lo, this is our God ! we have waited for him, and he will save us.' "

" Save them from what ? "

" From all the oppressions and miseries inflicted upon them by the rulers of this world; and more, from all the evils under which humanity has been groaning ever since the fall.   Then will strike the hour of the world's freedom. That will be the time when the bridegroom cometh, and they that are ready will go in with him to the marriage. Don't you think they will be glad? who have been waiting in darkness and weariness for so long? Then comes the marriage supper, and the everlasting union between Christ and his church. Should not the church be glad?"

"You said, 'they that are ready.'"

"Yes."

"Who are they?"

"Do you remember the parable of the marriage supper? Don't you recollect, one man had not on a wedding garment?"

"But what *is* the wedding garment?" said Flora, who looked as if she had some difficulty to keep her composure.

"Shall I answer you in the words of one of old time?—'I will greatly rejoice in the Lord, my soul shall be joyful in my God; for he hath clothed me with the garments of salvation, he hath covered me with the robe of righteousness, as a bridegroom decketh himself with ornaments, and as a bride adorneth herself with her jewels.'"

"Then it is something given"—said Flora slowly.

"Given, by the King to the guests; a free gift, Miss Flora, to all who accept the King's invitation."

Flora asked no more, but lay still on her couch of pine branches, looking out on the calm and glorified hills. Nobody else broke the silence; I think

22

Fenton was gone to sleep; and the others were quiet.

"The shadows are going the wrong way," said Flora at last. "I wish this day would last longer!"

"'A thing of beauty is a joy forever'"—said Meredith.

"Don't quote such a dreadfully hackneyed senti- ment!" said his sister. "How comes, it Mr. Mur- ray, that beautiful things in nature never grow hackneyed?"

"They are always fresh. No two days in one's experience are just like each other."

"There never was a day in my experience like this one," said Flora. "Ditto, aren't you going to read some more?"

"It will be a variety, if I do."

"We are made to like variety—as Mr. Murray has just reminded you."

Meredith guessed that his sister cared more about putting off the hour of departure than about the reading in the abstract; and he opened his book again, for nobody else made any objection to Flora's proposal.

"I shall read you," said he, "the story of a pas- tor and a farmer."

"Those are the people your stories are generally about," said Flora. "I hope the variety will lie in the treatment. Go on. I don't care what you read."

"'In a certain country, that I am not going to name, there is a parish village. In the parsonage lives a pastor; it is not I however. This pastor faithfully serves our beloved church with the word of God, which he preaches in truth, and with the holy sacraments, which he administers as he ought. And wherever this is done, the fruit will not be wanting; for God has promised it, and he keeps his word still, although among men there is little truth or faith any longer to be found.

"'With temporal goods, however, this pastor is not specially well provided; and were it not that he has a living God in the heavens, he must many a time grow anxious and dispirited; which in truth he does not always escape, as he himself humbly confesses. For if you have a small benefice, a large family, and a couple of children at school to boot, sometimes that gives even a believer the headache; though indeed there is no need for that, were faith but strong and prayer simple enough. Now there are cultivated fields belonging to the living; but as the pastor cannot drive the plough spiritual and the plough agricultural both at once, he hires out his ground; that he may give himself the more diligently to the cultivation of hearts. From these hired-out acres comes not a small part of his scanty means, and therefore it becomes a very desirable thing that he should dispose of his ground suitably. With most of his fields, indeed, this is not difficult, for they are fruitful and favourably situated and easy to get a good tenant for them. But one of his pieces of ground, and a pretty large one, lies on the slope of a hill which is wooded at the top; this field nobody will take, because in great rains loose earth and stones come rolling down over the slope from the hill above, and in this way the whole crop may easily be destroyed. It comes to my mind that the fault probably lies at the door of the beloved Enclosings. In the course of them it might well happen that too much wood has been cleared from the hill and sold. By that means the soil has been laid bare and the rain floods can wash it off anywhere they come. At any rate, nobody wants the field; and it always gives the pastor a stab in the heart when he comes past it; and he does not content himself with thinking, but he prays too, and promises that he will give to the Lord Jesus, for the mission, a portion of the hire of the field, if only a tenant may be found for it.

"'And He in the heavens has heard the pastor's prayer. Not long after, there comes a man of the parish, who is not in possession of ground enough to make his farming suffice for the wants of his family, and who therefore would willingly hire some more acres. He offers to take the neglected field off the pastor's hands. The upright pastor does not hide from him the reason why the field has hitherto found no tenant. But this man, who loves the Lord Jesus, and who therefore is a hearty friend of his pastor, declares that he has already quietly considered all that; and he has thought among other things that it must be very important to the pastor to let out this field, for to be sure the boys cost money; and it is very desirable for himself to hire a field, since he also has a great many mouths to feed. So both of them would be the better off. The Lord must have the care of the thing, and that he is well able for; he himself also would pray the Lord faithfully to this end, and he would make it the one stipulation with his beloved pastor, that he would stand by him and help him in faithful prayer. The two men gave each other the hand upon that. The man hiring the ground had also told the Lord that he would give him a portion of the produce of the field for the conversion of the heathen, and that all the same whether the produce were much or little. But the man had said nothing about this to his pastor, and he again on the other side had said nothing to the man about his own contract with the Lord; so that each of them had thus kept in his heart a secret for himself, which was known to the Lord alone. But surely I know that the Lord thereupon looked kindly on both the men.

"'Now in the autumn the farmer sets himself vigorously to work to get the field in order; and the Lord gives his blessing upon it; up comes the seed merrily, and the winter does it no hurt; the Lord has graciously sheltered it. With a wet summer the corn really shoots up, and stands so fine that it is magnificent to see. Both pastor and farmer are heartily glad at the sight, and both at the same time have a secret recollection of their vow, and are still more glad. But many of the peasants, who are not lovers of the Lord, and therefore also not lovers of their good pastor, and of the good farmer as little, feel no pleasure, but a regular hateful grudge in their hearts; for indeed there is everywhere a plenty of envy and spite to be found among unbelievers, because they make their god out of what is earthly and that is all they care about. However they comfort themselves with the thought that when the thunder-showers once come with their violent rain-pours, then surely there will be stones and soil enough rolling down upon the field from off the hill in the end to destroy all that is standing upon it. Verily that is not a godly sort of satisfaction, but a true Satanic delight, for Satan rejoices when any evil happens to people.

"'And at last, the wish of the peasants seems to be fulfilled. There comes up an uncommonly violent thunder-storm; the rain pours down from heaven in streams, as if the clouds had burst; so that regular brooks are flowing down the village streets. Then the envious people triumph; there is no mistake about it, the field lying so exposed on the slope of the hill, must be thoroughly laid waste. Those two men, it may well be, tremble too, for the storm is too frightful; but lose heart they do not; on the contrary the need drives them to more ardent prayer: "Lord, help, and do not let the field be spoiled. Thou art the strong, almighty God of Sabaoth, and thy hand is not shortened, but thine arm is stretched out still." So they prayed; and when the storm was past they went confi-dently up to the field, a good many accompanying

them; and as they were going, and while the many
who went along could hardly hide their delight,
they were singing in their hearts the hymn—

"'"Was mein Gott will gescheh allzeit,
Sein Wille ist der beste;
Zu helfen ist Er dem bereit,
Der an Ihn glaübet feste."'"

"Ditto, we don't understand that."

"It means about this. 'The will of my God be
done always. His will is the best. He is always
ready to help them who rest on him in firm faith.'"

"'With that, they are able to look up cheerfully
and they are of good courage. And when they
arrive at the field, what do they see? The entire
field is unharmed. The stalks of grain lift their
heads up bravely, as if they too would give thanks
for the beautiful rain which has so refreshed them.
But on both sides of the field a whole stream has
poured down from the hill, and nothing is to be
seen but a wild mass of rocks and stones. Whose
is the strong hand which seized the rain flood and
parted it just before it came to the field and so gently led it down on both sides of the field? Moved
to the depth of their hearts, our two friends were
constrained to cry out—"The Lord, he is the God!
The Lord, he is the God! Give our God the glory."
And it is to be hoped that many of the unbelievers,
if not aloud yet quietly, joined in the prayer with
them.

"'And now, when the harvest was finished, and
the farmer brought to the pastor what he had prom-

ised to give the Lord of the produce of the field, and then also the pastor's vow was made known to the farmer, the two fell upon their knees again and thanked the Lord for his goodness, because his mercy endureth forever. Must not such gifts to the heathen go with God's special blessing resting upon them?'"

"Is that all?" said Maggie.

"That is all," said Meredith smiling.

"I do not know what to make of that story," said Flora.

"Why?"

"Storms come from natural causes."

"O do they!" said Meredith. "You do not believe then what the psalm says—"'He commandeth and raiseth the stormy wind'—"

"But that is poetry."

"So is this," said Mr. Murray,—"'Who hath divided a watercourse for the overflowing of waters; or a way for the lightning of thunder; to cause it to rain on the earth, where no man is; on the wilderness, wherein is no man; to satisfy the desolate and waste ground; and to cause the bud of the tender herb to spring forth?'"

"Well," said Flora a little abashed, "is'nt it poetry?"

"I do think, Flo," said her brother, "you have forgotten all our talks around the breakfast table in Florida and elsewhere."

"Here again," said Mr. Murray,—"'He saith to the snow, Be thou on the earth; likewise to the

small rain, and to the great rain of his strength.'
It won't do, Miss Flora, to resist the fact. And I
would remark, that the highest poetry is the highest truth also."

"But do you think, Mr. Murray, if it is so, that
God will change his arrangements just for men's
asking him."

"I don't *think*, I know it, Miss Flora. It is precisely the Lord's way. But we can not stop to talk
about that now. My friends, do you see where the
sun is?"

"O must we go?" cried they all.

"It is a pity, isn't it? But this would hardly do
for a night's lodging; and if we are to sleep at
home, we must take the necessary steps."

Slowly they gathered themselves up from their
pine bushes, and shook themselves; literally and
figuratively, I might say.

"What are you going to do with your oyster-shells, Fenton?" his uncle demanded.

"I don't want to do anything with them, said
the boy.

"You always want to be a gentleman."

"What has that to do with it?"

"A gentleman never needlessly annoys anybody."

"Nobody comes here," said Fenton grumblingly.
But they all laughed so at him that he pocketed
his ill-humour and took his share in carrying the
wrecks of the feast down to the creek side.

Then with the tide they swept up the river. I
can never tell you how pretty it was. The day

had kept its character of clear quiet beauty without change; and now as the sun began to get lower in the western sky and shadows stretched along under the shore on the river and fell in lengthening patches or lines from hill-tops and trees, it did not grow cold. Quiet and sweet the air was, even on the water; and the rowers dipped and raised their oars in steady time, and in silence. Nobody wanted to talk. They passed the island or promontory a little above Fort Montgomery, passed on and on, keeping the mid stream now, passed Gee's Point, saw the boat-house looming up before them,—and were at home.

The very next day it rained.

Finis.

530 BROADWAY, NEW YORK,
November, 1876.

ROBERT CARTER & BROTHERS'

NEW BOOKS.

Forty Years in the Turkish Empire.

Memoirs of Rev. William Goodell, DD., late Missionary at Constantinople.   By E. D. G. Prime, D.D.. 2.50

Dr. Goodell was the first American Missionary at Constantinople, his wife the first American lady that ever visited the Turkish Capital, and they both remained at this post in labors of usefulness, until in their old age they returned to this country to die among their kindred.   This volume is largely autobiographical, being compiled from Dr. Goodell's Letters and Journal, containing also his personal Reminiscences written during the last year of his life.   He was inimitable as a letter writer, and everything that came from his pen was marked by spirituality, a peculiarly apt use of Scripture language, and a spice of wit that enlivened his conversation and his writings to the day of his death.

Autobiography and Memoir of Dr. Guthrie.

2 vols., 12mo. 3.00; Cheap Edition, in 1 vol..................................... 2.00

" His stories which give sparkle and zest to the narrative, and greet us on almost every page, are woven together in a picture of Scottish life that is wonderfully graphic." *Harper's Magazine.*

The Life and Works of Thomas Guthrie, D.D.

10 vols. In a box. (The volumes are sold separately)...................15.00

D'Aubigne's History of the Reformation.

In the TIME OF CALVIN. Vol. 7.. 2.00

D'Aubigne's History of the Reformation.

In the TIME OF CALVIN. 7 vols..14.00

D'Aubigne's History of the Reformation.

5 vols. in 1. 8vo., 3.00; in 5 vols., 12mo.. 6.00

Without doing violence to historical truth, he seems to invest history with all the charms of romance, and with the enthusiasm and skill of a poet he sketches on the historic page his fascinating and life-like pictures.

Hugh Miller's Life and Works.

New edition, very neat. 12 vols., 12mo..18.00
FOOTPRINTS OF THE CREATOR................................ 1.50
OLD RED SANDSTONE... 1.50
SCHOOLS AND SCHOOLMASTERS......................... 1.50
TESTIMONY OF THE ROCKS.................................. 1.50
CRUISE OF THE BETSEY... 1.50
FIRST IMPRESSIONS OF ENGLAND..................... 1.50
POPULAR GEOLOGY... 1.50
TALES AND SKETCHES... 1.50
ESSAYS. HISTORICAL AND BIOGRAPHICAL.................. 1.50
HEADSHIP OF CHRIST... 1.50
LIFE AND LETTERS. 2 vols................................. 3.00

"There is in HUGH MILLER'S geological works a freshness of conception, a depth of thought, and a purity of feeling rarely met with in works of that character."— *Professor Agassiz.*

Hugh Miller's Life and Letters.

By PETER BAYNE. 2 vols.. 3.00

Mr. BAYNE carries the absorbed reader with him through the whole period, unfolding leaf after leaf of the history of a life, certainly one of the most interesting and striking as well as useful of this century.

By the Author of "The Wide, Wide World."

THE LITTLE CAMP ON EAGLE HILL...................... 1.25
WILLOW BROOK.. 1.25
SCEPTRES AND CROWNS...................................... 1.25
THE FLAG OF TRUCE.. 1.25
BREAD AND ORANGES... 1.25
THE RAPIDS OF NIAGARA.................................... 1.25

The Say and Do Series.

Comprising the above 6 vols. on the Lord's Prayer. In a neat box 7.50

"Every new work of fiction by this gifted author we receive with a cordial welcome, for we know that it will be an addition to that pure, elevating, and delightful class of books which we may love as the fireside literature of our country. She writes for the home circle."—*N. Y. Observer.*

By the same author:

The Story of Small Beginnings. 4 vols. In a box.............. 5.00	House of Israel.................... 1.50
Walks from Eden................... 1.50	The Old Helmet..................... 2.25
	Melbourne House.................. 2.00

Elsie's Santa Claus.

By Miss JOANNA H. MATHEWS, author of the "Bessie Books.".... 1.25

Miss Ashton's Girls.

By Miss JOANNA H. MATHEWS. Comprising "Fanny's Birthday Gift," "The New Scholars," "Rosalie's Pet," "Eleanor's Visit," "Mabel Walton's Experiment," and "Elsie's Santa Claus." 6 vols. In a box... 7.50

By the same author:

The Bessie Books. 6 vols...... 7.50	Little Sunbeams. 6 vols........ 6.00
The Flowerets. 6 vols.......... 8.00	Kitty and Lulu Books. 6 vols 6.00

"The children in Miss MATHEWS' stories are perfectly natural. They get into trouble and get out of it. They say sweet things, and sharp things, and funny things, yet all the time childish things. They illustrate the right and the wrong, but in either case in a manner to attract to the former."—*Albany Express.*

Dare to Do Right Series.

By Miss JULIA A. MATHEWS. 5 vols... 5.50

"Miss JULIA A. MATHEWS' boys are as live and wide-awake as any one could wish, into mischief, now and then, like the majority of boys, yet frank and manly withal, and not ashamed to 'own up' when they find themselves in fault."—*Hearth and Home.*

Coulyng Castle; or, a Knight of the Olden Days.

By AGNES GIBERNE. 16mo.. 1.50

By the same author:

Aimee; a Tale of James II.... 1.50	The Curate's Home................. 1.25
Day Star; or, Gospel Stories... 1.25	Floss Silverthorn................... 1.25

The Odd One.

By Mrs. A. M. MITCHELL PAYNE. 16mo...................................... 1.25

By the same author:

Cash Boy's Trust................... 1.00	Rhoda's Corner..................... 1.25

Fred and Jeanie: How they learned about God.

By JENNIE M. DRINKWATER. 16mo.. 1.25

By the same author:

Only Ned............................ 1.25	Not Bread Alone.................... 1.25

Brentford Parsonage.

By the author of " Win and Wear."   16mo............................... 1.25

By the same author :

WHO WON?... 1 25
MABEL HAZARD'S THOROUGHFARE.................................. 1.25
DOORS OUTWARD... 1.25

Win and Wear Series. 6 vols. 7.50 | Ledgeside Series. 6 vols....... 7.50
Green Mountain Stories. 5 vols 6.00 | Butterfly's Flights. 8 vols..... 2.25

Imogen ; a Tale.

By EMILY SARAH HOLT... 1.50

By the same author :

Isoult Barry. 16mo.............. 1.50 | Ashcliffe Hall. 16mo............ 1.25
Robin Tremayne. 12mo........ 1.50 | Verena. 12mo..................... 1.50
The Well in the Desert. 16mo 1.25 | White Rose of Langley. 12mo 1.50

Mind and Words of Jesus, Faithful Promiser, and Morning and Night Watches.

By J. R. MACDUFF, D.D.   All in one vol.   RED LINE EDITION.
Handsomely bound in cloth, gilt... 1.50

By the same author :

Footsteps of St. Paul............. 1.50 | Hart and Water Brooks......... 1.00
Family Prayers.................... 1.25 | Memories of Olivet............... 2.00
Memories of Gennesaret........ 1.50 | Noontide at Sychar............... 1.50
Memories of Bethany........... 1.00 | Memories of Patmos............. 2.00
Bow in the Cloud................. 0.50 | St. Paul in Rome................... 1.25
Grapes of Eschol................. 1.00 | Tales of Warrior Judges......... 1.00
Sunsets on Hebrew Mountains 1.50 | Comfort Ye, Comfort Ye......... 1.50
Thoughts of God................. 0.50 | The Healing Waters of Israel.. 1.25
Prophet of Fire................... 1.50 | The Gates of Prayer............. 1.00
Altar Incense..................... 1.00 | A Golden Sunset................... 0.35
Shepherd and his Flock......... 1.50 | Clefts of the Rock................. 1.50

The Pilgrim's Progress.

Twenty full-page pictures.   Handsomely bound in cloth.   Gilt
and black, 4to... 2.00

" The CARTERS have done a good service to the cause of juvenile literature in publishing the 'Pilgrim's Progress' in a style more attractive for boys and girls than any other edition before the public."—*Christian Observer.*

Nurses for the Needy.
By L. N. R... 1.25

The Golden Chain.
By Miss Marsh.. 0.90

Four Years in Ashantee.
By Ramseyer and Kuhne... 1.75

Twelve Months in Madagascar.
By Dr. Mullens.. 1.75

Little Brothers and Sisters.
By Marshall.　16mo... 1.25

New A. L. O. E. Books.
AN EDEN IN ENGLAND.　16mo., 1.25; 18mo...................... 0.75
FAIRY FRISKET... 0.75
THE LITTLE MAID... 0.75
THE SPANISH CAVALIER.. 0.75

Alice Neville and Riversdale.
By C. E. Bowen.　4 illustrations....................................... 1.25

All about Jesus.
By Rev. Alexander Dickson.　12mo...................................... 2.00

"I have read it with the delight which every reader of the 'Pilgrim's Progress' recalls. Compared with the current literature of the time it produces a feeling akin to that of one who passes from barren sand into the verdure and fragrance of a spring garden, when each lily and rose is still touched with the morning dew, and rejoicing in the early sunshine."—*From Judge John K. Porter.*

This book has been re-printed in England at the earnest request of Mr. Moody, who gave away nearly 100 copies to friends in Great Britain before parting, each containing his autograph.

Nature and the Bible.
By J. W. Dawson, L.L.D., Principal of McGill University, Montreal, Canada.　With ten full-page illustrations......................... 1.75

"It contains the well-considered opinions of one who is a student of nature, and of the sacred record as well. The questions considered are of interest to a great many, both in the religious and scientific world."—*Presbyterian.*

The Shadowed Home, and the Light Beyond.

By Rev. E. H. BICKERSTETH, author of "Yesterday, To-day, and Forever.".. 1.50

By the same author:

Yesterday, To-Day, and Forever.

12mo. edition, mor., 5.00; full gilt, 3.00; cloth......................... 2.00
Cheap edition, 16mo... 1 25

The Reef, and other Parables.

By Rev, E. H. BICKERSTETH. 16 illustrations....................... 1.25

Dr. Williams on the Lord's Prayer.

12mo... 1.25

Dr. Williams on Religious Progress.

12mo... 1.25

The Suffering Saviour.

By F. W. KRUMMACHER... 1.50

The Works of James Hamilton, D.D.

Comprising "Royal Preacher," "Mount of Olives," "Pearl of Parables," "Lamp and Lantern," "Great Biography," "Harp on the Willows," "Lake of Galilee," "Emblems from Eden," and "Life in Earnest." In 4 handsome uniform 16mo. vols....... 5.00

Earth's Morning; or, Thoughts on Genesis.

By Rev. HORATIUS BONAR, D.D........................... 2.00

The Rent Veil.

By Dr. BONAR.. 1.25

Follow the Lamb; or, Counsels to Converts.

By Dr. BONAR.. 0.40

*Carters' Cheap S. S. Library. No. 1.

Fifty vols. in neat cloth. In a wooden case. Net....................20.00

*Carters' 50-volume S. S. Library. No. 2.

Net...20.00

These fifty choice volumes for the Sabbath School Library, or the home circle, are printed on good paper, and very neatly bound in fine light-brown cloth. They contain an aggregate of 12,350 pages, and are put up in a wooden case.

The Wonder Case.
By Rev. R. NEWTON, D.D. 6 vols. In a box.......................... 7.50

The Jewel Case.
By the same. 6 vols. In a box....................................... 7.50

Golden Apples; or, Fair Words for the Young.
By Rev. EDGAR WOODS. 16mo................................... 1.00

The Scottish Philosophy. Biographical, Expository, Critical.

By JAMES McCOSH, LL.D., President of Princeton College. 8vo... 4.00

By the same author:

Method of Divine Government 2.50	Logic.................................... 1.50
Typical Forms...................... 2.50	Christianity and Positivism.... 1.75
The Intuitions of the Mind.... 3 00	Royal Law of Love. Paper... 0.25
Defence of Fundamental Truth 3.00	Reply to Tyndall.................... 0.50

Christian Theology for the People.
By WILLIS LORD, D.D., LLD. 8vo................................... 4.00

Christianity and Science.
A Series of Lectures, by A. P. PEABODY, D.D., of Harvard College 1.75

A Lawyer Abroad.
By HENRY DAY, Esq. Twelve full-page illustrations.................. 2.00

The Period of the Reformation—1517 to 1648.
By Prof. LUDWIG HAUSSER. Crown 8vo........................... 2.50

*Songs of the Soul.
Gathered out of many Lands and Ages. By S. I. PRIME, D.D.
Elegantly printed on fine paper, and sumptuously bound in Turkey Morocco, 9.00; cloth, gilt... 5 00

Thought Hives.
By Rev. T. L. CUYLER.. 1.75

The Empty Crib.
By Rev. T. L. CUYLER.. 1.00

Cheap Editions of Important Theological Works.

CHARNOCK ON THE ATTRIBUTES.. 3.00

McCHEYNE'S WORKS.   2 vols. in 1.. 3.00

DR. CHALMERS'S SERMONS.   1105 pages.............................. 3.00

LEIGHTON'S COMPLETE WORKS....................................... 3.00

DICK'S THEOLOGY.   2 vols. in 1.. 3.00

JOHN NEWTON'S WORKS.. 3.00

*JOHN HOWE'S WORKS.   2 vols., 8vo.............................. 6.00

THEOLOGICAL SKETCH BOOK.   2 vols. in 1...................... 3.50

DR. JOHN BROWN ON THE DISCOURSES AND SAYINGS OF
     OUR LORD.   2 vols. in 1.. 8.50

*MURDOCK'S MOSHEIM'S CHURCH HISTORY.   3 vols......... 6.00

*THE WORKS OF JONATHAN EDWARDS.   4 vols., 8vo.........12.00

DAVIES' SERMONS.   3 vols... 3.75

SETS IN BOXES.

A. L. O. E. Library.   37 vols..28.00
*Cheap S. S. Library.   No. 1..20.00
*Cheap S. S. Library.   No. 2..20.00
The Jewel Case.   6 vols......... 7.50
The Wonder Case.   6 vols...... 7.50
Win and Wear Series.   6 vols. 7.50
Green Mountain Stories. 5 vols 6.00
Ledgeside Series.   6 vols....... 7.50
Butterfly's Flights.   3 vols.... 2.25
The Bessie Books.   6 vols....... 7.50
The Flowerets.   6 vols.......... 3.60
Little Sunbeams.   6 vols....... 6.00
Kitty and Lulu Books.   6 vols 6.00
Miss Ashton's Girls.   6 vols... 7.50
Drayton Hall Series.   6 vols... 4.50

Golden Ladder Series.   6 vols 3.00
Dare to Do Right Series. 5 vols 5.50
Tales of Christian Life. 5 vols 5.00
Tales of Many Lands.   5 vols. 5.00
Ellen Montgomery.   5 vols... 5.00
Stories of Vinegar Hill. 6 vols 3.00
The Say and Do Series.   6 v. 7.50
Story of Small Beginnings. 4 v 5.00
Young Ladies' Biog. Lib'y. 5 v 5.00
Ministering Children Library.. 3.00
Little Kitty's Library.   6 vols. 3.00
Harry and Dolly Library. 6 v. 3.00
Rainbow Series.   5 vols......... 3.00
Primrose Series.   6 vols........ 3.00
The Lily Series.   6 vols........ 2.00

HELPS TO BIBLE STUDY,

PUBLISHED BY

ROBERT CARTER & BROTHERS.

---

*MATTHEW HENRY'S COMMENTARY ON THE BIBLE.

In 9 volumes, 8vo., cloth, - - - - $27.00

In 5 volumes, quarto, sheep, - - - 25.00

It would be easy to name commentators more critical, more philosophical, or more severely erudite; but none so successful in making the Bible understood. In the words of the late JAMES HAMILTON, D.D., who has done as much as any man to promote the circulation of HENRY'S Commentary, "It has now lasted more than one hundred and forty years, and is at this moment more popular than ever, gathering strength as it rolls down the stream of time; and it bids fair to be the Comment for all coming time. True to GOD, true to nature, true to common sense, how can it ever be superseded? Waiting pilgrims will be reading it when the last trumpet sounds, Come to judgment!" Or, in the words of Dr. ALEXANDER, "Taking it as a whole, and as adapted to every class of readers, this Commentary may be said to combine more excellence than any work of the kind which was ever written in any language."

*POOL'S ANNOTATIONS ON THE BIBLE.

3 volumes, royal 8vo., - - - - - 15.00

RICHARD CECIL says "Pool is incomparable."

EDWARD BICKERSTETH says "Judicious and full."

T. H. HORNE says "He who wishes to understand the Scriptures will rarely consult them without advantage."

*HORNE'S INTRODUCTION TO THE STUDY OF THE BIBLE.

One volume, royal 8vo., sheep, - - - 5.00

"An indispensable work for a theological library. * * * It is a work of gigantic labor. The results of the research and erudition of scholars of all countries and in all time are here faithfully garnered."—*Evangelist.*

KITTO'S BIBLE ILLUSTRATIONS.

4 volumes, 12mo., - - - - - - 7.00

"I cannot lose this opportunity of recommending, in the strongest language and most emphatic manner I can command, this invaluable series of books. I believe for the elucidation of the historic parts of Scripture, there is nothing comparable with them in the English or any other language."—*John Angel James.*

DR. HANNA'S LIFE OF CHRIST.

3 volumes, - - - - - - - - 4.50

"We can most heartily commend the 'Life of our Lord' by Dr. HANNA."—*Congregational Quarterly.*

"Sabbath-school teachers will find Dr. HANNA's work very helpful."—*S. S. Times.*

"From a perusal of these volumes we believe that the sympathetic reader will carry away a more distinct image of the character and life of Christ, and his relation to his contemporaries, than he can gain from the more brilliant page of PRESSENSE, or the more elaborate discussions of NEANDER.'"—*North British Review.*

DR. JACOBUS' COMMENTARIES.

Genesis, 2 volumes in one, - - - - 1.50
Exodus. Part I, - - - - - - 1.00
Matthew and Mark, - - - - - - 1.50
Luke and John, - - - - - - 1.50
Acts, - - - - - - - - 1.50

The value of Dr. JACOBUS' Notes is evinced by the fact that over ONE HUNDRED THOUSAND VOLUMES of them have been sold in this country alone, without counting the circulation in Great Britain.

Drs. HODGE, GREEN, and others of Princeton, say: "The excellent Commentaries of Dr. JACOBUS have deservedly attained a high reputation. They present, in a brief compass, the results of extensive erudition, abound in judicious exposition and pertinent illustration, and are, moreover, distinguished by doctrinal soundness, evangelical character, and an eminently devout spirit."

RYLE ON THE GOSPELS.

7 volumes, 12mo, - - - - - - -	10.50

OR SEPARATELY:

Matthew, - - - - - - - -	1.50
Mark, - - - - - - - -	1.50
Luke, 2 volumes, - - - - - -	3.00
John, 3 volumes, - - - - - -	4.50

"We know of no comment that, as a whole, gives as much satisfaction in the study of the Divine Word as this."—*Christian Instructor.*

"Those who are engaged in teaching others will find in them a treasury, full of edifying and instructive suggestions."—*Episcopal Register.*

BONAR'S BIBLE THOUGHTS AND THEMES.

Genesis—Earth's Morning, - - - -	2.00
Old Testament, - - - - - -	2.00
Gospels, - - - - - - - -	2.00
Acts and the Larger Epistles, - - -	2.00
Lesser Epistles, - - - - - -	2.00
Revelation, - - - - - - -	2.00

"The condensed riches of Bible truth."

DR. HODGE'S COMMENTARIES.

Corinthians, 2 volumes, - - - - -	3.50
Ephesians, - - - - - - -	1.75

"Dr. Hodge's Commentaries ought to be in the hands of all readers of the Bible, in families, in Sabbath-schools and Seminaries."—*Observer.*

DR. CROSBY ON JOSHUA,   - - - -   1.00

DR. GREEN ON THE BOOK OF JOB,   - -   1.75

"The thanks of the christian public are due to the scholarly and devout Prof. W. H. Green, of Princeton, for a modest, but as we think, exceptionably valuable little treatise on the Book of Job."—*Congregationalist.*

HORNE ON THE PSALMS,   - - - -   2.50

BRIDGES ON THE PROVERBS,   - - -   2.50

HAMILTON ON ECCLESIASTES. (Royal Preacher). 1.25

MISS NEWTON ON THE SONG OF SOLOMON,   1.25

BROWN ON THE DISCOURSES OF OUR LORD, 3.50

ARNOT ON ACTS. (Church in the House).   -   2.50

HALDANE ON ROMANS, -   -   -   -   -   3.00

CHALMERS ON ROMANS,   -   -   -   -   2.50

*BROWN ON ROMANS,   -   -   -   -   -   2.00

McGHEE ON EPHESIANS,   -   -   -   -   3.00

LILLIE ON THESSALONIANS,   -   -   -   2.00

*SAMPSON ON HEBREWS,   -   -   -   -   3.00

MISS NEWTON ON HEBREWS, -   -   -   -   1.50

DR. BROWN ON FIRST PETER,   -   -   -   3.50

BUTLER ON THE APOCALYPSE,   -   -   -   1.50

THE BOOK AND ITS STORY, -   -   -   -   1.50

FRESH LEAVES FROM THE BOOK AND ITS STORY, 2.00

BOWES, THE SCRIPTURE ITS OWN ILLUSTRATOR, 1.50

DRUMMOND ON THE PARABLES, -   -   -   1.75

DYKES ON THE SERMON ON THE MOUNT. 3 vols., 3.75

THE WORD SERIES. By Miss WARNER. 3 vols., 4.50

THE FOOTSTEPS OF ST. PAUL. By Macduff, 1.50

FRASER'S LECTURES ON THE BOOKS OF THE
    BIBLE. 2 volumes,   -   -   -   -   -   4.00

THE CHRIST OF HISTORY. By JOHN YOUNG,   1.25

NATURE AND THE BIBLE. By DAWSON,   -   1.75

BLUNT'S COINCIDENCES AND PALEY'S HORÆ
    PAULINÆ,   -   -   -   -   -   -   -   1.50

PALEY'S EVIDENCES, Edited by Prof. NAIRNE,   1.50

www.ingramcontent.com/pod-product-compliance
Lightning Source LLC
Chambersburg PA
CBHW030100130726
47902CB00018B/1417